THE FAR HIMĀLAYA

THE FAR HIMĀLAYA

a novel

PHILLIP ERNEST

The following is a work of fiction. Many of the locations are real, although not necessarily as portrayed, but all characters and events are fictional and any resemblance to actual events or people, living or dead, is purely coincidental.

Prepared for the press by Carmelita McGrath
Cover photographs: David Ernest
Cover design: Debbie Geltner
Layout: Tika eBooks
Printed and bound in Canada

Library and Archives Canada Cataloguing in Publication

Title: The far Himalaya : a novel / Phillip Ernest.
Names: Ernest, Phillip, author.
Identifiers: Canadiana (print) 20190066717 | Canadiana (ebook) 20190066741 | ISBN 9781988130972 (softcover) | ISBN 9781988130989 (EPUB) | ISBN 9781988130996 (Kindle) | ISBN 9781773900001 (PDF)
Classification: LCC PS8609.R54 F37 2019 | DDC C813/.6—dc23

The publisher gratefully acknowledges the support of the Government of Canada through the Canada Council for the Arts, the Canada Book Fund, and Livres Canada Books.

Linda Leith Éditions
Montréal
www.lindaleith.com

for A

Questo d'ignoto amante inno ricevi.

1

It may have been around 4 o'clock when the rain started. Ben didn't have a watch, so he couldn't be sure. Thunder had been brewing for some time, and in his half-sleep he had felt the air change as a current of coolness flowed in and pushed aside the muggy July heat that had possessed the city for some days. He had returned to sleep, and slept better for the coolness, turning onto his back on the bench (one of the comfortable ones, with spacious flat boards), until a huge raindrop shattered on his face, wresting him into consciousness. The rhythm of the drops accelerated quickly: *splat splat,* on him, the bench beside his, the pavement of the Innis College plaza around him, the leaves of the plants in the wooden planter that separated the plaza from the sidewalk of St. George Street.

He rose, lifted his book-crammed knapsack from under the bench by the shoulder-band that was already looped over his left arm, and stumbled round the planter onto the sidewalk. By now, the heavens had opened, and the deluge was pounding the street. Every few seconds, there were flashes of day-making lightning and simultaneous shattering cracks of thunder. His longish hair clung to his head and face. Streams ran under his collar, and he could feel that his clothes were already almost completely soaked through. He was worried about his books, thick and strong though his knapsack was. None of the narrow spaces that the college or the library afforded would give real refuge from rain like this. The nearest adequate shelter would be the back porch of the Religious Studies Department, an old house, like many of the departments and centres on St. George Street.

He walked briskly up the sidewalk, stepped into the ankle-deep current flowing down the street, crossed to the driveway between the department and the adjacent building, and climbed the porch stairs. Then he lay down in a corner of the unlit porch, against the brown brick wall, beneath a window, with his head against his knapsack. One minute under the rain had soaked him through, but he was still exhausted and not fully awake. The fresh air that had brought the rain was sweet relief after several restless heatwave nights, and he was soon deeply asleep again.

A sharp blow to his lower legs propelled him back into consciousness. He opened his eyes to a form silhouetted against the dull morning light of a rainy day. Another blow. He cried out in pain. Someone was kicking him. And there was singing. The person who was kicking him was singing.

I wanna dance,
I wanna dance with someone
in the summer rain ...

Ben scrambled to a sitting position against the wall, hugging his legs, which were burning with pain. His assailant was a campus cop, one he had never seen before: a tall, large, middle-aged brown man with metal-framed television-screen glasses. He was grinning.

"*What* the..." said Ben, frightened and appalled. In his more than two years of living on campus, he had come to know the university cops well. They were ugly souls, but never in the often ironic theatre of cat-and-mouse antics that he shared with them had he encountered violence.

The cop kicked him again, this time in the left hip, drawing his leg back and swinging it as he held his arms out for balance, a serious strong kick. Ben cried out, stumbled to his feet, stood at bay behind his massive knapsack in the corner of the wall.

"Get out of here, you piece of shit," said the cop.

The colloquial profanity was weirdly incongruous with the precise and incorrect enunciation of his heavy Hindi accent. His grin had faded, but remained as a trace that coloured the expression of disgust and hate that now dominated his face. He kicked Ben's knapsack, which barely budged. Ben stooped, grabbed it by one of its shoulder-straps, hoisted it heavily onto his back, all the while looking up at the cop. With his back first to the wall, then to the railing, he moved cautiously round the edge of the porch towards the wooden steps, warily circling the cop, watching him as he stood watching. When Ben turned his face from him to descend the steps into the now milder but steady rain, the cop kicked him in the ass, sending him stumbling down the last two steps and sprawling onto the wet pavement of the driveway under his knapsack. Ben groaned, scrambled with difficulty to his knees and then to his feet as the cop slowly descended the stairs.

"I never want to see you again," said the cop.

Ben moved towards the street. Behind him, the cheerful singing resumed.

... in the summer rain,
with someone who loves me.

Ben was quaking with rage and humiliation. Across the street, a beautiful girl in a T-shirt and track pants, with blonde hair dishevelled from sex and sleep, was standing in front of the opened door in a fraternity house's sheltered doorway at the top of several stone steps, watching blankly. She smiled, and Ben realized the smile was not for him. He felt the cop behind him.

"Good morning," the cop called cheerfully. The girl smiled again.

At the sidewalk, where the campus police car was parked, Ben turned. The cop was a couple of paces behind, grinning again. He raised his right arm to point towards Bloor Street. "Get off the campus and don't come back."

Looking him grimly in the eye, Ben held up a pointing, minatory hand, and spoke:

tathā smārayitā te'haṃ kṛntanmarmāṇi saṃyuge

The cop's grin collapsed into an expression of confusion and rage. Ben turned and walked towards Bloor in the pouring rain.

2

“Do you think he had any idea what you were saying?” Moksha Das asked. He and Ben were sitting side by side on plastic chairs in the Scott Mission chapel’s fecal stench.

It was about 10:30, half an hour before the second sitting, and because it was still early in the month, and people hadn’t yet blown their welfare checks, the crowd was sparse and consisted mainly of the wretchedest of the wretched—the people who survived on begging and charity alone.

Moksha was a tiny man, and this smallness combined with his cropped hair, pointed beard, and one-eighth native complexion to give him a striking resemblance to his declared guru, the south Indian sage Ramana Maharshi. This in spite of Moksha’s huge tortoiseshell glasses, rumpled suit, thick aura of body odour, tobacco, and booze—and lack of upper front teeth.

“A meathead cop?” said Ben, smiling with disgust. “Obviously not, but I could see that he sensed it was probably Sanskrit.”

“What was it again?” said Moksha.

“tathā smārayitā te’haṃ kṛntanmarmāṇi saṃyuge. Can you make that out?”

“What a memory!” said Moksha grinning, with an exaggeratedly histrionic tone of admiration that indicated that his inebriation had already reached cruising altitude. "Wait: *tathā …"*

"tathā … smārayitā … te … 'ham … kṛntan … marmāṇi … saṃyuge," Ben repeated slowly.

Moksha listened attentively, thought a moment, then shook his head violently, grinning his toothless grin, laughing with the sniffling, nasal laughter of his drunkenness. "OK, I give up!" he said. "Translate it!"

"I will remind you of this when I cut open your guts in battle," said Ben. "It's from the *Mahabharata*. Bhima says it to Duhshasana after he's dragged Draupadi around the assembly hall."

"Oh, *well,* the *Mahabharata,"* said Moksha with theatrical scorn. "No wonder I didn't know." He took an orange juice bottle from a jacket pocket, twisted off the cap, and took a swig of the amber liquid. "Can I offer you some? I know it's a bit early … "

"Yes, it's too early for me," said Ben. "You're on holiday today, I take it?"

"Yes, I made a killing at work yesterday," said Moksha. "I got a twenty and a ten, plus the usual take. So I celebrated: Spanish Amontillado and Bushmills Irish whiskey. Half of the Bushmills is still left." He took a swig.

Ben was looking at the bottle, frowning. "Let me smell it."

Moksha handed him the bottle. Ben raised it to his nose and sniffed, lowered it, sat looking at it for a moment, troubled. Finally, he said, "No, I can't. Not today. Bushmills is *amṛta,* nectar of the gods. But not today." He handed it back.

"Well, I can understand," said Moksha, taking another swig. "But we can always buy Bushmills whenever you join me on the street again. We're always a hit when we play together. You still have your recorder?"

Ben nodded.

"Don't get out of practice," said Moksha. His gaze lingered caressingly on Ben for a moment too long.

They were sitting in the fourth row of the chapel: prime seats, later in the month, and even now prime enough that they began to fill up as 11 o'clock approached. The early morning's rain had ended at around 9, the clouds had dispersed, and the heat had again begun to rise.

An Anishnabe man, probably not more than five years older than Ben, but as decrepit and hobbling as if he were sixty, came and sat on the chair to Ben's right, bearing along with him the familiar miasma of piss, shit, sweat, and Chinese cooking wine. Despite the heat, which was barely mitigated by two large humming fans, he wore the long winter coat of brown-stained tweed that must have kept him alive through the winter, and whose protection would soon be welcome again in the post-heatwave nights of August and beyond.

Though he was several days unshaven, his full head of straight black hair was combed into a fairly neat Beatles-style mop. His full-lipped, moist mouth was slackly open. His eyes were those of a suffering child already resigned to a life of incomprehensible despair: not one of the dangerous ones, thought Ben, recognizing him.

An Anishnabe woman, whose wrecked youthful beauty made it similarly difficult to estimate her age, turned into their row and sat next to the man. They began to talk in the soft tones of their language, like cautious footsteps in the forest undergrowth, probably the Ojibwe of the majority of the natives on Toronto's skid row.

"Did you see the books?" asked Moksha. "There's a new bumper crop at the front. Someone interesting must have died. Look at what I found."

He bent down to reach the shoulder-bag on the floor between his feet—his worn, dirty Indian *akṣamālā,* or bead rosary, hanging forward from his neck—and with a clunk of what must have been the bottle of Bushmills, took out four books and began showing them to Ben.

"This one is a history of mathematics that was a bestseller a few years ago, which I've been meaning to steal from Coles for some time. And here's an excellent historical novel about Mary Queen of Scots that I read when it was new, some thirty years ago. It's about time I reread it. Here's a beautiful find: a *first edition* of Robert Graves's *The Hebrew Myths!* Do you know it?"

Ben shook his head.

Moksha continued: "If I were still in the used book business, I could get at least twenty bucks for this at Atticus. I guess I'll take it there when I'm finished rereading it, but you should read it first. And this is a bilingual edition of Rimbaud."

He reached down into the bag again and took out an ancient little brown hardbound volume, carefully opened the brittle, tea-coloured pages, and held it up to Ben. "I also found this," he said, "in case you're interested. Is this ancient or modern Greek?"

Ben took the book from Moksha's hands, looked at the spidery archaic font, and turned a few pages. "It's modern Greek, actually, which I can't really read, but it's evidently a commentary on an ancient Greek text ... poetry ... which is quoted throughout. It's in dialect ... probably Pindar .... " (He turned to the title page) "... yes, Pindar. Thanks for thinking of me. I'll take it, even though I won't have time to do more than browse it, and then I'll leave it on Atticus's doorstep. You know, I'm finished with Greek. But who else here could get anything out of it?" He closed it and put it into his jacket pocket. "I'll check out the books after lunch, but there's no urgency: I've got more than enough to read now for a few hundred rebirths."

It was to the book bin that Ben and Moksha owed their meeting a couple of weeks after Ben had begun coming to the Mission. That was more than two years ago, when Ben was fifteen and still illegally homeless. On that day, Ben, lacking a watch, barely made it to the second sitting at 11 o'clock. He shuffled into the dining room with the last stragglers, holding Gore Vidal's *Kalki,* which he had found in the bin the day before. The dwarfish stranger who happened to be behind him in line ostentatiously mimed interest in the book, tipping his head to look at the cover.

"Kalki," said Ben. "The last incarnation of the Hindu god Vishnu."

"Yes," Moksha said with a condescending smile and a look sharpened by what might have been fascination, or desire. "I know who Kalki is."

Now the organist, a squat, round-bellied, white-haired old man wearing the white apron of the kitchen staff, emerged from the chapel. He sat down at the electric organ and began to play the drunkenly lurching music that accompanied the diners' entry. He had a repertoire of about four hymns, and this morning it was *Were You There When They Crucified My Lord?*

Someone—an amorphous, faceless heap of homeless humanity dressed in the standard all-season costume of the street—was still lying asleep across three seats in front of Ben and Moksha. All the other seats in the row were taken. A hulking Anishnabe youth turned in from the centre aisle, pushed past the knees of the first three people, and smacked the sleeper's head.

"Get up," the hulk said. He had cold eyes and imbecilic features framed by long dishevelled hair.

The form stirred, looked up—revealing itself to be a white man of about fifty—and, recognizing his peril, scrambled into a sitting position on the last of the three seats he had been occupying. As the hulk was about to sit down, he noticed Ben.

"Hey, pretty white boy!" said the hulk, looming over him, his tiny round mouth spreading in a sneer of rotten, jumbled fangs. "Come sit next to me! Be my pillow."

Ben looked up at him with suppressed fear.

"You know this guy?" murmured Moksha.

"As well as I need to," Ben replied softly.

The hulk laughed, a low, malevolent *ho ho ho*. The Anishnabe man to Ben's right looked up at Ben's antagonist with furtive, fearful eyes.

"Hey, leave him alone," came a voice from the left. It was Big Frank, the Mission's bouncer, who was an enormously brawny-fat man with a tiny head, slicked-back hair, and chubby face that gave him the look of some obscene, gigantic infant. He was sitting off to the side of the rows with the wispily-bearded troglodytic youth who was probably his current Ganymede. (On the day Ben first appeared at the Mission, Big Frank had casually asked him "So, you like girls?", and was visibly disappointed with his affirmative reply.)

The hulk sneered at Big Frank and sat down. No one came to occupy the seat to the right of him.

This morning's MC was a bespectacled, cheerful young chap from the office whom Ben knew by sight alone. He was probably studying for the ministry, like many of the upper echelon of the Mission, which had been founded by a Jewish convert to evangelical Christianity. He emerged from behind the sitters, hurried up the left side of the chapel, and stepped up to the podium as the organist brutally truncated the hymn with a swelling cadence.

"Good morning, gentlemen," the MC said loudly, smiling diffidently. "I see it's the beginning of the month. Not too many people here this morning. Announcements ... ? This morning we received a large donation of books." He looked to his right, where they lay in and around a large cardboard box beside the stage. "I see that you've taken many of them already. I know a lot of you guys like books. Other than that ... bag lunches at the side door at two o'clock ... razors and soap in the office ... That's about it. So

let's say grace, and we'll go in. Heavenly father, we th
all your blessings upon us, and we give thanks to you fo
we are about to receive. Ay-*men! Bon appeteet,* gentlemen
The first row stood up with a rumble of chairs. One
kitchen workers pushed back the accordion-curtain, and th
gan sprang into the invariable incidental music for this momen
sprightly rendition of *The Saints Go Marching In*.

The first, second, third rows, then the fourth with Moksh
and Ben, filed to the end of the scrambled columns of chairs, past the box of books, and into the dark dining room, where the tables stood ready with ten sets of battered cutlery and yellow plastic cups, a jug of coffee, a loaf of Wonder Bread, a tub of margarine.

The diners poured round each table. As Moksha and Ben neared what was by now clearly going to be their table, Ben saw the hulk standing at the end of it, watching them.

"I'm sitting next to these ones," he announced gruffly. To Ben he added, sneering, "I want your meat, boy."

Ben had foreseen this.

"No," he said. "No way. I give my meat to who I want."

He felt a light furtive touch on the back of his shoulder. It was the other Anishnabe, the gentle one he had been sitting next to. "Brother, just give it to him," he said softly, frightened.

"I'm gonna sit next to who I want," Ben declared, raising his voice.

The hulk stepped swiftly towards him, his mouth a tight little O of menace.

"Would you please just fuck off," said Moksha, who was in front of Ben in line.

"Shut up, old man," said the hulk, shouldering Moksha aside, so that he stumbled and almost fell. The flow of the line was stalled. There were murmurs of irritation, yet no one attempted to move past the disputants and sit down. Peripherally, Ben saw

ervising the entry from inside the din-
he stalled line of men and lean his
hapel.
ed at Ben. He was almost shouting,
strange deep-woods subduedness that
racterized Anishnabe voices. He grabbed
der and thrust him into the space between the
s. Ben crashed into the empty chairs and tumbled
floor with his heavy knapsack. Murmurs and shouts of
se and outrage rose from the seated diners who felt the im-
act on their backs.

"Oh for Christ's sake," Ben heard Moksha say. He raised his head from the floor just in time to see an enormous dark object flash horizontally through space. Shouts of amazement, confusion, and admiration filled the dining hall. Holding onto chairs and the table, Ben got to his feet and saw Big Frank lying face-down on the floor. He had completely smothered Ben's tormentor, whose hands and feet protruded from under his bulk.

Big Frank rolled off his crushed quarry, dragged him to his feet, and hustled him to the side door by the scruff of his coat. "Barred for the rest of the month," he announced in a voice that betrayed no trace of exertion, as he rammed open the door and pushed the hulk into the lane. The door whipped closed with a metallic clang.

"A little dinner theatre this morning, gentlemen," the MC joked as he supervised the seating of the last of the diners. Moksha and Ben sat down at the end of the row of chairs that Ben had knocked over, and the gentle Anishnabe and then his woman friend sat down next to Ben. There was an immediate rush of ten pairs of hands for coffee, bread, margarine. One of the two sitters at the head of the table ladled out the soup, the standard greasy mess of chicken body parts, potatoes, and remnants of past main courses.

"None for us," said Ben, at which the Anishnabe man laughed softly, without malice, and said to his companion, "The vegetarians!"

At the head of the aisle, a towering cart had appeared, as awesome as the central apparatus in some religious ritual, and trays rumbled and clattered as the kitchen staff slid them out and leaned them on the tables' ends so that the head sitters could begin handing down the battered plates with the standard trinity of some kind of meat, some kind of vegetable, and some approximation of salad.

"Yer in luck today," Ben said to his neighbour. "Just take the meat."

"*Megwech,* brother," the Anishnabe replied, forking the two desiccated hamburger patties onto his own and his female companion's plates, and handing the severely diminished meals down to Ben and Moksha.

"Too bad," said Ben to Moksha. "The hamburger patties are one of the few palatable dishes here."

"Ethics is sacrifice," said Moksha. "Pass the salt."

3

Ben had been asleep on the sofa in the panoramic corner classroom in the East Asian Studies department on the fourteenth floor of the Robarts Library when he met Aditi. Her quiet watching presence roused him, and he opened his eyes to see a tiny brown woman staring at him with enormous birdlike eyes. The full lips of her large mouth were parted in surprise. She might be five years older than his twenty-two years (he would later find out that it was seven). She wasn't conventionally beautiful, with her sharp physiognomy, large cheekbones and long nose framed by curly hair, but Ben never forgot the instantaneous completeness of his passion at the moment he opened his eyes upon her.

It was a warm September day, and she was dressed in a white short-sleeved shirt open to the breastbone, knee-length beige shorts, and sandals. Her piled hair was bound back at the temples with a clip, with ringlets spilling round her neck. She was carrying a towering styrofoam cup of coffee from the cafeteria downstairs.

For a moment, Ben stared at her as she came into focus. Then, feeling how closely his track pants were clinging to his morning erection, he scrambled into a sitting position, buttoning his suit jacket over his lap.

"Are ... you a student?" she asked.

"Uh, yeah," said Ben, shaking his head to hasten the process of waking up, then looking up to stare at her again. "Sorry, I was here all night ... working. I'm, uh, a Sanskrit PhD candidate."

"Oh, Sanskrit," she said, not smiling, but raising her eyebrows in a manner that cautiously acknowledged interest without conceding any loss of equality. *"I'm* doing an MA in Sanskrit. I just started. I'm from Edmonton. I did my BA at the University of Alberta. I didn't know Professor Boylan had any PhD students." Her Hindi accent was strong, her voice a commanding midrange in pitch.

"I'm ... not his student," said Ben, lowering his eyes. "I'm Professor Chamberlain's student. His only student."

"Oh," she said, her huge eyes widening a little, her face brightening with growing interest, but still not smiling. "He's a very distinguished scholar, very famous."

"Yes," said Ben. "And he almost never comes here anymore. He's very old, can barely walk."

She put the coffee down on the table, drew out a chair, and sat. Ben crossed his legs and unbuttoned his jacket, the embarrassing prominence in his crotch having by now subsided. He realized he was allowing himself to be led into possible danger. He should stand up and politely leave now, before he embellished his standard self-fictionalization with an unsustainable degree of detail that could get him into trouble. But he couldn't leave. Just a little longer. He glanced up at the clock: it was not yet 9 o'clock, well before 10, the opening time of the carwash on Spadina where he worked. He sat back and stretched out his arm along the sofa's back.

She looked at him again, and crossed her legs as she saw him staring, his eyes moving involuntarily from her face down to the rest of her—her small bra-less breasts, the dark nipples not too faintly visible against the translucent fabric of her shirt, the slender buttocks which his eyes followed as far as they could up the tunnel of her shorts.

Raising his eyes to her face again, he flushed violently, to which she responded first with a look of irritation that would later become deeply familiar to him, then with a forgiving, cautiously inviting smirk. She turned her head, raised the cup to her lips, and sipped.

"You seem a little young to be a PhD student," she said, still smirking a little.

Ben flushed again. "What's your area?" he asked. "You must be planning to do a PhD yourself?"

"I'm working on the *Mahabharata*," she replied. "Yes, I'll be doing a PhD. I'll probably stay here, with Professor Boylan. Or I may go somewhere else. But he's very reputable."

Ben's face darkened a little with some unexpressed concern. "Are there any other MA students?" he asked. "You must be here for a class?"

"There are two others," she said. "We're about to have a reading session with the professor. You don't know all this? It's a small enough Sanskrit culture at this university that I would have expected everyone to know everyone and everything."

"I'm not really involved in what goes on in the department," he replied. "I'm very much on the periphery, like Professor Chamberlain himself."

"Hm," she said, with what he uncomfortably took to be a note of skeptical amusement and a knowing smile. She looked him in the eye, and he flushed yet again and looked down. "And what's *your* topic?" she said.

"The *Mahabharata* too, believe it or not," said Ben, more at ease now, suddenly on firm ground.

"Oh!" she said with real interest. "What aspect of it? What's the title of your dissertation?"

"The title is *History and the Individual in the* Mahabharata," he said. "I'm studying the way Vyasa comes to rely more and more on individual characters, their individual psychologies, as a storytelling tool over the course of the epic's narrative."

"That's really interesting," she said, looking him seriously in the eye, and this time he did not drop his gaze. "That connects with what *I* want to write about, but I want to focus on female characters. Well, this is very interesting! I had no idea that there was anyone else here working on the *Mahabharata,* and not just that, but approaching it from a perspective so similar to mine. We should really get together and talk more—if you're not concerned about sharing your ideas ... "

"Oh no, not at all," replied Ben quickly, "I'm not concerned about that at all. Yes, let's meet again. We'll definitely meet again, here in the department..."

Someone else came into the classroom through its other door, a dopey, bespectacled chap whom Ben had seen before. "Hi Aditi," he said, smiling sheepishly and nodding at Ben.

"Hi, Andrew," she said, and glancing at Ben, "This is ... "

"Benjamin, Ben," said Ben.

"Benjamin," she continued. "He's Professor Chamberlain's PhD student."

"Oh, Professor Chamberlain!" said Andrew with innocent wonder. "I didn't know he still had any students."

"I should get going," Ben said, rising from the sofa and hoisting his book-heavy knapsack onto his shoulder.

"Do you have an email address?" she asked, with a hint of alarm.

Ben paused, confused, then said, "Yes. Do you have a piece of paper?"

"Just a moment," she said, rummaging in one of the pouches of her shoulder bag and taking out a folded page. "Here."

He took the page from her, put it on the table, wrote on it with his own pen, and handed it back to her. She looked down at the address: *yadbhavishyati@hotmail.com.* "*yad bhaviṣyati* . . . ." she murmured. He saw her react with what looked like recognition. This was part of a familiar phrase that recurred in various forms in the *Mahabharata* and other texts: *yat yat bhaviṣyati tat tat bhaviṣyati,* "Whatever shall be, shall be."

"We'll meet, definitely," he said, looking down at her with an almost ludicrously frank fascination that he had not permitted himself until now. It was agony to leave her. *Aditi:* her beautiful name, the name of a goddess, echoed in his mind's ear.

Still looking at her, he moved towards the door through which she had entered, and collided with a ruined old man who was coming through it at the same moment.

"What the *fuck?*" shouted the man, tottering perilously with hands slightly outstretched for balance, as Ben stumbled backwards, almost pulled off his feet by the weight of the library on his shoulder. Except for the fact that he didn't smell of piss and shit, the man could easily have been one of Ben's fellow diners at the Scott Mission. He was short, seemingly quite frail, despite the belly visible through his shirt. He had a full head of wild, curly snow-white hair and an ugly, sullen face palled with the unmistakable wear of the alcoholic. And he did, in fact, smell of booze, though doubtless it was booze of a higher grade than the toxic Ontario pseudo-sherry and Chinese cooking wine that perfumed the Mission's clientele.

"Sorry, excuse me," muttered Ben, regaining his balance and momentarily meeting Boylan's eyes with a look of disgust before rounding a bend in the hall and standing against the wall, within earshot.

"Who the fuck was that?" he heard Boylan ask.

"He said he's a PhD student of Professor Chamberlain," said Aditi.

"Like hell he is," he said. "That old cocksucker can't even find his own asshole to wipe it anymore, let alone supervise a PhD. He could be dead right now, for all anyone knows. Or cares." He snuffled a laugh. Then, looking around: "Where's the other guy? The Jewish guy? There are three of you, right?"

"He ... hasn't arrived yet," said Aditi uncomfortably.

"Well, to hell with 'im, let's get started," he said. His eyes rested on Aditi's face, then dropped. "Have you considered wearing a bra?"

She started, looking at him with irritation and cold contempt. Already this was not new to her. It was enragingly new to Ben, but no surprise.

Weeks passed before they saw each other again. Ben was consciously avoiding her, taking care to slip out of the department as soon as the cleaning staff opened it at around 7 o'clock, rather than lingering until the working day began.

He had been haunting the place for years, periodically hiding at the summit of one of the fire escape stairwells as the building was cleaned and locked up after midnight, then re-descending to the fourteenth floor, where he sat reading and writing in the South Asian Studies library and sleeping in the corner classroom. This was a trick he had learned from Moksha, who had taught himself Sanskrit in the library during the seventies. Moksha's deepening alcoholism had eventually made such stealth too difficult and risky for him, and he now did his work in the Sigmund Samuel undergraduate library—"Sig Sam"—during the day instead, between lunch at the Scott Mission and playing the recorder for booze and book money on Bloor Street in the evening.

So Ben avoided her, in resigned despair, conjuring up her image during his daily masturbation sessions at the Harrison Baths or in one of the library washrooms after finishing work at Malcolm's carwash, but entertaining no expectation of ever talking to her again. He had no real correspondence with anyone from his email account, which he had set up on a whim one day on one of the library computers, and which he rarely checked. But now he deliberately did not go to it, in case he should find a message from her which he could not bring himself to answer.

And yet why not? If he could pass himself off so effectively as a PhD student to various university employees over the years, and now even to an actual graduate student, if he could teach himself Sanskrit to a level of fluency that placed him above most Sanskrit professors—if he could pull off such an effective impersonation, why on earth did he need to pretend? Why not actually become what he so effortlessly appeared to be? There were ways it could be done. Yet he knew that he couldn't, he couldn't dare. Because he knew that he was *not* what he appeared to be, and that the appearance was thin and fragile enough that it could be shattered in a moment.

It was a cold night in November when he saw her again, in Philosopher's Walk, where the dead lawns cleared of fallen leaves waited for the first snow. He had left Moksha drunk under what Ben had dubbed his "Troll Bridge"—the concrete steps of the first-floor fire escape of the Royal Conservatory of Music at the top of the Walk—and was on his way south to his current regular sleeping place in Kensington Market, this not being one of his nights in the library.

Ahead of him, by the bridge-like passageway to the music faculty's entrance, he saw two people who appeared to be struggling, and as they came into focus through Ben's uncorrected myopic haze, this turned out to be true. One of them was Aditi, and the other was an Indian man of about the same age, who had grasped her by the wrists and was trying to force her to sit down on one of the two benches beside the paved path.

"Just let me go, Sujay, let me *go*," she was saying, furious, vigorously resisting him.

Ben was far enough away that they had not noticed him. He took off his knit winter hat, threw it and his knapsack on the grass beside the path, took off his scarf and wound it round his face, leaving a slit for the eyes, then walked towards them rapidly and steadily. The man looked up when Ben was two paces away. Ben punched him squarely in the face, and he fell sprawling onto the path. Ben stepped forward and kicked him hard in the gut. He groaned and writhed.

"Wait!" said Aditi. "It's ... it's enough."

Ben turned to her and looked her in the eye, and knew that she knew him, but he did not speak. She was breathing hard, recovering her breath. She zipped up her coat, re-bound her hair.

"Thank you. Could you ... could you just please walk me up to Bloor Street?" she said, trying to control the tremor in her voice.

Ben paused, nodded, then turned back to the man, who was slowly trying to get to his hands and feet. Ben got down on his haunches, grasped him by the hair, violently turned his head up so that his terrified eyes were looking into Ben's, held him this way for a long moment, then roughly let him go and stood up.

"Don't call me, Sujay!" Aditi shouted, her voice trembling. "It's *over.*"

She and Ben turned together and walked up Philosopher's Walk—he stooped and picked up his hat and huge knapsack, an unmistakable marker of his identity, if there had been any doubt—walked past the Royal Conservatory, where Ben saw the blanket-covered feet of the drunkenly sleeping Moksha under the fire escape, up the concrete stairs at the end of the Walk, onto Bloor.

"I live this way, in the graduate residence at St. George," said Aditi, gesturing westward with a turn of her head. "If you could just walk me that far ... "

They proceeded along the deserted sidewalk, a tiny intense brown woman a head shorter than her companion.

In front of the residence, they stopped and faced each other.

"This is where I live," she said. "Thank you. He ... Sujay... he ... just turned out to be an asshole. I think he'll probably leave me alone ... now. Thank you."

Ben nodded, holding her gaze, then looked down and set off again, walking west, leaving her standing there.

The next morning, when she opened the door of the corner classroom, he was sitting on the sofa, looking directly into her eyes, suffering. She smiled softly, relieved, happy.

"Come," she said.

4

Tonight, four years later, as he lay spooned against her, Ben swelled slightly in the cleft of her buttocks, remembering that first day together. It had been beyond belief for him, everything, that day and the days that followed. She was only his second, and the first who had loved him. It was the most beautiful thing either of them had ever known. And what a price they had both had to pay for it.

It had begun to snow yesterday afternoon, and the snowfall had continued steadily into the night—one of his nights out—until he had felt the temperature plunge, and had clenched himself tighter in his blanket, where he lay on a flattened cardboard box in the sheltered lower-level doorway of a Chinatown tofu manufacturer. This was his preferred bedroom this winter, not least because of the shop's cat, who, sitting at the glass door, benignly watched him come, sleep, and go, and evidently enjoyed his company as much as he enjoyed hers.

When he had climbed the steps to street level at dawn, violently shuddering himself warm, the sky was a brutal clear arctic blue, and his misted breath played about his mouth and nostrils, spiking a foot in front of him when he exhaled. It was almost like home, a day like this, as close as Toronto ever got to the snow-piled 40 below of his native north-eastern Ontario, where the snow, cold, lake, forests, and country roads were nearly all that he missed.

Now, at 10 p.m. of the same day, it was a delicious 25 below, but Ben was glad he wouldn't be sleeping out tonight. His boots creaked on the sanded sidewalk as he walked along Bloor to make another pass in front of the graduate residence at St. George, an unrenovated old three-storey brown-brick building with a façade like the lower half of a capital H and the entrance set back from the street in an open half-courtyard. At this hour, almost no one was out of doors.

He had walked past the residence about five minutes before, but there had been two people, a man and a woman, going through the glass-walled antechamber where the intercom was. So he had kept walking, turning back at the Bloor entrance to Philosopher's Walk where Moksha would be sleeping under the concrete steps of the Royal Conservatory's fire escape. When he reached the residence again, the antechamber was empty, and he went to the door.

There was a dull audio crack, and Aditi's voice came on the intercom, distant and flattened: "Yes?"

"vallabhaḥ te āgataḥ asmi," he said.

The door clacked and buzzed, and he opened it and walked through.

"'My lover has arrived,' hm?" she said, opening her door and laying her arms over his shoulders as he pushed it shut behind him. He loomed over her as she smiled up at him, her rich curly hair piled and bound high behind her dark brown face.

He said nothing, but immediately began kissing her, devouringly, holding her by the waist, gently walking her backwards towards the bedroom, at the bedroom door reaching down to hold her buttocks as she raised her legs and crossed them behind his back, clinging to him. Falling onto the bed with her, laying her down, he began to descend, kissing and sucking her neck, biting her small breasts through her sweater, unbuckling her belt with trembling hands, pulling off her jeans and underpants, kissing and sucking her thighs, burying his face in her sex, ravenously sucking and licking her as she moaned and writhed and caressed his head. He thrust his hands under her sweater and shirt, grasping and kneading the belly, ribs, breasts of her spare body, laughing with her as she cried out "Oh! Cold hands!"

He sat up, unbuckled his pants, released his penis, cut and youthfully large, and already rock-hard. "Are you safe?" he gasped, holding it with his hand and pressing his swollen glans against her wetness.

"We need a condom tonight," she murmured. "Sorry."

"Suck me," he gasped again.

They lay long afterwards, dozing face-to-face in each other's arms. The cool lunar light of the streetlamps on St. George Street bathed them and the landscape of the bedclothes. Finally she stirred, kissed his face, which was almost buried under her tumbling hair, slowly raised herself off his still half-hard penis with a wince, lay down beside him, pulled from her vulva the leaking condom that had slipped off of him and remained inside her when she rose from him, tied it off, and tossed it onto the floor.

She sniffed his armpit, smiling. "You didn't even shower first."

"You didn't ask me to," he replied. "It'd been, what, a week? Too long. And anyway, I'm clean, aren't I? I actually went to the Harrison Baths just before I came."

"Hm," she said, sniffing his armpit again and kissing his shoulder, "you're clean." Propped up on one elbow, with her other hand she slowly stroked his thigh, pensive, as he lay on his back with his head raised on the pillow.

"I have some more of the translation," he said. "I got it from

Moksha yesterday, worked on it yesterday and today after work, and now it's ready."

"Hm, good," she said, unsmiling, looking down, continuing to stroke him.

"And the sleeping dog?" he asked.

"He's still sleeping," she said.

"*ciram svapitu,*" he said, and she laughed bitterly and replied, "Yes, long may he sleep."

He laid his hand on her stroking hand, squeezed it, looking at it, not her. She squeezed back, kissed him on the lips, then said, "Come on. It's hot in here. I'm thirsty."

Naked, they went into the sitting room, where there was a sofa, a coffee table, a wooden desk and chair, a bookshelf. She picked up a half-empty bottle of orange juice from the coffee table and took a swig. "It's warm," she said with a wince of disgust, "but I don't want to put clothes on and go to the kitchen."

"Let's go out as we are," he said, smiling. "Come on, it'll only take two minutes, and look, it's ... 12:30, so everyone's asleep or drunk or fucking, and anyway who cares if we're naked. Where do you think we are?" He unlocked the door.

She laughed, horrified. "Ben, for god's sake, no!" she said in an urgent half-whisper, "you'll get me thrown out of here!" But he had already opened the door and gone out, and was walking down the hall towards the kitchen. As he came back with a large bottle of orange juice, his still-heavy penis flopping back and forth, she was peeking round the door, grinning in mock horror. "Hurry up! Run!" she called to him, whispering. He reached her, kissed her, and they went back in together, pulling the door softly closed behind them.

He sat cross-legged on the sofa, and she on the wooden chair, scanning the pages he had brought.

"Moksha lays down the basic translation, then I revise it, as you know," said Ben, sipping orange juice from a glass. "It's good for him. I hope it'll lead him back to his own work, his translation of the *Yogavāsiṣṭha*. He's rusty, and he's forgotten things, but his deep knowledge and his gift often flash into view in brilliant intuitions. I'm glad he can do most of the work. I wouldn't want to have to do it all myself, with this kind of text, *yogaśāstra*. That's his thing, not mine."

She perused the handwritten pages silently, English with fragments of the original text in *Devanāgarī* script, then put them down on the desk and looked at Ben. "It's so strange and sad, this man who knows so much, who knows Sanskrit so well that he's actually doing the work of the professor of Sanskrit at this university. And there he is, on a night like tonight, sleeping under a stairway in Philosopher's Walk, drunk. And you, who speak Sanskrit like it was your mother tongue ... It's so bizarre and tragic, so ... wrong."

She looked at him with love and pity, and he returned the look.

"You know," she continued, "there is this thing called the Transitional Year Program—its office is just down St. George here—for people who didn't complete high school. We could easily get you into that ... "

"Aditi," he said, sadly and earnestly, "I am so sorry you love me so much. You can never understand how terrible I feel about what your love has cost you." He felt his eyes shining. "But we'll get you out of this. I swear it. *idaṃ satyaṃ bravīmi te,* I tell you the truth."

5

Ben felt the drag of gravity on his guts as the elevator, much more rapid than the one in the Robarts Library, propelled him upwards to the thirty-third floor. The scrambling red numbers flashed through their changes in the digital display above the door: *fifteen … twenty … twenty-five …* When had he last been here? About two months ago, he thought. Thank god there was no one else in the elevator today. Ben had learned early on in his decade on the street how to make himself "pass," yet even though he didn't stink like the homeless person he was, his vaguely bohemian appearance would be enough to arouse suspicion and mild disgust in such an atmosphere of rarefied poshness.

Thirty-three.

The elevator stopped with an almost imperceptible bump, and the door whispered open to reveal a soft-lit windowless carpeted hallway lined with doors. He walked to the end and knocked on the last door on the right.

Within a minute it opened, and in the gap appeared an Indian woman in a Western-style dress, obviously very old, but moving without the sluggishness of old age.

"Come in, Ben," she said, and he followed her in and closed the door behind him. "The professor will be with you in about five minutes," she said as she led him through the spacious apartment, through a dining area and towards a cluster of furniture by a long window. Her movements were strikingly youthful, her English unaccented. "Would you like something to drink? Or to eat?" she said as they reached the seats by the window, which looked out over the expanse of Lake Ontario, a miles-wide margin of white ice followed by shining open water as far as the horizon.

"Uh, if there's coffee, that would be nice. Black," Ben replied. He wasn't hungry: with freezing hands and misted breath, he had eaten an entire loaf of dense wholegrain bread while walking along the deserted windswept parkland that fringed the lakeshore as far as the mouth of the Humber River, where this monolithic apartment tower stood in striking isolation.

She went to the kitchen, and Ben put his knapsack down beside one of the enormous padded armchairs and went over to the wall of glass. Directly below his feet was the rocky shore assailed by massively heaped buckling ice, and to his left, the black pool of water where the Humber ran into the frozen lake. Further to the left, the shore along which he had walked led back past Parkdale's sparse apartment towers to the thrilling apparition of the CN Tower, the city centre's aspiring cluster of glittering skyscrapers, the islands, the harbour, the infinite urban shore.

This was the only such grand vista he had ever seen as an adult, not having seen the sea, or mountains, or prairie, or tundra, or any vast natural expanse since he had left his childhood home at fifteen. What he remembered of that region's relatively humble natural beauty, and of the prairie, sea, and mountains that he had seen as a child lacked the lustre of awe in which they would have appeared now to his soul deepened by maturity and suffering. This rare sight of the city from above, with its whispers of infinity, always troubled him deeply with the earliest stirrings of a regret that he was not yet old enough to consciously feel, but which the events of his life darkly intimated. It was really the losses of Aditi, seven years older than him, that had begun to make him aware of his own. And her losses were his fault.

"Good morning, Benjamin."

At the sound of the patrician British voice, Ben turned his head to see Professor Chamberlain. He was bald-pated and white-bearded, sad-eyed, small and frail in his maroon dressing gown, and his hands were folded over the golden knob of his wooden cane as his wife pushed him slowly forward in his wheelchair.

Ben turned towards him. "Good morning, Professor."

"How goes the battle?" asked Chamberlain, as his wife parked him and went to the kitchen. "There is really just the one battle nowadays, isn't there? Aditi's battle? With you and ... Moksha, Moksha Das, as her allies."

Ben sat down in the armchair. "The battle. It goes on," said Ben, "on the same two fronts. Moksha and I are translating and annotating this extremely boring text—boring for me, anyway—the *Yogayuktadīpikā,* and that frees Aditi to work on her dissertation. She estimates that she should be finished within six months, if Boylan doesn't wake up and take a renewed interest in thwarting her."

Chamberlain's wife returned and put a tray with two coffees on a low table. "Thank you, Pallavi," said Chamberlain, "I can reach that from here." She retired.

"What is Boylan's current condition?" Chamberlain asked.

"He's still unconscious or semi-conscious most of the time," said Ben. "He's remarkably unobtrusive, at this point, not like that period a couple of years ago when his final descent began, and he was causing quite a lot of trouble in the department, collapsing in the halls and picking fights with people. Now he stays in his office, when he comes to the department. He's so quiet that people don't even know he's there, because most of the time he's lying stupefied on the floor. It may have something to do with a change of drug. It looks like he's using some kind of hallucinogen these days. Maybe he isn't drinking at all anymore." Ben lifted his coffee and sipped.

"Ah, tenure," said Chamberlain, smiling ironically and looking out over the lake's almost blinding brightness. "It's always a gamble. If we had known … "

They paused. Then Ben continued, "As I mentioned to you in my last email, Aditi had a great success in October at a conference at the School of Oriental and African Studies in London. Her paper caused a sensation, and she met some important people. She had to get the money together herself for the conference and trip. We knew from past experience that if Boylan found out about it, he would not only refuse to apply to the university for funding, but would do everything he could to prevent her from going. So that paper was published in the proceedings, of course, and she's had two others published in major journals. The first one appeared in *The Journal of American Indology,* and it went unnoticed by Boylan. In retrospect, this was not really very surprising—I'm sure he hasn't even read a newspaper in years—but we were very scared when she submitted it. She had just reached a point where she couldn't stand it anymore, she had to start taking risks, because there was almost nothing left to lose. And thank god she did, because the risks have been paying off. She published another paper, went to this conference. People know who she is now. She's recognized as an important upcoming talent, and major universities have postdocs and professorships ready for her when she's finished the PhD … Unless something goes wrong … "

Chamberlain was still looking out over the lake. "Yes," he said, "I remember much of this from your last email—you know I don't often read my emails. I'm very happy for Aditi. I've been very impressed with everything you've told me about her over the years. Perhaps ... I'll find the strength to help her in the future, but happily, it sounds like she won't need my help, at this point."

He paused, moving his gaze from the lake to the floor in front of his feet before speaking again. "Professor Ian Boylan is a sick, evil man. Through his invidious machinations, psychopathic antics, and breathtaking professional misconduct, he has single-handedly destroyed Sanskrit studies at the University of Toronto. We had one of the largest, greatest Sanskrit departments in the world when we made the enormous blunder of hiring this buffoon, swayed by the bombastic lies in his CV. And one by one, over several years, he drove our brilliant faculty away, gathering whatever power was left into his own hands—though for a time, one of us stooped to engage with him, and came close to beating him at his own ruthless game. It's always surprised me that no one in Edmonton warned Aditi of the situation in Toronto, but the University of Alberta was as much of a backwater as the University of Toronto has become, so far as indology goes, so I suppose there was really no one there who knew. And then, of course, she was unable to escape even when she finished the MA."

Ben looked out over the lake.

"It's a great tragedy," Chamberlain went on, "a very cruel fate. What is it that the two of you always say? *daivaṃ hi balavattaram*—fate is stronger. I have always wished there were more I could do to help. But now it is looking like she will finally prevail, without my intervention."

"The last great moment of peril will be the viva," said Ben. "The way things are going, we should be able to quietly slip the dissertation under his nose. So long as he doesn't know about her publications, and about her consultations with senior scholars at other universities, he won't even read it. But the viva situation offers the possibility of a kind of drama he might find irresistible. He would love to toss that kind of surprise at her. And then it would be her against both her supervisor and her co-supervisor. Chen is useless, and neither knows nor cares what Aditi's dissertation is about, so she'll just follow Boylan, whatever attitude he takes. He could oppose anything and everything, even demand a complete rewrite."

Chamberlain was looking down, his expression serious. "None of the senior scholars Aditi has met has been willing to replace Chen as her co-supervisor?" he asked.

"There's been no point in asking them," said Ben, "since even suggesting such a thing to Boylan would be suicide, and it would be impossible to do it without his approval. If he even knew that she's been talking with other scholars ... "

Chamberlain nodded.

"There *is* one person I can think of ... the *only* person," he said softly, as if to himself, apparently troubled, remembering. "But I don't know where he is." He gave his head a sharp, tight shake, and looked up. "We shall have to see what fate offers," he said, "and for the time being, hope for the best. No problems with your card, by the way? With the authorities?"

Ben shook his head, smiling.

Chamberlain took up his cup and finished his coffee, and Ben did likewise. Chamberlain's wife appeared from the kitchen and took the cups.

"There are a few passages that I want your opinion on," he said to Ben. "They're in a forgotten *kāvya* of the seventeenth century. No translation, not even a commentary in Sanskrit or any other Indian language. *Devilishly* difficult. Would you wheel me into the study?"

This room also looked out over the lake. A large desk faced the window, and bookshelves covered two of the walls. A stone sculpture of an almost nude *apsarāḥ,* a celestial nymph, tall as Ben's shoulder, stood to the right of the desk.

"Here's the *kāvya*" said Chamberlain, taking up a fragile old volume that lay open in the centre of the desk and putting it into Ben's hands. "This is the only printed edition, 1931, one of the dozens of late *kāvyas* I've been reading in recent years for the last volume of my history. Nobody reads them anymore, not in India, not anywhere. I'm the first one in centuries to be reading most of them. It's thrilling, a new frontier. As with any literature, most of them are dull, a few are execrable, and a few are masterpieces. This one is a masterpiece. Here are the passages that have stumped me," he said, drawing a hard-covered black notebook into the centre of the desk. "As always, your insights may be valuable."

Ben was perusing the book, murmuring one of the poem's verses to himself. He put it back down on the desk and took up the notebook, leafing through pages filled with stanzas and fragments of stanzas in handwritten *Devanāgarī* script, with words underlined here and there. Looking at the most recently copied passage, he said, "I think this has to be a printing or copying error." With his finger on one line, he bent down to show the page to Chamberlain. "This might not be a present participle. If you just amend *tu* to *nu* ... I think it all comes together."

Chamberlain looked at the passage, silently mouthing a few words to himself. "Yes ... I think you're right," he said, beginning to smile. "I wouldn't have thought of something as simple as that."

"I'm not at all sure I'm right," said Ben, "but this is what immediately occurs to me. I'll go through these pages right now and just put down these impressions."

"Yes, that will be good," said Chamberlain. "That's been a great help in the past. And as usual, you will of course be credited. Readers of the last volume may have begun to wonder about this non-doctor Benjamin Doheney non-PhD."

Ben sat down in a nearby armchair and began going through

the pages of the notebook with a pen from his jacket pocket, while Chamberlain sat looking at the lake across the vast desk. After some minutes, Ben finished and handed the notebook to Chamberlain, who leafed through the pages, nodding and commenting from time to time. "Yes, of course." "Yes, why didn't I think of that?"

At last, laying the notebook on the desk, he said: "I must make my usual comment that it is a great shame that your talent is ... not exactly *going to waste,* but not being fully realized because of your isolation. You wouldn't necessarily have to earn degrees in order to find some place in the culture of Sanskrit scholarship. I am still a powerful man."

"My future is absolutely dependent on Aditi's," said Ben. "If she lives through this PhD, I'll follow her wherever she goes. As long as I live, however I'm living, I will always be a scholar. I used to live for that, being a scholar. Now, it's just what I am: what I live for is her. If she succeeds, I will be a scholar with her. If she doesn't succeed ... there's nothing for either of us to think about. Her success, her *survival,* is all that matters."

Chamberlain looked down at his hands resting on the knob of his cane. "I believe you have found the path that will lead her to success," he said. "If she faces a challenge at the end of it, I may intervene. But you know that that will be very dangerous for me, and that I have everything to lose. As a scholar, Ian Boylan is a fraud, but as a fraud, he's a genuine master, with a special gift for the art of blackmail—as Aditi knows." He looked up at Ben. "But at this point, as I say, it doesn't look like Aditi will need my help."

Ben looked out at the lake. "I hope you're right," he said.

6

The young April night smelled of spring, but it was already cold as Ben made his way up Philosopher's Walk towards the Royal Conservatory, where he expected to find Moksha Das already ensconced in the recess beneath his Troll Bridge. Ben was more than usually eager to talk to him tonight: at the tail-end of his reading session in the Robarts Library, he had written a poem, his first non-Sanskrit poem in several months, and was looking forward to hearing the old editor's opinion of it.

Philosopher's Walk was deserted, as usual at this hour, and the Conservatory was silent as he approached its shadowed bulk, the last late-night practicers—pianists, violinists, flautists, singers—having long since been forced to vacate the three storeys of study-cells from which fragmented, obsessively repeated music poured through the windows and onto the Walk throughout the day. He was feeling good after a day of daydreaming labour at the carwash, a massive plate of mixed vegetable and tofu noodles at Buddha's Vegetarian Restaurant on Dundas, two hours of exceptionally smooth reading of the *Mahabharata,* and the unexpected inspiration of this poem. Its arrival would not have been quite as perfect on an Aditi night, since Aditi cared less for poetry than Ben and Moksha, and in any case she was always more or less distracted by anxiety over her doctorate, a years-long ordeal that was hopefully soon to end.

Reaching the Conservatory, Ben turned aside from the paved path onto the recently thawed lawn, cold and damp. The Walk's last dim yellow lamp was ahead, at the bottom of the staircase up to Bloor Street; another was behind. Here, all was more or less dark: trees, bushes, the benches against the Conservatory wall. As he approached the concrete staircase of the fire escape, he saw a shadowed figure standing beside it, someone far too tall to be Moksha. He stopped.

The person was talking: a man's voice, one that Ben recognized.

"If you won't come out on your own, I'll drag you out myself."

That Hindi-accented voice, with the menacing and implacable cheerfulness of the professional bully who loves his job ... Ben restrained his impulse to step forward immediately. He had nothing on him yet.

The figure moved, suddenly and violently, and there was a dull sound of impact, and Moksha's grunt of pain, and the voice: "Get up."

Swiftly and silently stepping forward, Ben emerged from the darkness, standing close to the figure, staring. The cop snapped his head round to glare in alarm and indignation at Ben's shadowed face, a few inches higher than his own.

"What do *you* want?" he said sharply.

"You kicked him," said Ben calmly. "I saw you kick him."

"Who are *you?"* said the cop. The sharp features of his broad face were ugly with hate. "This person is trespassing on university property. So are you."

Moksha had raised himself into a sitting position, and was looking up at them from under his Troll Bridge. Ben glanced at him. He was in the most advanced stage of inebriation, a state in which it would be very difficult to influence his behaviour. His mouth was slack. He was clearly about to begin babbling, and his babbling would reveal too much.

Ben muttered sharply, *"tūṣṇīm āssva," keep quiet.*

Amazingly, despite his condition and his somewhat limited spoken Sanskrit, Moksha got the message: his toothless mouth comically snapped shut.

Surprise and confusion darkened the cop's face, and he began to scrutinize Ben's.

"No, I'm not trespassing," Ben said flatly. "I'm a student at this university."

"Show me your student card," the cop said without missing a beat.

Reaching into his already unbuttoned overcoat, Ben took a cloth wallet from his suit jacket's inner pocket, opened it to reveal a blue and white student card behind its plastic window, and handed him the wallet. The cop suspiciously inspected Ben's photo, several times looked up again at Ben's defiantly serene face, then took the card out from behind the plastic window and turned it over and around, examining it with ostentatious care. Ben put out his hand, and the cop placed the wallet and the card into it, glaring at him through his television-screen lenses.

"You could be a professor or the head of a department," said the cop, "and it would make no difference. Homeless people are not allowed to take up abode on university property. This man is a trespasser, and it is my job to remove him."

"You assaulted him," said Ben calmly. "You kicked him. I saw you."

The cop was looking at him with naked hate.

"And I've seen you before," said Ben.

A touch of fear flickered into the cop's face.

"Moksha Das is my friend," said Ben. "After spending the day in the Robarts Library writing my PhD dissertation, I've come here this evening to relax and have an enjoyable conversation with my friend. Is that all right with you, officer Ganesh Malhotra? Or do you need to consult with your superior Professor Boylan first?"

Officer Ganesh Malhotra stood silent for a moment. Then he stepped back, still looking at Ben with a face dark with brooding revenge, turned, and walked south on Philosopher's Walk. Ben watched him until he disappeared into the darkness.

"What was *that* about?" said Moksha in the nasal, drawling voice that characterized his stage-four drunkenness.

"An old acquaintance," said Ben. "You know, I've mentioned him before: the Indian one, the one who literally kicked me off the steps of the Department of Religion when I was eighteen, and then assaulted me on a bench in Queen's Park in the middle of the night a couple of years later. And Aditi once saw him talking with her professor, so the two old scumbags know each other. You once told me you'd never had any experience with him."

Moksha wagged his head violently back and forth. "What do I know?" he said. "I didn't even see the person who kicked me just now." And this was true. How many mornings had Ben met Moksha in the Scott Mission chapel, bloodied and bruised in some assault of the night before that Moksha couldn't remember. For all they knew, Moksha and officer Ganesh Malhotra might go way back.

Raising himself to sit cross-legged, Moksha reached into the darkness of the recess under the concrete staircase, brought out the familiar juice bottle, twisted off the cap, and took a swig, the sherry making a delicate little splashing sound as he tipped the bottle back and returned it to his lap. Ben already knew that the enjoyable conversation with his friend that he had been so looking forward to would have to happen on another night.

"So what are *you* doing here?" Moksha slurred. "I had given up on you for tonight. I assumed you must be porking your girlfriend ... what's her name ... *Aditi.*" He laughed his sniffling drunken laugh, grinning toothlessly. "I can never get used to these Indians with their names of gods and goddesses. Aditi mother of the gods, mother of the sun, and her boyfriend Benjamin Doheney." An extended burst of sniffling.

"No, I'm outside tonight," said Ben. "I pork Aditi Monday, Wednesday, and Friday, and Saturday if she's still horny." Moksha guffawed, which pleased Ben, though he felt bad about acquiescing to the crass banter into which Moksha always tried to drag Aditi, a veiled expression of hostility to his victorious rival. "Other nights, she works on saving herself from the clutches of that psychopath Boylan."

"I've never really understood what all that is about," said Moksha, slumping his head on his chest as if the effort of holding it up had become too great. "This is the person for whom we translate this *Yogayukta* whatever the hell it's called, right?"

"Right," Ben said, "the person who will then take credit for translating it himself, when it's published as a book, as he's taken credit for our previous work when it's been published in the form of articles in scholarly journals. Though he thinks it's Aditi who's doing all this work, and has no idea that you and I exist."

Moksha remained slumped in the same attitude of dejection or indifferent disgust. Finally he said, "You know that the only reason I'm helping you with this is because I love you and lust after your body." He took another swig. "I must have asked you before why you don't just do it all yourself."

"I don't have time," said Ben. "I actually have to earn a living. I have my own reading and writing. And I don't know *yogaśāstra,* which you do. And that's why this work is good for you, too: to get you out of the morass of alcoholism and despair into which you've sunk, and back to translating the *Yogavāsiṣṭha,* and your other writing." Moksha remained silent, looking straight down at the bottle in his lap. "It'll be *puṇya* for ya, Moksha," Ben said, now jocular, "get ya a better rebirth in a less shitty *loka."*

"Hm, and what about *your* merit?" said Moksha. "What about *your* rebirth in a less shitty world?"

"I'm actually hoping to be reborn in this one," said Ben, almost to himself. "After I've made it a little less shitty."

7

It was evening, a warm May evening, perhaps, perhaps the moment when the last trace of twilight has just vanished in the western sky. Ben was walking up one of his favourite lanes, between Robert and Brunswick Streets, towards the lane-side rear of Harbord Bakery. He was feeling good, feeling the peace of the evening and the season. He could hear a voice, probably his own voice, singing a song which had been a huge hit a few years before:

Take my hand, take everything.
There's nothing I wouldn't die for,
with you by my side.

As he walked, he imagined himself with a guitar, singing this for Aditi, invisibly present. He rounded the corner into the second lane, but the fragrance of bread that usually emanated from the bakery's tall blue plastic recycling bins was absent. Ahead of him, where the lane met Robert Street, was a spot that he loved: the first house on the block, on the right, had a beautiful garden-like front yard with a huge ancient tree and a trellised, ivy-covered gate. He could hear the tree breathing the night breeze. The singing had stopped, and a voice (his voice, probably) was speaking: *What have I done to you, poor child? What have I done to you, poor child?*

A dark figure was standing on the sidewalk in front of the trellised gate, admiring the ivy. The cold hand of fear clutched his heart. He couldn't see the shadowed face. It was a woman. Far back in his mind, there was a scream, perhaps his own. His own voice was saying, *I'm sorry, I'm so sorry.*

She turned her face to him, innocently surprised. It was her—his mother. Nothing but space between the two of them, three paces and she could touch him, or he her. Horror and panic flooded him like freezing water, swirling almost audibly, propelling him violently upward through the waters of darkness, out of the darkness, awake.

He lay on his back with pounding heart, staring up into the night-breathing shadows of the trees. The sky showed no hint of dawn. He shifted onto his side on the wooden bench, so that he was looking towards the church, his mother's church, on whose sanctuary-giving grounds he was sleeping on these lovely May nights. On the grass next to the College Street sidewalk, someone was sleeping on his side in a posture that suggested alcoholic collapse. There was still no traffic on the streets, except for the occasional taxi. The clock tower of the fire station across Bellevue Avenue would not resume sounding the hours until 7 a.m.

The song was still sounding in his mind. He continued to feel himself singing it, fingering the chords.

Take my hand, take everything.
There's nothing I wouldn't die for,
with you by my side.

Beautiful. Vulgar but beautiful, and expressing a simple wisdom that would have saved him and Aditi years ago, if he had been capable of it.

Aditi. Working alone this night, now collapsed in her bed alone. Seventeen, eighteen more hours. His penis stirred and began to stiffen, but he turned from the impulse, not wanting to sully his newly bathed cleanliness and fresh underwear. Shifting onto his back, he saw the sky was now tinted with the first degree of dawn. He closed his eyes and drifted off again.

His shallow sleep was broken by a voice that was marked with the characteristically soft gruffness of the Anishnabe: "Brother, you got a smoke?"

Opening his eyes to full daylight, he saw a man stooping over him, one he knew by sight but not by name, waving twinned fingers before his lips in the street's familiar dumb show of smoking.

"No, sorry, I don't smoke," Ben mumbled.

"Don't smoke! A *skid* that doesn't smoke!" said the man in surprise and disgust, turning sharply away, as Ben sat up and leaned forward with his arms on his knees.

He shook his head, paused to gather his consciousness, then sat back, stretching his arms out on the bench's backrest. Another gorgeous May day. The sharp, rapid note of the clock tower's small bell began to sound: *three, four, five, six, seven*. The Corner, a drop-in centre for the homeless that was nowhere near a corner, would be opening right now on Augusta Avenue, five minutes away in Kensington Market.

Ben stood, hoisted his heavy knapsack onto the bench and then onto his back, and set off south on Bellevue Avenue. Reaching one of the Market's old synagogues at Denison Square, he turned left, walked to Augusta, and crossed to The Corner, which occupied the upper half of a dismal split storefront. Four or five skids were standing on the broad sidewalk outside, smoking and drinking coffee from small styrofoam cups. Inside, he climbed the stairs, entered the already crowded space, and poured himself coffee from an urn on the counter. Two of the drop-in's employees were busy preparing and dispensing wretched sandwiches of white bread and baloney.

On any other day, he would have turned round and gone out to stand on the sidewalk, sipping his foul black coffee alone. But today, above the grumble of the motley crowd seated at tables in the dark space further in, above the fitful shouting and commercial music of the television, there was another sound, surreally incongruous: someone was playing the ancient battered upright piano, which normally stood against the wall ignored, its rounded keyboard covering lowered.

The music was Beethoven, the slow movement of the *Appassionata* sonata, the first variation, music so simple and slow that one who did not know might even take it for the tentative and halting experimentation of a child. But Ben knew, having worked on this piece himself when he was twelve. He looked towards the piano and saw that the pianist was a black man, good-looking, about his own age, whom he had seen on skid row over the years, always quiet and alone, never speaking to anyone, like Ben himself.

Seeing him now, hunched obsessively over the keyboard, watching his hands as if he had not played in years, Ben was struck by the bizarreness of it. Who could have guessed? Who could have guessed that this nondescript skid was actually carrying the sonatas of Beethoven in his hands? But this was by now a familiar kind of epiphany for Ben.

Who could have guessed that the stinking dwarf lying in a drunken coma on the grass of Philosopher's Walk or under the Conservatory fire escape was a published poet and performed playwright, the founder of a still current major poetry journal, once an auditor with a prosperous middle-class income—the first in his working-class family to have one—a onetime Catholic monk and many-times resident devotee in several Canadian Hindu and Buddhist temples, a proficient self-taught musician, a proficient self-taught scholar of the ancient sacred language of India, and a onetime translator of the difficult philosophical poem *Yogavāsiṣṭha*—besides being an impoverished, self-destroying alcoholic and multiple failed suicide?

Who could have guessed that Ben was what he was? And Moksha and Ben were actually not that extraordinary on skid row, which had a substantial subclass of once highly accomplished people whose lives had been derailed by tragic circumstances. Again and again over the years, Ben had heard some bum or bag lady open their mouth and utter words that provided a glimpse of such a tale of shattered potential, superficially incongruous with their present form. Who could have guessed?

And now, here was another one, playing music of Beethoven which in its course from childlike simplicity to virtuosic difficulty almost seemed to be the spontaneous self-expression of the pianist, finding his talent again after who knew how many years of silence.

Ben leaned against the wall with his cup in hand, watching the pianist from well behind him. The low-range notes of the tentative first variation, now nearing its end, barely penetrated the television's shouting and mumbling. Most of the others in the room's catacomb-like dimness showed no sign of having noticed the music yet, though one or two had looked over at the pianist with mild curiosity or irritation, having no idea that the sounds he was creating were anything but the doodlings of a lunatic. Then, like a vision, the second variation began, where the music blossoms into fulfilment and self-confidence, carried forward by the right hand on a stream of loveliness and grace whose radiance even this ruined piano's hollow out-of-tuneness could not smother.

"What the hell *is* this?" came from one of the adjacent tables: it was a man bloated with the unwholesome fat of poverty who was turning a hostile gaze from the television towards the piano. Several others did the same.

The pianist was no longer hunched over the keyboard, looking at his hands. He was sitting up, back straight, with his head slightly raised and eyes closed. At a moment when he shook his head slightly in the trance of creation, Ben saw that his face was streaked with tears. Someone snorted derisively. As the man began the yet more animated third variation, with its rapid notes in the right hand, he again hunched over his hands to monitor them.

By now the music had reached a pitch of beauty that the room could no longer tolerate. "Shut the fuck up!" someone shouted. "We can't hardly hear the TV!" A balled paper napkin sailed over the heads at the table nearest to the pianist and struck him in the back of the head, ricocheting onto the floor.

He started violently, his hands instantly springing from the keyboard, and whirled round in his seat, staring with a face suffused with shock, hurt, outrage. And then he began to scream.

"Chopsticks! Chopsticks!"

He whirled round again, and beat his face and comically flailing hands against the keyboard, screaming.

"Can't even play... Chopsticks! The genius... can't even play... Chopsticks!"

People laughed. Someone shouted, "Shut up, nutbar!"

The bouncer, a frighteningly burly, pretty-faced Anishnabe youth with smouldering eyes and flowing long hair fixed with a bandana, strode out from behind the counter and past Ben.

"Get out," the bouncer said loudly, not quite shouting, stern-faced and unperturbed, advancing on the pianist, who sprang from his seat, knocking it backwards onto the floor, and circled away from him with his back to the wall, his eyes wild.

"Chopsticks! A genius! Can't even play Chopsticks!"

"Out!" repeated the bouncer, standing as if to block the pianist's path of return as he backed like an animal at bay towards the counter and the entrance beyond.

Still standing with his shoulder to the wall, Ben caught his gaze, wild with rage and confusion, as he passed, screaming.

"Can't play! The genius can't play! Not even Chopsticks!"

Laughter and shouts of *Shut up!* followed him as he scrambled out the door. Ben stood shaking his head, saddened, but too jaded to be really stricken. He thought of following him out, but what was the point? The bouncer strode back to the space behind the counter, smirking conspiratorially at the jeerers.

Ben went into the washroom, perched his cup on the top of one of the two small round urinals, took a piss, came out again, re-filled his cup, returned to his place at the wall. Someone else, a typical skid-row hillbilly, had just approached the piano. Standing bent over the keyboard, he began to plunk out a simple rhythmic figure on alternating hands. One of the sitters, a young woman, looked over at him with the excitement of recognition.

"Hey, listen!" she said to her companions. "He's playin' boogie-woogie!"

10 o'clock. Ben softly closed the door of the South Asian Studies library behind him. The hall was empty, like the library itself, and in this safety, he released what he could feel was a richly and densely fragrant fart which immediately surrounded him with its aura. He set off down the hall, rounded a corner, pushed through the first and second doors of the small washroom with its single urinal and toilet. Sitting, he leaned back on the cool perspiring metal of the flushing apparatus.

He was tired. He had slept well last night on his bench beside the church, a good, safe place which he would probably stick to until autumn forced him into one of his protected storefront sleeping places. But he had worked at Malcolm's carwash today, the usual eight mindlessly meditative, draining hours. He had put his head down on the table when he got to the library and dozed for some fifteen minutes, a rest that had invigorated him for a couple of hours.

Now the thought of the impending orgy of two with Aditi animated him like a shot of caffeine. His penis stirred and began to stiffen as he shat, swiftly and easily. The stink that arose—the product of that pricey multigrain bread—was a wholesome one, not the diseased foulness produced by Mission and drop-in food, which he rarely ate anymore, now that he had in effect become a regular salaried employee at the carwash. Why did he even go to The Corner and the Scott Mission anymore, he sometimes wondered. But of course, the answer was obvious: it was his identity as an outsider, as one of the injured and rejected, that continued to tie him to skid row, and always would, despite any superficial legitimacy that money or academics might invest him with now or in the future. The majority of skids were as alien to him as majorities everywhere, but they did at least share with him the common brand of damnedness. And besides, among them there were the prodigies like himself and Moksha, Ben's only true brethren in this world.

With his back against the flusher and his head leaned back against the concrete wall, he had drifted into an open-eyed reverie, Aditi riding him in reverse cowgirl position, her taut, sinewy, coffee-hued ass bouncing up and down on the saddle of his dick with a rhythmic slapping sound. His eyes shimmered into focus, and he looked down to see that he had become rock-hard. He glanced over at the paper dispenser to the right, and noticed his old graffiti in black ballpoint, faded but still indelible after several years, written on the cream-coloured paint of the metal stall wall just beneath the projecting next leaf of paper: *paṇḍito rākṣaso mukhamaithunaṃ karoti narake,* "Professor Demon sucks cocks in hell." He had spent a long time trying in vain to come up with a Sanskrit pun on Boylan, but the man himself would probably have gotten what he had actually written, and at this point, who else was there to get it?

He wiped himself with a leaf of the smooth paper, flushed, untied and removed his right shoe, rose from the toilet, stepped out of the right half of his pants and underpants, limped out of the stall, and twisted the lock of the washroom door. Then, half-sitting in the sink, on tiptoe on his left foot and with his right raised high and pressed against the wall, he washed his anus with soap and water, both a practical measure of street life and an approximation of what he understood to be Indian practice.

His heart froze when he heard the sudden boom of the first door being pushed open into the trapped air of the washroom's tiny antechamber, and someone thudded once and again against the second, locked door. "Shit!" shouted a voice, which was clearly Boylan's. Then the first door boomed again, and again there was silence.

Ben held still for a moment, then resumed and finished washing, re-dressed, unlocked the door, and went out into the empty hall. Boylan must have gone to the washroom on the floor's other side, if he wasn't too befuddled by tonight's drug to find his way around the labyrinthine passageways of the building's uncanny layout, arranged asymmetrically on the principle of the triangle.

Ben returned to the still empty South Asian Studies library, put the fourth and last volume of the *compact edition of the Mahabharata* back on the shelf, put on his knapsack, and went out into the hall, where he paused, then turned left instead of right. Like some of the other floors lower down, at its periphery the fourteenth floor was split into two sub-levels of offices. Concrete staircases of five steps led to upper and lower sub-hallways set off from the main hall by a concrete parapet for the upper one and a concrete wall for the lower, both punctuated by gaps, all in the Robarts Library's brutal battlemented style.

Boylan's office was on the upper row of the west-facing wall. Ben strolled down the hall, and saw through one of the gaps that Boylan's door was open. He approached the gap, stopped, listened, looked both ways. Was Boylan still in the can? He continued walking until he came to the next staircase, climbed it, slowly walked towards Boylan's open door, passed it, glancing inside surreptitiously out of the corner of his eye, stopped, and came back to stand in the doorway.

Boylan was lying on the floor in front of his desk in an attitude of collapse. His chunky, worn face, framed by dishevelled curly white hair, was mashed against the floor, and he was drooling, apparently unconscious. In the region of his crotch, his pants were stained dark with wetness, and a pool of piss on the floor reflected the harsh fluorescent light. The aroma of fresh shit hung in the air. Ben stepped cautiously forward.

"Hey, are you all right?" he said, knowing that there would be no reply. Standing above Boylan, he saw that he had indeed just shat himself: the seat of his pants was stained brown.

Ben looked around the office, which reflected the story of Boylan's decline. On the bookshelves that lined the walls, stray books and papers lay in the gaps between the upright volumes along with styrofoam cups and other trash from the second-floor cafeteria. Similar junk was strewn on the desk around a desktop computer, though there was no visible drug paraphernalia: the professor had retained at least that much good sense.

Ben's mind was racing: this was a now-or-never opportunity to find the pictures with which Boylan had been blackmailing Aditi for years, with which he had cornered her into wrecking her life by staying on to do her PhD in this worthless, ruined department instead of fleeing to one of the top-rank schools that would have welcomed her like royalty. Though Ben himself, too, had been a factor in that disastrous decision. Could he redeem himself now?

But they could be anywhere, and Boylan must certainly have made copies of them, maybe even on the computer, expert as he was in Machiavellian institutional politics, if nothing else. And Ben was in great danger here. If someone looked in at this moment, he would easily be able to talk himself out of it—he was just walking by when he happened to see the professor lying on the floor, etcetera—but if he started rifling through papers and drawers ...

No, he could get away with it, with cunning and caution. And the opportunity was too precious to let pass.

He walked back to the door and softly closed it just as the first announcement sounded from the PA system, the touchingly mournful voice of the black girl who sat at the information desk on the second floor: *The library will be closing in forty-five minutes ...* He was gratified to see that Boylan had papered over the door's narrow rectangular window.

Ben turned and began rapidly looking over the contents of the shelves, running his gaze over the spines of books and the contents of the gaps between. Books in Sanskrit, German, French ... The old fraud had once been at least a convincing bullshit artist in his field, which in itself required a certain level of intelligence, not to mention guile. Newsmagazines, pornography, file folders, sheaves of papers punctuated the rows of books. Various miniature sculptures of Hindu gods, an *akṣamālā,* a long-dead potted plant, empty bottles of various kinds of liquor, including two 750 millilitre bottles of Bushmills Irish whiskey, Ben's own onetime favourite, a sad framed picture, no longer standing, of the smiling professor with a smiling woman who was probably his ex-wife, taken probably twenty years ago, a picture of him as a young man handing a *laḍḍu* to a cautious stern-faced monkey poised on the railing of an Indian house's verandah.

Ben removed and opened one of the file folders. Inside were papers relating to an attempt by the university to fire Boylan about a decade earlier, and his successful contestation of the attempt. Ben leafed through the pages, some of them grouped with paperclips. One paragraph mentioned a large body of official complaints made over the years against Boylan by staff and students, a fact of which Ben was already aware through Aditi.

As he read, he heard from behind him a soft gurgling, spluttering sound: the professor was puking.

"Choke on it," Ben muttered.

He put the folder back and moved on to another that was wedged vertically between books on a shelf at the level of his head. Opening it, excitement and fear surged up in his breast when he saw Aditi's name: these papers related to a confidential complaint that she had made four years ago to the head of South Asian Studies, Narendra Kulkarni, towards the end of her MA program. This had been a *confidential* complaint, which she had made in mortal fear for her academic future, in her despair revealing even the material with which Boylan was blackmailing her, trusting Kulkarni with her secret. Ben was sure that Kulkarni, a good man who hated Boylan, must have kept that secret, and kept the complaint from Boylan's knowledge.

Yet here was the report on it, in the possession of the complaint's subject himself. Ben raced through the pages superficially, since they described matters he had known directly from Aditi since that time: Boylan's grossly unjust assessments of her work, his plagiarization of it, his insulting and sexually loaded language, his frequent intoxication and outrageous antics.

Most of the text related to the bureaucratic mechanics of the complaint process. Unlike innumerable other complaints that had been made against Boylan over the years by both students and faculty, the university had deemed this one to be strong enough to be taken forward, thanks to the charge of sexual harassment.

But Ben already knew that in the end, it had *not* been taken forward, and the last item in the folder was the reason why. Despite its dismal over-familiarity, he felt the nausea of rage and despair well up in his guts when he saw it again, for the first time in years.

It was a photograph that had clearly been taken during the 1993 assault on the Babri Masjid in Ayodhya, India, showing a group of about ten people in the foreground, facing the camera, and in the background, the famous scene of the mosque's dome surrounded and mounted by triumphant Hindutva activists. The people in the foreground were a mixed group of men and women in traditional Hindu attire. They had their fists raised in a gesture of triumph and were shouting. One of the women, a smiling girl in her mid-twenties, was Aditi—Aditi after finishing her BA in Edmonton and before beginning her MA in Toronto. And Ben knew that this was not the only such picture, and that others, taken minutes after this one, were far more damning.

He put it in his jacket's inner pocket.

At this moment he heard Boylan groan and begin to mumble. He looked over at the frail, soiled figure lying on the floor, and felt himself possessed by an almost overwhelming impulse to kick him to death.

Discernible words emerged from the mumbling. "Where ... where are you? Don't go ... don't ... go ..."

Despite everything, an unwelcome spasm of pity contaminated Ben's hate. This man was a monster, but Ben knew that monsters, like everyone, are created by karma, and that in the domain of karma, the chosenness and ownership of what is presumably one's own action is anything but clear. Yet there *was* such a thing as choice and responsibility, deeply mysterious, ambiguous, and compromised though it was. At least Ben was tortured by remorse for the disastrous consequences his actions had had for Aditi. But what evidence of remorse had Boylan ever shown? Even now, these pitiful words reflected only concern for himself.

Ben turned back to the shelves and continued to scan them. If only he had more time! Would he ever be able to get in here again?

The second closing announcement came, muffled, from beyond the door: *"The library will be closing in thirty minutes ..."*

"Dammit," Ben muttered sharply. He turned to the desk, began opening drawers. Here was the drug paraphernalia, both illicit and licit. He recognized the boxes and strips of antidepressants and tranquillizers from his own brief adolescent psychiatric experience. There was a syringe, a crack pipe, a sheet of acid tabs printed with a purple picture of the seated Buddha, and other material that he didn't recognize. Packages of cookies, unopened, half-consumed and stale, or empty. More pornography and other magazines, a few indological journals, more papers, both loose and collected into folders. Ben took out one of the folders, glanced through it: this was one of the instalments of his and Moksha's translation of the *Yogayuktadīpikā*. He put it back and took out another. Opening it to the first page, he saw Chamberlain's name: Anatole Chamberlain. This was a detailed account of his life, beginning with his education at Cambridge and Bonn, moving on to his years of work at research institutes in Varanasi, Pondicherry, and Mysore. There were about twenty pages. Underneath, there were several pages of photocopied photographs. On the first were pictures of a middle-aged Chamberlain, heroically tall and robust, with a number of Indian men and women.

Boylan groaned again.

Why not just take these, Ben thought. Look at this fool, he'll never notice.

He closed the folder, hastily returned to the shelf, and took down the one in which he had found the picture of Aditi. As he did, a stray picture fell onto the floor. He bent over and picked it up. It was Aditi as a teenager, standing in front of a car with an equally young Indian man. Her hair was much larger, unbound and permed in a way she never wore it anymore. Both were smiling, happy to be together. This must be Sujay, who had been her betrothed in Edmonton, and whom Ben had knocked down in Philosopher's Walk. Aditi had already told Ben everything about Sujay, but seeing this picture for the first time, and finding it in the possession of this manipulative wretch, electrified Ben with a violent rage that he was no longer able to master.

He stepped towards Boylan and kicked him savagely in the gut. Boylan shook slightly, groaned, rolled onto his back. His eyes fluttered open, unfocussed and swimming, and looked up at Ben, who recoiled, stepping back and turning towards the door, cursing himself for succumbing to such a dangerous impulse and not making the most of an opportunity that might never recur, and which he could never dare to take advantage of now even if it did.

"The library will be closing in fifteen minutes …"

He left the door open behind him, rushed down the five steps and down the hall, rode the elevator alone down to the nearly vacant second floor, and at two minutes to midnight pushed through the revolving door into the cool sweet spring night.

He was in the shower, and he was already hard.

He came out of the washroom and entered the bedroom, erect. The cool light of the streetlamp bathed him, shadowing his hard sex against his abdomen. She was lying front-down on the bed, legs spread, her head turned slightly to the right to look at him, beckoningly.

They fell asleep without separating, his face pressed against her hair and neck. With the typical randomness of dreams, he found himself in Kensington Market, at night, on his way to one of his old sleeping places, when he met his father.

"Is there room for me there too?" he asked his son.

"Yes," he replied, "but we have to find you some cardboard to sleep on."

So they walked down deserted Augusta Avenue, checking out the cardboard boxes, mainly full of rotting fruit and vegetables, in the trash heaps in front of the stores. A vague dread troubled Ben, but he was not aware that it was connected with his father, though he would have been deeply unsettled and confused if he had met him like this in waking life, for the first time in years. He looked like he was in his forties, the age he had been when Ben had last seen him, before fleeing home at fifteen. Tall, thin, mild-faced.

In one of the boxes, Ben found an intact, firm, unrotten avocado. "What a beauty!" he said, holding it up for his father so that he could join him in admiring it. "What's the etymology of avocado?"

His father said something in Latin, apparently an entire sentence, which Ben was no longer able to grasp.

The vision dissolved as Ben felt Aditi's ass stir and his limp penis slipped out of her vulva, slick with their mingled wetness. She murmured, and he moved off her to lie beside her as she shifted onto her back. The room was quite hot, though cool air flowed in from the open window.

As they lay on their backs holding hands, Ben dropped into sleep again. The thread of the previous dream had not been completely broken, but now his father was gone, and he stood on

Augusta alone, watching Reg Hartt staple his posters to a storefront, boarded for the night, on the other side of the street. Then, oblivion.

When he opened his eyes, the sky outside the window was grey with earliest dawn. He found Aditi's hand still in his, and squeezed it gently. She stirred, turned onto her side to cling to him with arms and legs. He kissed her forehead and caressed her hair and neck.

"Let's go out today," she murmured. "Just walk around. It's going to be a beautiful day, like yesterday. We're up to date with our work. The end is in sight."

"Hm," he said, and kissed her on the lips. "Hm, yeah. We can take the day off. I've got a fair bit of cash. I'll treat ya to lunch at Buddha's."

She smiled. "Where were you before you came here last night?" she asked. "I do believe that these are the first words we've said to each other since you arrived."

"Besides 'Are you safe?' and 'Don't stop!' you mean," said Ben smiling, and she giggled. "I was in the department library. My usual reading." He paused. "Boylan was there."

She was silent. Then she asked, "Where? In the library? That would be remarkable, nowadays."

"No," said Ben. "In his office. On the floor, comatose. The door was open."

"You didn't go in, obviously?" said Aditi, her voice slightly hard with anxiety.

Ben paused. "No."

They were silent. Ben caressed her buttock and hip, and his penis stirred and hardened within five seconds. Aditi meditatively caressed his balls. Her face, laid on his chest, was pensive. He shifted on top of her, pressing his glans against her still-dry labia. She winced slightly.

"It's as good, with me, isn't it?" he murmured, kissing her, studying her eyes. "I'm as good? As your others?" She was moistening rapidly, and he slipped in. "Even though I'm cut?"

"Baby, I've told you so many times," she said, a little breathless as he pulsed in and out of her, "I've never noticed any difference ... If you'd never mentioned it ... I'd have never even thought about it ... And I never do."

"Sujay was uncut ..." murmured Ben.

"Shut up. You're spoiling it," she said, a little sharply, and raised her legs to clutch him round the back.

It was around 10 o'clock when they left the graduate residence and set off west along Bloor, walking as far as Robert Street and then south. It was a splendid spring day, with cool air and aspiring white clouds that gave intermittent relief from the hot sun. Aditi wore her huge rock star sunglasses, jeans, a light jacket, and Ben his broad-brimmed brown cloth hat. He kept his hands in his jacket pockets as they strolled, and she held him by the crook of his right arm, a deceptively submissive-looking posture dictated by the almost comical disparity of their heights.

In this neighbourhood, the Annex, with its preponderance of university-related people, they looked completely at home, a couple of young grad students, or assistant professors, or professionals in one cultural domain or the other, and Ben felt the appeal of this apparent legitimacy, which from a practical point of view was so completely within his grasp. And how he yearned for it, as he would share it with her: the little house, the twin studies filled with books and music, the back yard with two lawn chairs where they would sit together, reading or talking, in the shade of some big old tree, no children (they were agreed on that, thank god), but a dog and a cat with hilarious ten-syllable Sanskrit names, a professorship for her, and for him some kind of worthy and remunerative work in which the talents people saw in him could be realized and appreciated, and which would be his more or less equal contribution to their shared life.

His eyes brimmed with tears. He looked straight ahead, widening them, lest the tears spill, removed his hand from his pocket and caressed her lower back, again looking her in the face and smiling. She smiled back, with a touch of inquiry at the tragic intensity of his expression, but asked nothing, since this was nothing out of the ordinary for him.

As they crossed Harbord, he looked ahead to the spot where he had seen his mother in his dream the night before last: an entirely plausible vision, especially today, Saturday, when he knew she was not at work, and was indeed very probably walking in this very neighbourhood, which was her own neighbourhood, after all. What would happen, at this point, if he did actually see her? *Perfect love casteth out all fear,* he thought, in the language of the religion into which he had been born and from which he had apostasized as an adolescent—*her* religion, not his.

The last time he had actually seen his mother, on College Street, he was already loving and being loved by Aditi. Was it really because of some imperfection in that love that he had been so shattered by that vision, so shaken that for three weeks he had not felt able to read, so shamed and emasculated that he had not felt able to make love to Aditi? Yes, he thought, it would be different now, after so many years of being loved by this woman, and of being taught to feel that he deserved it. By now, he felt an indignant rage on behalf of their love, on behalf of the whipped and humiliated child he had still been on that day, when he had seen again the terrorizing, pursuing face of his oppressor.

It was this rage that made the difference between now and those early days, when the defining tragedy of their relationship had also occurred. As the end of her MA with Boylan approached,

Aditi—not yet trapped in Toronto— was preparing to apply to other universities, if only Ben would agree to come with her. Tortured by the certainty of his worthlessness and the fear that he would drag her down, he had fled the university, disappeared from the scene of their shared life, convinced that he was suicidally sacrificing himself to free her, the woman for whom he lived. But when he had returned weeks later, to his horror—and to his secret, appalling relief—she was still there, having been unable to choose freedom without him.

They had sacrificed their freedom to his fear, and enslaved their love to it. But now that slavery was about to end. Together, they were about to be free. And as for himself, these years of love had finally taught him the truth—that he deserved to be loved—and had fostered the strength he would need to stand before the one who had taught him to hate himself, the next time she should appear before him. He was ready. His eyes scanned the street before them.

"We'll walk past your carwash?" she said.

"Yes, definitely," he said. "You should see it, already. It's been a long time since we came this way together."

At College they walked the one block east to Spadina. At the corner, a few skids stood against the white cliff-like wall of the bank, or headed towards the Scott Mission, just to the north on Spadina, for the 11 o'clock sitting.

"The Mission is just up this way, isn't it?" said Aditi. "Can we just go up, for five minutes? I want to see it again."

They strolled north, past the Waverly Hotel, once the boozy home of Ben's early hero, the skid row poet Milton Acorn, and now a drug and prostitution den owned and operated by a family of Punjabis like Aditi, where in the early days of his job at the carwash, before he had met Aditi, he would splurge from time to time, and blow several days' pay on a room for a week of relatively spa-like rest and relaxation.

The air was already heavy with the Mission's characteristic atmosphere of bad cooking and stinking human bodies. Still linked to Aditi, Ben paused in front of the Silver Dollar Room to read the names of upcoming bands on the poster board, as skids young and old, mostly male but some of them female, stood around or moved about. The two of them moved on, past the Mission's mirrored windows, towards its main entrance. Ben was uncomfortable with the idea of *looking*.

"Is that ... Moksha?" Aditi asked.

Ben looked up to see Moksha hurrying across the street from the large circular island of manicured land to the Mission's north, the grounds of an impressive old university building round which the avenue parted and flowed as Spadina Circle, joining again to the north of it.

Approaching the Mission's entrance, Moksha recognized Ben. "Oh, hello," he said, with the usual friendly upturn of his voice at the end of *hello,* pausing to stand in front of Ben and Aditi, nodding genteelly to Aditi. Ben recognized in his voice the characteristic tone of his sobriety, a reserved cordiality thinly covering a crackling potential irritation.

"Hello, Moksha," said Aditi with genuine friendliness. "It's been a while since we last met."

"Yes," said Moksha, who almost certainly did not remember the last time they *had* met, all three of them: a pleasant evening last September in Philosopher's Walk, when Moksha had been smashed but charming, a miraculously unlikely combination owed, no doubt, to a tenuous foothold on good sense that made him anxious to avoid outraging Ben by directly exposing Aditi to his usual envious salaciousness.

"Yes, it's been a while. Ben should bring you over to the Walk one of these evenings, so we can all catch up. But ... I've got to move or I'll be late for the 11 o'clock." He bowed slightly to Aditi, smiling with mouth closed, glanced up at Ben with a sharp and mysteriously significant eye, then hurried past them towards the Mission doors.

Ben and Aditi turned and began to stroll back south. A few of the skids who were lounging and smoking on the Mission's rail-enclosed porch looked curiously at Ben, possibly recognizing him, possibly marvelling a little that this aloof, pretty youth whom no one really knew was, after all, heterosexual, and had somehow managed to score this gorgeous, respectable looking brown chick.

As they passed the Silver Dollar again, a man Ben knew slightly, a wiry, rather neanderthalic but intelligent chap of about his age, walked past and said, loudly and admiringly, using the title with which he always hailed him, "Hey Pro-*fess*-or! Got a girlfriend!"

Aditi giggled and tightened her grip on his arm. Then she said thoughtfully, "You really are at home in this world."

"It must seem so," Ben replied. "It's probably truer than I want to realize. Intellectually, I feel so deeply alienated here, so bored. And I feel so at home in the library—so far as the books go. But the students, the people: a far deeper gap separates me from them than from ... this scum, this trash, these skids, of whom I am absolutely one. And the thing is, too, that there are others like me here—Moksha, but others too: double outsiders, because we're both rejects of the middle class intelligentsia and freaks amongst the damned. But there are enough of us that we form a small but permanent subspecies of skids."

He paused, afraid that he had already gone too far. "But ... I couldn't actually *stay* here, not even if I hadn't met you. Even now, I don't go to the Mission anymore. Even if I hadn't met you, I would eventually, now, be moving upwards, a little, to the simple and frugal life that suits me, at the bottom of the working world: a menial job, an apartment full of books ... maybe a girlfriend, from time to time, though I've never met any girl in this *loka,* this world, who wouldn't have quickly tired of me."

They had reached College, and were waiting for the light to change. It changed, and they began to walk across.

Aditi said, "I know how you used to worry about the disparity, the strangeness of our relationship. And I know you've realized, at this point: I've felt for a long time that you're not afraid anymore. It was written in our destiny, Ben," she said, reviving a phrase that she had used often in their early days, which reflected the karmic fatalism of her birth religion.

Ben was struck by how strange and incongruous it sounded now. How much was left of her belief? How deeply she had changed and changed again over the years since her adolescence, travelling from the mild traditional piety in which she had been raised, to a fanatical radicalism that had shocked and alienated her family, on to the bitter apostasy whose steady deepening Ben had witnessed. But something of the old *dharma* was still left in her, something so deeply fundamental and inescapable as to be almost invisible to her, if not to him. Something was always left: Ben knew this well. And what remained of her *dharma*—a quiet kernel of faith burnt down to its essence in the purifying fire of her disillusionment—resonated with the youthfully idealist philosophy that he had constructed in his solitary study of the ancient texts, and this shared spirituality formed one of the strongest fibres of their love.

Proceeding down Spadina, passing Chinese restaurants that were the outliers of Chinatown to the south, they reached Malcolm's carwash at the corner of Oxford Street. At that moment a car had just come through the mechanical rollers and brushes and was parked on the sidewalk, where Ben's colleagues were wiping it dry with rags. Larry, a troll-like, mildly hunchbacked middle-aged man in a red lumberjack shirt and knit winter hat, was standing at the side of the car exit, holding his rag.

"Ben!" he said, his sullen and scowling features brightening as much as their nature allowed. "What are you doing here? *This* is your girlfriend? Holy shit!"—these last words uttered with a hushed incredulity and wonder that Ben found simultaneously hilarious, touching, and deeply gratifying.

"No, this is just an escort I rented for an hour to impress you guys," said Ben. The three men working on the car looked up, smiling with similar astonishment. "Aditi, the guys. Guys, Aditi," he said. She smiled.

Malcolm, a tall Jamaican in his thirties, approached from within the building's sepulchral darkness. "Ben," he said. "This is your lady? Pleased to meet you," he said to Aditi. "I've been thinkin' of makin' this guy my partner, he's been here so long." He laughed softly, glancing at Ben with what might have been a conspiratorial smile of congratulation. "Out for a walk?" he continued. "Beautiful day."

"Yeah, we're goin' down to Buddha's to eat," said Ben.

"Ah," said Malcolm, turning back to Aditi. "I guess you're vegetarian too? You're Indian?"

She nodded.

"I'm *West*-Indian," he said, with another soft laugh. "See you Monday, Ben," he said, slapping him on the shoulder.

At Baldwin they turned into Kensington Market, still uncorrupted by gentrification, walked past storefronts with their tables of wares—fruits and vegetables, dried fruits and nuts, fish—traversed the park, and reached Dundas via sidestreets and lanes.

The yellow sign hung over the street, just in front of the hostel for destitute women: *Buddha's Vegetarian Restaurant/ Hong Kong Style/ founded 1991*. This had been a precious find for Ben when he was graduating from vegetarianism to veganism, then still unknown to him by that name. Even now, the place had not been "discovered," and as usual, there were no non-Chinese faces in its narrow, no-frills space. Round one of the larger tables sat a group of old women, probably just come from the nearby Buddhist temple on Bathurst, who shouted at one another in Cantonese as they worked on an enormous bowl of noodle soup crowned with vegetables and tofu, ladling it into their individual small bowls. At one of the small tables, a young couple sat across from each other, sipping jasmine tea and talking in Cantonese as they waited for their emptied bowls and plates to be cleared away.

As soon as Ben and Aditi sat down at one of the small tables, a waitress, late middle-aged with curled grey hair, brought menu cards, a slip of paper and a pen, chopsticks, and a white ceramic pot of tea with a rushed but pleasant greeting of *"Ha, ya, hallo."* Ben poured steaming tea into their two small ceramic cups as Aditi perused the menu, in Chinese with sometimes bizarre English translations.

"I think ... I'll leave the ordering up to you," she said finally.

Ben glanced over his menu card, and wrote down three items on the slip of paper, which the waitress immediately retrieved. *"Aha, ya, thank you."* She quickly came back bearing a plate with a thick sheet of crispy, succulent, yellow-brown material cut into narrow strips, and a tiny bowl of brilliant red chilli sauce. Aditi looked doubtfully at the disturbingly meatlike object before her as Ben immediately took up chopsticks, skillfully pulled off a strip of "imitation roast duck," touched it to the chilli sauce, and devoured it. "Oh god," he said, "I never get tired of this food. *Amṛta!"* (using a Sanskrit word for the ambrosia of the gods). Noticing Aditi's hesitancy, he said, "It's not meat! It's made of tofu. We've had this before."

She picked up the chopsticks, fumbled with them a bit. "I

would really rather not have to ask for a fork," she laughed.

"Here, like this," said Ben, holding up his sticks and rapidly clicking them together several times as if they were his own fingers. "Position them like this."

She studied his hand, imitated the hold, and tentatively but determinedly pulled off a strip of the tofu duck. "Hm, it's great!" she said, chewing. "Yeah, I remember this stuff."

The waitress brought a bowl of red hot-and-sour soup, then a plate loaded with thick fried noodles topped with mixed chopped vegetables and mushrooms large and small. Ben ladled the viscous liquid into one of the two smaller bowls, and took a spoonful, still in ecstasy. *"Amṛta, amṛta!"*

Manipulating the chopsticks with great care and attention, Aditi succeeded in grasping a large, slimy black mushroom and slowly guiding it towards her mouth. Then she lost control of the sticks, which clattered onto the plate and table as the rubbery mushroom bounced into her lap. Ben ducked and held his hand to his mouth, suppressing a burst of laughter that would have sprayed Aditi and the vicinity with hot-and-sour soup, and she was laughing too as she vigorously wiped with her napkin at the slime on her jeans. It was funny, and beautiful, a beautiful scene on a beautiful day. They were in love, they were happy, and on the verge of a future that promised the long-awaited fulfilment of their happiness. They knew that everything was about to change.

8

"Sweet Jesus!" said Moksha, sitting cross-legged under his Troll Bridge. "I haven't seen this much acid in one place since San Francisco in 1967."

Despite being first-stage drunk, he said this in a moment of ludicity that made him sound cold sober, so great was his astonishment at seeing the complete page of Buddha-stamped acid tabs in the open folder that Ben held beneath his gaze.

"You're *giving* me this?"

"Yes, but ... it's very illegal, isn't it?" said Ben hesitantly.

"Forget about *that,*" said Moksha, with both hands lifting the page with extreme gentleness and wonder, as if he were handling the ur-manuscript of the *Yogavāsiṣṭha*. "Sweet Jesus!" he said again, almost whispering. "There's enough here to keep me in *samādhi* until I die of old age!" He looked at Ben, his face an almost comical portrait of amazement. *"Where* did you get *this?"*

"It was in this folder that I took from Boylan's office, like I was telling you," said Ben. "I saw other pages like this in the same drawer. I had no idea that there was one of them in this folder, which contains material about Chamberlain—that's why I took it."

"*Other pages* like this?" said Moksha incredulously. "No wonder the guy is lying face-down on the floor. And you're giving this all *to me?* Look, a single tab of this is your *salvation!* You've been mad for as long as I've known you, and *miserably* mad. *This is the stuff* that will give you *mokṣa—liberation!*—from your madness! Come on, drop a tab with me. I'm an excellent guide, I've done acid about twenty times over the years. Believe me, this is the stuff that will *free* you—if you do it with *me*. This one page is equivalent to a *lifetime* of sitting meditating in a cave in the Himalaya."

"Moksha, I just can't," said Ben with a sad smile. "I know my madness. It's not the type that can be dissolved by an acid trip. I'm extremely delicately balanced. I would just go screaming mad, never to return. I might even kill myself, kill you, kill anyone."

"You don't know what you're talking about," said Moksha, shaking his head. "It's precisely people like you who need this stuff most, you people who live in your delicatedly poised card-castles of self-protecting bullshit. I'll be your Virgil. With my help, you can climb out of the hell you're stuck in."

He reached back into the darkness under the Bridge, dragged out his shoulder bag, rummaged among its clinking mass of books and bottles—from which Ben had known all manner of unexpected objects to emerge—and brought out a yellow plastic Coles bag containing a large pristine hardbound volume, *The Himalayas: Land of the Gods*. Folding the page of Buddhas in half with tender care, he placed it between the two halves of the opened book, and returned the book to its bag.

"Well, I don't know about you, but *I'm* gonna drop a tab of this tonight," he said. "You can come along. I don't exactly need a Virgil, and you couldn't be my Virgil anyway, but I haven't done acid in twenty years, so I could use the company."

"But ... isn't it a pretty serious undertaking, dropping acid?"

asked Ben with concern. "I mean, all that jumping-off-rooftops, *I am Indra* stuff ... People can just completely lose touch with common reality, right? They can even kill themselves and other people. I've heard about the Leary book, the thing about setting limits before a trip: *I will not harm another, I will not harm myself.* That sounds just terrifying, Moksha. This can't be the kind of thing you can do while walking around outside."

"That doesn't happen to me," said Moksha with a superior smile. "That only happens to stupid punks who think acid is just an especially potent party drug. Idiots. They *should* jump off the roof, and I guess they do it precisely because acid holds up the mirror to their own vacuous worthlessness for the first time. But now that you mention it ..." He looked down in a way that suggested disappointment in Ben. "Yes, it wouldn't be a good idea for *you* to do a tab tonight, out here. *You* would be ... a lot of work. We would have to go out to Douglas's place on Woodbine for a few days, or better, up to my *āśrama* on his property on Lake Simcoe. *That* would be ideal. We really should plan to do that. I'm telling you," he said, looking up at Ben seriously, "this is a tremendous opportunity for you, and I want to help you seize it. Not poetry, not Sanskrit, not philosophy, not sex, not booze: none of this can heal a soul as sick as yours is, none of it can do more than merely bandage the gaping, stinking wound. It's all just flight and denial: you're running from the demon of the void, inside your own head, and you'll never find true peace and happiness until you turn and face it. But someone like you can't do it alone, or else, yes, you'll be devoured, you *will* go screaming mad, never to return, you *will* kill yourself. The encounters with the void that you've had already were *nothing* compared to what you're gonna see when you do this. They weren't even encounters, they were mere whispers, the faintest intimations. And even so, they were so overwhelmingly terrifying to you that you couldn't bear to live with what they implied, what they meant. *This* will give you the courage, it will give you access to the spiritual resources that will allow you to face the void and survive—and *triumph*. To become the man your destiny intends you to be. To realize your *svadharma,* your true nature."

Moksha had not taken a swig from his juice bottle in some time, and the intense earnestness of this appeal, delivered in a voice from which the tell-tale nasality had almost completely disappeared, reflected the thinning of his inebriation.

Ben was touched, and irritated. "Moksha," he said gently, "you've been reading religion and philosophy since you were six years old. You've spent years of your life deeply and earnestly studying and translating one of the great books of Hindu philosophy, which you call a handbook for enlightenment. You've practised what you call yoga for years. And you've dropped acid twenty times, which you're telling me is a royal road to enlightenment and freedom. And look at you. With all due respect, look at you."

Moksha bowed his head, probably less in shame than in resignation to the evident futility of his attempt to persuade Ben.

"But go ahead," said Ben. "Drop a tab. The night is young. Assuming that you really are the old hand you claim to be, and that this stuff won't make you completely unmanageable, I look forward to hanging out with you for a while, as usual."

Moksha was silent, sitting cross-legged and with head bowed like a despairing yogi, his chin nearly touching his chest above his *akṣamālā,* his Indian rosary-necklace. Then he took his juice bottle from his jacket pocket, checked that the cap was twisted tight, put it into his shoulder bag, again took out the book wrapped in the yellow Coles bag, and opened it to the page of Buddhas. He paused for a few moments, looking down at the page.

"You know," he said, "quite apart from *samādhi* and *mokṣa* and all that, you could have made a fortune just selling this stuff."

Then he carefully detached one of the stamps along its perforated border, placed it on his tongue, and closed his mouth.

He sat in silence for about a minute as Ben watched anxiously.

"What are you expecting?" he said finally, looking up with a sly smile. "Eyes rolling up in the head? Foaming at the mouth? Instantaneous dissolution into the eternal Brahma?" He grinned. "The eye of Shiva opening in my forehead?" He laughed softly, in a way that simultaneously conveyed both a profound peace and a trembling, volatile excitement. "You know enough about this stuff to know that it doesn't work that way. Basically, it's like karma: you get what you expect, what you're ready for."

His voice was strange. Ben had never heard him sound quite like this. The nasality and slurring of drunkenness were gone by now, but instead of the prickly reticence that normally characterized his sobriety, there was a benign openness, apparently free of the negative side effects of alcoholic release.

Moksha raised his head and looked around. "What a beautiful night!" he said softly. "I want to walk. You like walking. Let's take a stroll and see where it leads us."

Moksha raised himself to his feet and hoisted his bag onto his shoulder. They set off down the Walk at Moksha's usual pace, which Ben always found frustratingly slow. But tonight he felt more envy than frustration, as he glanced from time to time at Moksha in what seemed to be his free-flowing communion with the loveliness of the cool spring night. A young couple coming from the other direction paused in their conversation and looked at them a little curiously as they passed. Moksha looked directly at them, smiling beatifically, another weird deviation from his usual closedness.

At the bridge across the ravine to the music faculty, the site of Ben's chivalrous defence of Aditi years before, Moksha stopped.

"Some music would be good right now," he murmured, looking at Ben.

"Music is always good," said Ben stupidly, "but I highly doubt that there could be any rehearsals going on at this hour."

"What is the hour?" said Moksha.

Ben was about to look at the watch strapped to his belt, when Moksha repeated "What is the hour?" and Ben realized that the hour he meant was not the time of day.

"At what hour will we finally understand that the truth we are forever seeking is not to be found in books," Moksha said as softly and fluently as gently running spring-water. "It is not to be found in cold solitary analysis in book-lined studies, nor in arid discussion in university seminar rooms and bohemian cafés. It is not to be found in the earnest study of ancient texts in the scriptoria of the temples of the great faiths of the world, nor in mastery of the primeval holy languages of the gods. It is not even to be found in decades of deep meditation on the rugged cave-gouged flanks of the holy Himalaya, nor in self-mortifications in the heart of the ascetics' forest, devoid of men, and haunted by elephants, deer, lions, tigers, leopards, jackals, hyenas, *śarabhas,* rabbits, mice, guinea pigs, vultures, buzzards, eagles, hawks, storks, crows, chickens, bees, wasps, ants, crickets, apes, and bats."

Moksha glanced over at Ben with a benevolent eye.

"At what hour will the lost child humanity finally realize that the guidance she is ever seeking is to be heard in the voice of the breeze of the spring night breathing through the harp-strings of the trees' budding branches"—he stopped and stood; the wind breathed—"and is to be seen in the oceanic depths of the stars"—he looked up—"superficially chaotic, but in reality arranged with ultimate order and significance by the hand of God"—he looked at Ben—"could we but see it."

Ben felt a rising hilarity that he could scarcely master, but at the same time he felt himself being drawn into a vicarious experience of Moksha's state of mind. He felt the world around him beginning to deepen with a not quite visible quality of hallucination, as if another dimension of it—a conscious presence, an *ensouledness*—were becoming perceptible to him for the first time. The breathing trees, the cool flowing night air, the wild looming and retreating shadows, the oceanic depth of the cosmos above thundered inaudibly in his senses like rising water, and an exhilarating sense of the tremendous *significance* of everything, verging on terror, threatened to sweep him away into what he feared might be irrecoverable madness. And he hadn't even taken a tab! If he had ... No, he had been right: he was too fragile for such an adventure. But for Moksha—messed up but not mad, and an old master of this form of recreation—this would be a mere romp in the playground of the psyche. The drug could do him no harm.

Moksha was laughing a deep silent laughter that soon became audible.

"What?" Ben said, smiling in confusion.

Moksha recovered himself and smiled patiently, with a touch of pity. "This stuff doesn't even begin to work until after about an hour," he said, sounding dead sober. "I'm no more stoned than you are—maybe a little less, actually, seeing how into it you seem to be." He began walking again.

"Bullshit!" Ben muttered, frowning.

They continued in silence until they reached Hoskins Avenue, where Moksha paused, then they crossed the street and walked round the corner onto Queen's Park Crescent. They had reached the point where the Crescent branched, and Moksha was about to cross into Queen's Park when a breeze-broken fragment of harmonic sound wafted towards them from Hart House's Great Hall, a wall of shadow behind tall trees. Moksha stopped, and they both listened as more fragments cohered into a tattered fabric of symphonic music.

"It's the Hart House Orchestra," said Ben, "a performance, or maybe a rehearsal." He paused. "I don't recognize this piece. It sounds like it could be mid-period Stravinsky, neo-classical Stravinsky."

"Let's go in," said Moksha.

"Moksha, I would really rather not," said Ben, "not just because you're certainly stoned, despite what you say, but because I hate Hart House, as you know. The guards, the watchdogs ... "

"To hell with 'em," said Moksha softly, turning. "I need music. This is destiny-sent."

Ben reluctantly followed Moksha down the two steps to the paved area in front of the Great Hall. Someone, maybe one of the musicians who had come out for a smoke, had left the heavy wooden door ajar. Ben pushed through the door and held it open for Moksha.

The hallway was dimly lit and deserted, and it echoed with the sound of the orchestra. It must be Stravinsky, thought Ben, one of his symphonies from the thirties and forties he had listened to once and never again. But as uncongenial as the music was to him, this was an *orchestra*. It could be playing anything: simply being in the presence of an orchestra was orgasmic for him.

He had been to Roy Thomson Hall once, years ago, before Aditi, to hear Mahler's Ninth, in the early days of working at the carwash, when he was richer than he had ever been in his life. It had been a transcendent experience and had led to an obsession with Mahler, the composer and the man.

After he met Aditi, he had never found time to go back—she didn't care for Western classical music—though he had occasionally had the good fortune to hear student orchestras rehearsing in the Music Faculty, where he used his fraudulent student card to listen to recordings in the library as often as he could find time. So the sound that now echoed around them in the dimly lit hallway was sonic nectar to him, and undoubtedly to Moksha too, no less an idolator of music than Ben, and by now probably experiencing distortions of sense and consciousness that could only increase the rapture.

Standing at a distance, Ben looked into the first of the Great Hall's two arched stone doorways. The orchestra was set up at the south end, near this door. The conductor was visible, not a student himself but a professor whom Ben had sometimes seen in the Music Faculty, short, rotund, bald, and with a vigorous, focussed conducting style that seemed somewhat incongruous with his middle age and apparently un-athletic physique. Ben led the way down the hallway to the second door, and they entered silently.

The Great Hall was a high chapel-like space of carved stone and wood lit by four dim yellow lamps that hung on long cables from the vaulted ceiling. Huge portraits of unknown worthies of the university's past hung high overhead on the walls, above a painted line of text from Milton's *Areopagitica* that circumscribed the room. The heavy wooden dining tables had been pushed to the walls on three sides, and their wooden chairs had been set in rows, in preparation for the concert they were now rehearsing for. Ben and Moksha sat about halfway back.

The music, now involving the whole orchestra, was nearing what was clearly the climax of the final movement. Ben was looking forward to the end of this piece, and hopefully the beginning of something more appealing. He was at least enjoying the generic orchestral experience: the sense of being surrounded and consumed by complex layered sound, the fascinating mechanics of the orchestra's organism, the conductor's choreographed language.

And Moksha was behaving himself. Perhaps what he had said about the drug's delayed effect had not just been a mean trick:

if Ben hadn't known otherwise, there was nothing in Moksha's silent demeanour at this moment that would have indicated that he was flying high on acid. He sat watching the orchestra with what appeared to be the ordinary careful attention of his sobriety, though from time to time he slightly nodded or shook his head in an odd way, as if he were listening to a lecture whose words he could discern but Ben could not.

The music reached its culmination, marked by the conductor's conclusive slashing gestures and the musicians' emphatically nodding heads. The final *tutti* hung dissolving in the Hall's resonant air for a couple of seconds, the conductor and musicians frozen in their final position. Then, release, smiles, murmurs of approval and mutual congratulation.

"Very nice," said the conductor smiling.

Ben had been assessing the beauty of both female and male musicians, identifying particularly ravishing girls and potential imaginary rivals in the various sections. For the first time, he realized how much older he was than most of the students around him on campus—*kids,* he now thought, this word occurring to him for the first time, with a mild shock. People who noticed him took him to be what he claimed to be when forced to declare himself: a PhD student. When he had met Aditi, at twenty-two, this claim had sounded unlikely, coming from someone who was obviously still so young, as young as these kids before him tonight. Now, at twenty-six, there was nothing suspicious or unnatural about it, but there soon would be if he continued to live like this, as an aging scholar-gypsy haunting the university's dark corners.

The orchestra was not packing up, so the rehearsal was evidently not yet over. One of the first violins, an East Asian kid, had stood up with his instrument and begun chatting with the conductor with a levity that could not completely conceal his nervousness. Ben leaned his head slightly to the right and murmured to Moksha, pointing in the general direction of the likely soloist with a conversationally raised hand: "The next piece is going to be a violin concerto, I believe."

"Why ... why this silence?" said Moksha out loud, perplexed. "There is no silence. Silence is the lie."

The conductor, the violinist, and several of the musicians turned and looked into the darkness towards Ben and Moksha. Could they see them?

"Moksha, for god's sake keep your voice down!" Ben said in a strangled whisper. Moksha turned his head and looked at Ben with the same innocent perplexity. There was no doubt now that the drug had begun to take effect, Ben thought anxiously. What was he going to say next? Or do?

But Moksha merely turned back to the orchestra, which was rapidly recomposing itself for the next performance, Moksha's philosophical question evidently not having been assessed as a threat. The violinist, now quite obviously terrified, had indeed stood in the soloist's position to the conductor's left, and the conductor stood poised above the silent, expectant orchestra. His hands broke into movement, and with the first rhythmic notes in the *pizzicato* double basses and rippling higher strings, Ben recognized the music: the Mendelssohn violin concerto, a piece he loved from childhood, when he had discovered it in his long exploration of his father's large, eclectic record collection. That mournful first theme on the violin, impatiently plunging right in in the second measure itself ...

Despite the young orchestra's embarrassing technical raggedness from time to time, the enveloping sound carried Ben away from his anxiety about Moksha, and in fact, for the duration of the performance, Moksha did not say or do anything to drag him out of his rapture. When the ecstatic final bars of the third movement had sounded, the orchestra broke into congratulatory applause, cheers, and laughter as the soloist, who had been brilliant, staggered forward, exhausted by effort and anxiety, and fell into the laughing conductor's arms, while still holding his violin and bow. Ben cheered and clapped too, and everyone looked with smiles of gratification towards their unanticipated audience of two.

Exhilarated, he finally turned to look at Moksha. Moksha was already looking at him. Ben's enraptured expression faded when he saw his face. He was unable to read it, but he seemed ... troubled. Added to the childish undefended openness that had been there since before the beginning of his trip, there was a chillingly unfamiliar element of fear.

"Moksha," said Ben softly, with concern, "are you going to be alright?"

Moksha paused, and then, in a hilariously significant tone, as if he were making another philosophical observation, said, "I'm just going downstairs to take a leak."

He rose to his feet slowly and carefully, holding on to the back of the heavy wooden chair in the next row as if he were balancing on a girder hundreds of feet in the air. Then he walked out the door in the same slow and careful manner, leaving his shoulder bag on the chair next to where he had been sitting.

Ben watched, and was about to go after him when he heard a woman's voice address him from his left: "How did you like the concert?"

He turned and saw a tall, bespectacled young woman. Beautiful despite noticeably uneven teeth, she had blonde hair drawn back in a long ponytail, and she looked vaguely familiar. She was pressing a viola case against magnificent large breasts smoothly outlined by a tight sweater. Behind her, the other musicians were packing their instruments in the cases they had left on the long dining tables pushed against the walls.

"I loved it," replied Ben, smiling and holding his gaze at face-level with conscious effort. "It's too rarely that I get to hear an orchestra live. This is the first time I've caught a rehearsal here. Which orchestra is this?"

"It's the Hart House Orchestra," she said, with an accent that Ben thought must be Slavic. "It's not very good," she laughed shyly, "not as good as the Music Faculty orchestra, but it's good for practice. I'm in the Music Faculty orchestra too." She paused. "I often see you in the East Asian Studies department."

Yes, Ben thought. He remembered now: he'd noticed her from time to time, but never talked to her, as he never talked to anyone in the department unless spoken to first.

"Yes," he said with what he hoped was not obvious caution, "I'm a PhD candidate there. Sanskrit. And you ... ?"

"Japanese," she said. "Undergraduate, fourth year. I'll be making my career as an orchestral violinist, but I love Japanese and want to keep it up. Maybe I'll apply for positions in Japanese orchestras." She laughed.

About ten minutes had passed by the time Ben managed to get out of the Hall, carrying Moksha's shoulder bag as well as his own backpack. Where could Moksha be, he thought, almost frantic, irritated with himself and the chance that had presented him with such an irresistible distraction. The first place to look was the washroom on the lower level. Hopefully he would still be there or somewhere in between, and hopefully still conscious and on his feet.

As he was rounding the carved stone corner of the echoing stairway, turning onto the second flight that led down to the lower level, he heard a familiar hectoring voice: *"Leave the building immediately."*

Ben felt a spasm of rage and despair. He was picturing the scene that would meet his eyes when he reached the bottom of the stairs. And indeed, there he was, with his back to Ben. A huge man, at least as tall as Ben's six-two, the guard was beer-bellied, sandy-bearded, with broad tinted glasses. He towered over Moksha, who was leaning against the brick wall by the washroom door, stooped, face bowed, wincing resignedly as if his assailant were pounding him with fists as well as words. His pants were stained dark: he had pissed himself. The hallway was otherwise deserted.

Ben advanced swiftly. "*What* is going on here?" he said with restrained fury, almost whispering.

The guard turned his face. "You keep a civil tongue in your head," he said in the same browbeating voice, ever so slightly tinged with surprise. Then, "Do you know this person?"

"This *person* is my friend," said Ben, "and therefore he is a guest of this house."

"Show me your student card," the guard demanded.

"I don't have to show you my student card," said Ben, pointing in his face. "I've been through this with you in the past. *'Hart House is your house'*—isn't that what you people tell us? Isn't it written all over this place? Why should I accept being subjected to a police interrogation in my own house? Why should I have to beg the Hart House Gestapo not to throw out my friend and your guest?"

The guard had now completely turned to face Ben, whom he certainly recognized from similar confrontations in years past. "You are abusing a staff member," he said in the pompous, declamatory tone of stupid people quoting official language, and with a just perceptible shade of tremulous excitement. "Come with me to the front desk. I'm going to have you barred."

"You couldn't pay me to come back in here, you self-important trash," Ben muttered, moving round him and approaching Moksha. "Even the washrooms stink, though I have to admit that they are the best place on campus to get your cock sucked by a stranger, if that's the best you can do. Hart House does at least provide a homey atmosphere for that."

He was giving his rage free rein, and knew that he had already let it carry him too far; as he bent over Moksha, he almost expected to feel the enormous battering-ram hands grasp his shoulders from behind and whirl him round.

"Moksha, are you alright? Did he hit you? What happened?"

Moksha did indeed look as cowed and anguished as if he had been hit, though Ben knew that this was almost impossible. In the Great Hall, he had looked like he was teetering on the edge of an abyss, and no doubt he had tipped over the edge when the guard confronted him.

"Let's just go," Moksha said, not raising his head, speaking very softly, as if he feared that even the sound of his own voice would hurt his ears.

"*Leave the building immediately,*" repeated the guard.

"Oh will you please just shut up, you wretched idiot," said Ben with disgust, gently taking Moksha's arm and beginning to lead him back towards the staircase. Moksha shuffled along like an eighty-year-old man, then took the stairs like a child learning to walk, climbing onto each stair with both feet before attempting the next. Their nemesis followed on their heels, looming over them with clownish menace. As Ben pushed open the heavy wooden door, he half-turned his head to shoot the guard a parting glance of contempt.

"If I ever see either of you in here again, I'll call the university police and have you officially barred," said the guard.

"Oh, drop dead," muttered Ben wearily as the door thudded closed behind them, followed by a ludicrously demonstrative clattering of the lock.

They stepped out of the arched doorway into the cool night. Up the stone stairs to their left, the musicians could be heard chattering and laughing as they came out by the door through which Ben and Moksha had entered.

"Can you carry your bag?" said Ben. "I have your bag."

Moksha stopped, nodded, took his shoulder bag from Ben.

He seemed to be recovering some fluency and awareness, so Ben pressed ahead. "Let's go this way," he said, moving towards the stairs. "That idiot *may* call the cops, and I really don't have the energy for another scene. And you don't have my immunity."

Moksha followed him up the stairs, this time climbing them like an adult. In the area around the upper entrance, a few of the musicians were standing about, talking or smoking, their instrument cases strapped over their shoulders or at their feet, while others left, turning towards Queen's Park Crescent or walking down the steps Ben and Moksha had just ascended. Some recognized Ben and Moksha, and smiled. The Slavic girl, who had told Ben that her name was Anna, was not to be seen, which was just as well, Ben thought.

They strolled back up the Crescent and crossed Hoskins into Philosopher's Walk. Moksha was silent. Could it be that the acid had already worn off? Ben didn't think so: he knew little about acid, but clearly its effect, whatever it was, had made the encounter with the guard traumatizing in a way it would not otherwise have been.

Maybe Moksha had been shocked back into sobriety, for a time, and would soon slip back into whatever state he had been in before, good or bad as that state may have been. Ben could smell Moksha's pissed pants. He glanced over at him. He appeared to be his usual sober self, until he turned his head and met Ben's gaze, and Ben saw a terrible fear and desperation in his eyes, like what he had seen just before Moksha had left the Hall, only much deeper.

And Ben became afraid too: for all that Moksha was evidently a tormented, fragmented character himself, like Ben, and like

Ben's long-lost father, nevertheless Ben had always experienced him as stable, superior and dignified in the ways that really mattered to him, one person whom he could always expect to find in his essentially immutable form, through Ben's own vagaries and breakdowns. Seeing him like this, apparently as confused and frightened as Ben himself had ever been, shook him deeply. What had Ben done to him? If he had known...

"For god's sake, Moksha," Ben murmured, "are you alright?"

"No," said Moksha, again looking straight ahead.

When they reached the Troll Bridge, Moksha put his shoulder bag into the darkness below, got down on his hands and knees, pulled out his cardboard mattress, and sat on it cross-legged, facing outward, as Ben had found him a couple of hours earlier. By now his movements had the fluency of sobriety, but his silence ...

"Moksha," Ben said, crouching, "I don't know what kind of state you're in, but ... do you want me to stay around here for a while? I could sleep on the bench over there." He nodded towards the one against the Conservatory wall.

Moksha shook his head. "No," he said, sounding normal, "I just need to sleep."

"Yes. Sleep," said Ben. "I need to sleep too." He paused. "You know, I know that person, that asshole in Hart House. He threw me out several times, years ago, before Chamberlain got me my student card, and he's come after me a few times in the years since. But he's not the only one, and I never liked the place, its pretentious pseudo-Oxbridge exclusivity, so I never go there anymore ... An *āsura* personality. You know, one of the demonic people. They rule. This is the world."

At this, Moksha smiled slightly. "Yes, this is the world," he said. "But it's not the only one."

Reassured by the banality of this reply, Ben rose and set off south, leaving Moksha sitting there, staring.

9

"You."

Someone addressed Ben from behind as he left the washroom and was walking back towards the South Asian Studies library. He turned his head and saw Boylan standing there, staring intently, pointing at him. Boylan advanced, still staring. His face radiated cold menace. Ben felt a surge of the cold nausea of fear. He turned to fully face Boylan, maintaining without much effort an expression of mild contempt.

"I've seen you here before," said Boylan in his sly, nasal voice, stopping in front of him, looking up at his face, which was the better part of a foot above his own.

Ben had been this close to him before—notably on the day when he had first met Aditi, and on the night when he had almost literally kicked the shit out of Boylan on the floor of his office—but he had never been the object of his gaze like this, and it was an ugly gaze. Over the years that he heard Aditi telling him, often with tears, about this man's tortures and machinations, he had come to think of him as a kind of evil clown, and since seeing him wasted on the floor of his office some weeks before, a minor element of pity had grown up alongside of the loathing, fury, and contempt. But before this moment he had never really, viscerally understood Aditi's *fear.* Because in his present aspect—cold sober, coldly hating, fully availing himself of the aura of his status—Ian Boylan was a fearsome sight.

"That's not surprising," said Ben coolly, "since I'm a PhD candidate in this department, and as such am here all the time."

"A PhD candidate," said Boylan. He looked down, his face fleetingly breaking into a mirthless snicker before he raised his eyes again to look into Ben's. "What's your subject? Who's your supervisor?"

"Sanskrit. Professor Chamberlain," said Ben, holding Boylan's gaze.

Boylan paused. "Professor Chamberlain," he said finally, and again looked down, snickering. "I'm surprised to hear he's still alive, never mind guiding a PhD. Or is he really guiding you? What is actually going on here. Show me your student card."

Ben's face twisted in disgust. "What is this?" he said, staring him in the eye, genuinely outraged. "I'm not going to be treated like this. I don't pay thousands of dollars a year to be interrogated like a criminal in my own department, as if I were some homeless person who'd just wandered in off the street."

Boylan continued to stare up at him, an almost imperceptible shadow of surprise and fury flitting across his face. "You know," he said, with a lilt of ironic levity that was clearly calculated to chill Ben's blood, "you're talking to a senior professor here. This may be the *Kaliyuga,"* he snickered, "but even in the Age of Decline there are provisions in place to deal with a student's openly insulting treatment of a faculty member."

"Oh yeah, I know about such provisions," said Ben, consciously giving himself as much rein as he thought he could get away with. "Like the ones that are in place to deal with a faculty member's openly insulting treatment of a graduate student. Powerful stuff, those provisions. I know about all that."

Boylan looked at him with what was by now naked hate. Then he said, "Say hi to Professor Chamberlain for me. And don't set too much store by your association with him. You know, a university employee was brutally assaulted on campus last night. Paranoia will be running high for a while, and suspicious people will look even more suspicious. And *you* are a suspicious person."

He began to walk off.

"*bhadraṃ te'pi bhavetsvāmin,*" Ben said, sneering: a spontaneous quarter-verse, *Good wishes to you too, master.*

Boylan shot him a murderous look as he rounded the corner.

"A Hart House guard. They found one of the Hart House security guards lying unconscious in the parking lot behind Convocation Hall with wounds to his head. They also found a deep blade wound on his calf. His attacker probably crept up on him while he was unlocking his car and stabbed him in the calf to bring him down, then repeatedly bludgeoned him on the head with a blunt object. He wasn't robbed. He didn't see his attacker. They have no idea who could have done it or why."

Aditi was lying on the bed, leaning her head on her left hand. They were both naked, as usual.

"You don't read the papers, I know, but there was an article about it on the front page of the *Star.*"

Ben was on his back with his head propped up against the headboard. Cool evening air flowed in through the window.

"You look troubled, baby," she said in a voice slightly dreamy with post-coital serenity, reaching over with her right hand and stroking his freshly washed hair. "It seems a little strange. What do you care if one of these people gets beaten up? I mean, I know how much you hate them, with your history, these guards and campus cops." She paused. "Obviously that's it, isn't it. You're worried that you might be suspected."

"That does trouble me, yes," he said, "though they would have nothing on me if they actually tried to pin this on me. I think I'm safe. I have my card. No one actually knows I'm not a PhD student. I have no criminal record. If there are any honest and decent campus cops, they could vouch for the fact that I've been known to them for years and have never responded violently, or even refused, when they've thrown me out of buildings or told me to get off campus. But ... " He looked over at her, "it's bad for me anyway, the cops and guard dogs will be paranoid for a long time to come."

"Plus, there's actually someone out there who attacked the guy," she said, widening her huge eyes with a mockingly ironic smile.

"Oh yeah, that. Well, as you suggest, I don't care about that. And you know me, you know why, you understand. Actually, from my point of view, he's welcome to share the campus with me and attack as many of these scum as he wants."

"Well, fortunately, you don't sleep on campus anyway," she said. "But Moksha ... "

"Yes, exactly. Exactly."

"So don't sleep under the Troll Bridge for a while. For a long while."

Moksha was sitting with his head slumped, as if staring at the juice bottle in his lap, an expression of irritated resignation on his face—the familiar signs of advanced inebriation.

"Well, I don't care about any of this," Moksha muttered. "They can arrest me if they want to. I have nothing to hide. And if they actually try to frame me, Douglas will get me off."

Douglas was Douglas MacLeod, now one of Toronto's pre-eminent criminal lawyers. He had been an old friend of Moksha's going back to 1970, when Moksha had been sleeping in a park across the street from the Robarts Library, and Douglas, who was studying in the university's faculty of law by day, was spending the nights—alone or with one of his innumerable girlfriends—in his van parked by the curb. MacLeod was a serious hippie indophile, and this had been a major element in their friendship, with MacLeod allowing Moksha to spend long periods of study and meditation in a cottage—Moksha's *"āśrama"*—on his property on the shore of Lake Simcoe.

"Well, quite apart from the assault," said Ben, "you're carrying around enough acid to get you put away for the rest of your life, *or* keep you in *samādhi* for the rest of your life, as you said."

He again glanced at Moksha's hands. Moksha grunted contemptuously, the grunt stirring his body like a belch. Yorkville's yuppiedom glittered and flowed around where they sat on a bench beside Cumberland Street.

"Speaking of Douglas ... " Ben said, and paused, thinking. "Yes ... yes, that's it, that would be perfect," he said finally, excited, with decision. "You go up to the *āśrama*. You've been saying for years that you want to go back. Now's the time. Because I'm telling you that you just can't stay in Philosopher's Walk anymore. The cops—both the campus Keystone Cops and the real ones—will be paranoid and trigger-happy for a long time to come, and extremely eager to find someone to pin this on. You're a sitting duck, Moksha, living under the Troll Bridge. And they *could* easily frame you. You *are* an extremely suspicious character. And what would your alibi be? And Moksha: *this was the guard we fought with just hours or minutes before somebody attacked him."* He paused, looking hard at Moksha. *"You* may not care, but *I* sure don't wanna be implicated in an assault that *I* certainly had nothing to do with." He grew warm. *"I* am on the verge of a new life with the woman I love. *I* wanna *live."*

Moksha remained slumped, the image of contemptuous indifference. Ben struggled to control his rising fury. "What are you going to say when they have you in interrogation?" he went on. "Where *were* you, Moksha, when this guy was attacked?"

"Nobody saw us," Moksha said softly in a voice so incongruously rational and sober that Ben was taken aback. "I may have looked like I was completely wasted, but that's actually not the state I was in. Nobody else was there when he confronted me outside the washroom, and nobody else was there when he followed us to the door. And why would he have mentioned such a trivial event to anyone afterwards?"

Ben paused. Moksha took the cap of the juice bottle out of his jacket pocket, twisted it on, and put the bottle in the shoulder bag that was next to him on the bench. Then he crossed his legs and leaned on the bench-back with his right elbow, half-turned towards Ben. In Moksha's current state, or what had seemed to be his current state, this was almost unbelievably responsive behaviour, a kind of declaration that he was available for serious discussion. Amazed and gratified, Ben collected his thoughts and prepared his presentation.

"OK," he said, "this *is* the right course of action. I want to go up to Seaton with you as soon as possible, in the next couple of days, probably the day after tomorrow. We'll take the bus up. I have the money. You have to call Douglas immediately and let him know. Once you're there, you apply for welfare in Seaton, right? The way you've done in the past."

"We don't have to discuss that part," said Moksha, shaking his head, still looking down, stroking his beard with his right hand. "I can take care of myself once I'm there."

Ben paused. This was all good, miraculously good, much better than he had expected, though his expectations hadn't been very clear. Just as his feelings about this event were still not clear. Moksha was his oldest friend, and in the years before Aditi had appeared, he had been his only friend (Chamberlain being more of a mentor, though his mentorship had the closeness and warmth of friendship). Despite the tensions in his relationship with Moksha—chiefly Moksha's resentful, frustrated physical longing for him, and his early molestations—Ben still loved him with the unshakable loyalty that was natural for him, and felt indebted to him for his early care and instruction. He hated the cops and guard dogs, as all their undeserving victims do. But Ben was not a violent man: on the contrary, he abhorred violence with the vehement conviction of one who has had to suffer it, who has been deeply shaped by the violence of others. Despite his show of cavalier callousness to Aditi, despite his special loathing for this particular Hart House guard, he felt no vengeful joy at the thought of the man lying half-dead in the parking lot at midnight. Moksha... Ben didn't know what he felt. All he knew right now was that Moksha was in danger, and that he had to save him. Because Moksha was his friend. And because Ben had been the one to give him the acid that may have driven him mad.

He glanced again at Moksha's hands, now empty and lightly clasping each other in his lap. Why be so delicate? He reached over, took Moksha's right hand in his own, and raised it to examine it. Moksha offered no resistance. The tiny gnomish paw was worn and leathery, but there were no obvious marks on it, no cuts or scrapes.

Ben glanced up and met Moksha's steady gaze.

10

"So Moksha, *uh-uhm,* what is the factor that is precipitating this sudden return to the *āśrama?*"

Thus the magnificently, sagely bearded Douglas MacLeod to Moksha, who was sitting in the passenger seat. Douglas, who during a high-profile drug trial had once been described by a *Toronto Life* writer as "Dickensian," was known, among other things, for his evolving panoply of Tourettes-like tics, and the currently dominant one was a soft, awkward clearing of the throat.

"It's the work we're all doing," answered Ben from the back seat, where he sat behind Moksha with his elbow out the open window and his hand holding Aditi's. "A translation of a yoga text. Actually, it's just me and Moksha who're doing the translation, without credit, for Aditi, who's supposed to be doing it without credit for her asshole of a PhD supervisor, who is the one who will actually publish it in his own name."

"I see," said Douglas. "But, *uh-uhm,* what's the connection with the *āśrama?* Won't it be more difficult for you to continue your collaboration, with Moksha up at the lake and you back in Toronto? *Uh-uhm.* You're not going to be co-inhabiting the *āśrama* along with Moksha, are you, Ben?"

"No," said Ben, "but we really will get more work done this way. Moksha has been feeling more and more discontented with the conditions of life downtown. This way, he'll be able to devote himself to translation all day. And the surroundings will of course be more conducive to a meditative state of mind: the lake, the woods. And he will be relieved of certain distractions..."

Ben hesitated on the cusp of frankly telling Douglas about the new danger to Moksha on campus. Why not? Besides being another old and loyal friend of Moksha, Douglas was a criminal lawyer, accustomed by his work to keeping grave secrets. But something held Ben back. Something about even giving voice to the idea that Moksha could be connected with this terrible crime. It would be tantamount to a request for an incredulous, dismissive denial, from Douglas, from Aditi... from himself. And he wasn't sure how genuine the denial would sound. And then, he would have had to go on to mention Boylan's acid, and how Moksha had gotten it... Anyway, Douglas had probably read the article in the *Star,* and figured it out for himself. Why complicate matters?

Moksha smiled silently, content to be spoken for. Leaning his elbow out of the fully lowered window as the wind punished his thin greying hair and flicked his *akṣamālā,* he watched the Southern Ontario landscape drift past, farmland and the occasional village and patch of woods. He wasn't smelling too bad today: the day before, in anticipation of this journey, Ben had bought him new pants and underpants to replace the ones he had pissed. Moksha had made an extremely rare visit to the Harrison Baths, too. So the car's atmosphere was tinted only by the composted sweat and smoke of his shirt and jacket and the stench of his shoes and socks.

Douglas looked up at Ben in the rear-view mirror, smiled, and cleared his throat again, a soft double grunt, before glancing over at Aditi, whom he had just met for the first time. His abundant hair was tightly bound in a black net that clung round the back of his head, the way he wore it on days that he went to court, but his attire was casual, a tie-dyed rainbow T-shirt and jeans. His flowing blond beard, though trimmed at the edges into a spadelike rectangle, was an insuppressible declaration of unconventionality, in court or out of it. His broad, handsome face, despite the clear first traces of middle age, radiated a childlike simplicity and ingenuousness which anyone might think incompatible with his work as a lawyer.

The same observer, watching him in court, would be surprised to see how these traits were on the contrary the very essence of his peculiar genius in that role, as Ben had been when, years before, he had attended Moksha's trial for theft. Moksha had been betrayed by the electronic alarm as he was leaving a Yonge Street Coles with a one-kilogram first volume of Proust's *Remembrance of Things Past* secreted in his underpants. Within ten minutes, Douglas effortlessly succeeded in making the Crown Counsel look like a philistine idiot (admittedly with a great deal of help from the Crown Counsel himself) and winning the judge's heart over for Moksha, without ever once showing the slightest hint of malice, mockery, or cunning. The trial had become the stuff of private legend between the three of them. "... while attempting to leave the store with a volume of *Prowst...*" the Crown Counsel had pompously declaimed. *"Proust"*, the judge had corrected him, softly, with a weary, condescending smile. Moksha had gotten off with a year's probation.

"So, Aditi," said Douglas, pronouncing her name with a correctness that somewhat startled her, unfamiliar as she was with his more than two decades of indophilia, *"uh-uhm,* I've heard about your troubles at the university. Really disgusting. It's hard to believe that a person who's supposed to be an expert in Sanskrit and its tradition could be, like, such a *rājasa* and *tāmasa* personality. I wish there were something I could do to help. *Uh-uhm."*

Aditi smiled, genuinely but uncomfortably, as Ben, still holding her hand, looked down scowling. "It's been very hard, yes," she said, "but we're coming to the end of it, finally. I'm almost ready to submit my thesis, and then the oral defence will happen as soon as the new academic year begins, in September. Barring some catastrophe, Ben and I will then go where opportunities lead me, which at the moment is looking like London or Cambridge."

Douglas glanced up at her in the mirror and smiled. "I'm glad to hear that. But, *uh-uhm,* it will be sad to see the two of you go. We never expected that departure from Toronto would be in Ben's future."

Ben looked out the open window, smiling grimly. "Well, we'll come back, from time to time," he said. "If only to see you guys, and a couple of other old friends. It hasn't all been bad."

The wind held back his hair and thundered in his ears. Journeys were on his mind today. This was the first time he had been north of Steeles since arriving in Toronto three months before his sixteenth birthday, more than eleven years ago. He had travelled west and east of Toronto during the first year, on foot and hitchhiking, to Hamilton, London, Sarnia, Ottawa, Montreal. But never north. North was the direction that mattered, the one he feared, the way back to everything he had fled and needed to forget.

In the early years, he had felt its nauseating, thrilling magnetism even during his occasional visits to York University, looking across Steeles to the endless expanse of cleared and parcelled land awaiting future decades of urbanization. Even then, at an age when mortality was barely even an abstraction, the sweep of space and time evoked a longing and sense of loss too deep for him to face or comprehend. Now, so many mostly wasted years of suffering later, he was able to articulate it: *So little time, how short our lives, how vast the eternity just beyond our reach*. And now here he was, deep in the midst of that once unreachable lost country, ready to face it at last. There was still time. It was still beautiful. He squeezed Aditi's hand.

From the highway that had carried them out of Toronto's northern suburbia and pre-urban clearings, they passed onto narrower and narrower roads running through farmland and forest. It was a landscape Aditi had never seen before, not too dramatically different from the flatter and more regularly parcelled-out prairie around Edmonton, but different enough that she went back to staring out the window when the conversation lapsed.

They rode in silence until the fields gave way to the town of Seaton and the northern horizon was possessed by the blue plain of Lake Simcoe. Within a minute they had passed through the town on a road that carried them past widely spaced lakeside houses on their left and more farmland and woods on the right. After a long stretch of lakeside forest—a provincial park—Douglas turned left onto a fading dirt road leading through grassy fallow fields to an isolated farmhouse.

"It doesn't look like it's been broken into, miraculously," he said as he pulled up and stopped in front of it. *"Uh-uhm.* I think you were the last human here, Moksha. How many solar cycles ago was that?"

"Oh, about fifteen," said Moksha, speaking for what may have been the first time that morning. His face shone with what looked like serene pleasure.

They got out and stood in front of the old white wooden two-storey house, peeling and almost visibly slouching, with windows so begrimed that the curtains were barely visible. Tall ancient trees and high grass surrounded it and covered the intervening space down to the lakeshore, where a decrepit wooden dock extended some ten paces out onto the water. To their right and towards the lake, the hut, the *āśrama,* was visible amidst a grove of trees, deciduous and conifer: the *tapovana,* the "ascetics' grove."

Shaking loose his Viking-length hair, Douglas walked up to the house, looking it over, made sure the door was locked, and peered into one of the windows, shading his eyes with both hands.

"I'll open it up in a minute," he called back to them. "Moksha, I'll give you the key, like last time, so you can go in and, *uh-uhm,* do your ablutions from time to time. Otherwise, you have the outhouse."

He walked back towards them and the car, looking round at the property, well advanced in its slow march back into nature.

"You know, *uh-uhm,* I may come up and spend some time here myself, take a few weeks off, me and Felicia, after this case is over. That's what I was thinking when I offered to drive you folks up here. I used to spend the summers here, you know, when I was growing up. If that wouldn't disturb you, Moksha, in your, *uh-uhm,* meditations?"

"No, not at all," murmured Moksha.

Ben and Aditi holding hands, the four strolled along the faded track to the *āśrama* through the deep grass on either side, under the undulating shade of the trees breathing with wind in the surrounding deep silence. The *āśrama* was evidently as old as the house, and built in the same style: a single-room cottage with a window and door in front, a window at the back, white-painted wooden siding, and a peaked shingled roof, worn but intact. Douglas unlocked the padlock, then the key lock, and pushed the heavy wooden door open. They followed Moksha inside.

Under the back window was a heavy wooden desk with a table lamp, a short stack of books, a coffee mug of pens, and a framed copy of the famous portrait of the south Indian sage Ramana Maharshi, barely visible through a thick shroud of dust on the glass. In one corner there was a heavy wooden bedframe with a folded blanket in the pillow's position. Against one wall there was a three-shelved wooden bookcase as high as the room, with a few more books, both hardbound and paperback, on the top shelf, and a small black stone figurine of the divine bull Nandi. The window looked through the grove to the lake beyond.

Taking a facecloth from the otherwise empty second shelf, Moksha went over to the desk, picked up the picture of Ramana Maharshi—eerily like an ideal image of himself—and wiped the dust from it. He picked up the first of the stacked books, with its obviously Indian binding, patted a cloud of dust from it, opened it, paged through it.

"So, Moksha, *uh-uhm,* this looks quite nice," said Douglas, taking a few steps around the room. "Even I'm thinking that I wouldn't mind, *uh-uhm,* doing a retreat here sometime. I'd kick you out, banish you to the *adharmic* luxury of the main residence." He laughed, a fluent, throaty laughter that illuminated his face, enhancing its already remarkable youthfulness.

Moksha smiled with raised eyebrows, a bit indulgently, still perusing the book.

Douglas went on: "I would think that you'll be able to accomplish higher deeds in this sacred space than, *uh-uhm,* sitting in Philosopher's Walk or the Harvey's across the street."

"Yes," said Moksha, "it will be good to get back to this."

They strolled down to the lake along another faint track through the trees. The water was slightly choppy, and low waves shushed rhythmically on the thin margin of pebbly beach. Three or four sailboats were visible far out, towards the vast Georgina Island, which dominated the vista on the right. On the left, much beyond, the small city of Orillia could just barely be seen on the far north-western shore. Moksha's last retreat at the *āśrama* had pre-dated Ben's arrival in Toronto by a couple of years, so Ben had never been here before, and now, seeing the place for the first time, he was regretting that he had not had the chance to spend time here before Aditi had appeared. This peace and beauty would have been such a consolation in that phase of solitary darkness and fear. It might have changed everything, might have begun to transform and free him in the way that only Aditi had been able to do. And then, how much more ready he would have been for her, how much more worthy of her, right from the beginning. He would have been able to understand what she was offering him, wouldn't have stupidly and insanely rejected it, shattering them both.

But then, if he had been here, if he had come here even once, how could he have met her? *What might have been is an abstraction/ remaining a perpetual possibility/ only in a world of speculation,* he thought—words he often recited to himself as a not very effective *mantra* against the remorse that often threatened to submerge him. As always at such moments, he tried, against the grain of his brooding, backward-looking nature, to redirect his attention to what was possible and real: it might be possible, now, for him and Aditi to spend time here together, in the house, a holiday of rest before they departed for wherever her newly favourable destiny was going to lead them.

He turned and looked at her. She was also gazing out over the lake as the shifting wind gently whipped the loose curls about her face. She smiled at him. His eyes glowed with intense, silent love. He let go of her hand, and leaving his sandals on, waded up to his knees into the water rising and falling with the mild pulse of the waves.

"It's cold!" he shouted, turning towards her, "but I'm goin' in. I can never say no to an opportunity to take a bath."

He rapidly splashed back to shore and removed everything but a pair of blindingly crimson jockey shorts, leaving his sandals and clothes in a heap where the pebbly sand began to fade into the grass.

"Do I have to leave these on?" he said, looking at Douglas.

"Um, I think it probably doesn't matter," said Douglas, "we're, *uh-uhm,* pretty isolated here."

Ben slipped off his shorts and dropped them on top of the heap.

"Ben, for god's sake!" said Aditi, laughing with embarrassment.

He was laughing too. "I won't even try to encourage you to come in," he said, smacking her ass through her tight jeans as he strode past her and Moksha, who was frankly staring at him. His dick flopping exuberantly back and forth, he rushed into the water up to his balls, then fell forward in a vigorous crawl, heading out into the deep, where he turned and faced them, treading water.

"It's wonderful!" he shouted, gasping. "Come on in, baby! You can leave your undies on! You too, you guys!"

He launched into a backstroke, pulsing along like a squid with a strong stopping-and-starting rhythm, his pale genitals alternately bobbing and being swept back like a water plant in a shifting current. Aditi took off her shoes and socks, with difficulty pushed the tight legs of her jeans above her knees, and waded tentatively into the water, looking as if she regretted that she could not bring herself to forget the presence of Douglas and Moksha, and join her lover in the nude.

"You know," shouted Douglas, "you two could come up here and, *uh-uhm,* stay in the house sometime. Just get in touch with me, and I'll transfer the key into your keeping."

"Whaddaya say, baby?" Ben shouted breathlessly, treading water. "We'll do it ... right? ... after your viva ... though the water ... will be even colder ... then."

"Yes, we'll come," shouted Aditi, standing up to her knees in the water. "It'll be beautiful."

11

Aditi sat watching Boylan's face on the other side of the desk as he perused the pages she had just presented. She wished Ben could be here, even just waiting outside the office somewhere, in the department lounge, or the library, but of course he was at work. She looked down at her hands, glanced around surreptitiously, without interest. It was hard to believe, and painful to remember, how awed she had been the first time she had seen this office.

She couldn't blame herself: it *had* been impressive, compared to what she had known at the university in Edmonton, where Indian Studies had been represented by a single faculty member, Professor Mrs. Kamala Joshi, who knew Sanskrit well, but whose provincial sensibility had barely been affected by her adult emigration from India. She was only superficially aware of modern scholarship, and not interested in it, teaching her small and mainly Indian-origin classes straight from the textbook. Even then, the poverty of her teaching style had irked and frustrated Aditi, who had read far more than Joshi in indology, not to speak of other modern literature, about which Joshi knew and cared nothing. But at the time, Aditi was chiefly focussed on becoming an incredible sanskritist, and on this level, they bonded strongly: Aditi's passion for the Sanskrit texts inspired Joshi's love and maternal solicitude, and made her willing to spend hours reading with her, mainly from the *Mahabharata* and *Ramayana,* while Aditi brooded in lonely silence on the implications of her private readings in modern scholarship.

The dark side of her isolation in Edmonton was that she had no *intellectual* mentor whose influence could have checked the drift of her thought towards a insidious error to which her naive fascination with authenticity made her vulnerable: the romantic idealization of India. The result was a disastrous lack of both intellectual and practical guidance, and a rudderless odyssey that led her first to Ayodhya, then into the clutches of the monster who now sat across the desk from her, plotting whatever last attempt to destroy her he could think of in the final days of her servitude.

Boylan was leaning back in his chair with his feet up on the desk, reading what Aditi and Ben expected to be the penultimate instalment of the *Yogayuktadīpikā* translation. His worn, froglike face, ugly more by attitude than by nature, expressed a mildly contemptuous indifference. Aditi knew that there could be nothing in the translation for even the most determined hostility to argue with, and the shade of irritation in Boylan's expression indicated that he saw that too. Finally, he tossed the printout onto the desk next to his shoes, whose soles stared Aditi in the face.

"Pretty good," he said with a concessive lilt in the soft voice he used to communicate his darkest shade of menace, "good enough that it won't embarrass me in print."

She raised her eyes and looked at him with unconcealed disgust, a boldness that she had rarely permitted herself.

Boylan's eyes alone registered the insult. "Pretty good," he said again, "especially considering that you're finishing your dissertation at the same time. That's not as good as the translation. In fact, it's worthless, and I could tear your thesis apart in front of your face right now and send you back to square one. But I won't, because I'm sick of reading it, and I'm sick of you."

He paused, perhaps expectantly, looking at her with a familiar slack expression that said *fuck you I don't give a shit*. She remained silent, more from boredom and contempt, at this point, than from any fear of what he could do to her. These were final days, and he knew it, and they both knew that the distribution of power had shifted slightly in her favour.

He went on, his words shaped by the nasal drawl of his scarcely eroded working class Newfoundland accent. "I don't know why I took you on in the first place, actually. I've never had the faintest interest in these comic books, the *Mahabharata,* the *Ramayana*. Literary theory. Feminism. In retrospect, it's obvious that you should have found someone to work with in the Comparative Literature department. This is not indology." He glanced at the typescript on the desk. "It's basically an English thesis about the Sanskrit epics. Any English MA could have written it, using existing translations."

He paused again. She remained silent, feeling no impulse to respond to these tiresome insults and provocations now, as she had in earlier years—when she would rise to the bait and indignantly defend herself, to his amusement.

"So *I'm* done with it," he said finally. "I'll pass it on to the rest of your committee, not that they have the faintest idea what you're talking about, or care, since none of them knows anything about indology."

His face darkened.

"You know, it really is too bad you didn't pass on Ayodhya and come straight here from Edmonton a few years earlier, when Chamberlain was still here. I know he would have liked you. He was a true scholar, of the old school, but he would have been nice to you, out of aristocratic chivalry, and would have cared enough to train you, to teach you how to whip this worthless pomo feminist gobbledygook into a respectable scholarly shape."

He paused. "I imagine you've probably met Chamberlain, haven't you. There's a guy in the department who says Chamberlain is supervising his PhD. You know the guy."

Aditi remained silent.

"He's your boyfriend, isn't he?" said Boylan, softly. "You've gotten Chamberlain to read and comment on your dissertation, haven't you? I can tell. It's garbage, but it's better than anything you could have written on your own."

It occurred to her to say something in Sanskrit, which always enraged him, because he couldn't, but why bother? It was almost over.

Leaving his office, she walked along the upper corridor, past doors that she knew had once been the offices of the eminent scholars that had made this university's indology department one of the greatest in the world. Where had she been then? A little girl growing up in a prosperous mercantile family in Delhi, an adolescent being educated in English by nuns in an elite convent school, then an immigrant, a high school and university student in Edmonton, sinking deeper and deeper into the delusional, romanticizing fascination with India with which she consoled her loneliness, falling ever more under the sway of Sujay and his fanatical relatives in Canada and India. And then the fatal misstep: her return, with Sujay, to her ill-remembered, ill-known homeland, to all the backwardness and misery that her practical, realistic parents had struggled and sacrificed to save her from. But by then this department had already been destroyed and dispersed, everyone but Anatole Chamberlain, a tragic relic of the lost golden age.

She rode the elevator alone down to the second floor and pushed through the revolving door into the warm June day. She walked down Huron Street, Russell, Spadina Circle, Spadina, her step slightly accelerating without her realizing it. Before Oxford Street, a car was standing in the middle of the sidewalk as three of

Malcolm's crew dried it with their rags. She slowed, approaching Ben from behind as he polished the side windows. Ben's two colleagues on the other side, skids older than Ben and worn with the years, looked up at her, frankly astonished, then smiled with suppressed laughter as she silently reached up and caressed the nape of Ben's neck. He started, whirled round, and seeing her standing below him, smiled with an unqualified joy that was rare for him. She stepped forward impetuously and embraced him, turning her head to press her cheek against his chest, and he reciprocated, laughing, still clutching his rag, smelling the fragrant curls on the crown of her head, while his two colleagues stood on the other side of the car, their smiles fading into a troubled perplexity as she wept silently, feeling the tears pool at the bottom of her sunglasses and slip down her face.

"Baby, believe me, you don't want to live in India," she said, taking a sip from a paper Coffee Time cup and putting it back down on the park bench. "We'll visit. But there's no way I'm ever going to live there again. And whether you know it or not, you don't want to live there either."

The Queen streetcar whispered into view from where they sat in Trinity Bellwoods Park, well back from the street. The high evening sun shone in the west behind them. People were strolling on the paved footpaths.

"It's just, you know, I need to have one foot there," said Ben. "I have to spend a lot of time there, at least, studying with *paṇḍitas,* travelling around the country. It would have been good to actually live there, but ... "

"But you met me. Wrong Indian!" She laughed. "But the truth is that almost any Indian you meet in Canada would be the wrong Indian for that. We're here precisely because we don't want to be there. Because we know."

She paused. "But that's not quite true. I did go back, after all. My story was a little unusual, I took things to an unusual extreme, characteristically. But lots of immigrants' children get ill-informed romantic ideas about Mother India. Even me, and I lived there until I was sixteen. I should have known better than kids born here who get their heads filled with their parents' nostalgic fantasies. A lot of them do go back—to visit relatives, say—and they generally smarten up very soon after they get off the plane. I wish it hadn't taken *me* so long." She shook her head. "What a waste of life," she said bitterly. "Precious years wasted on my idiot fanaticism, with those idiot fanatics."

She was silent for a long time, looking darkly towards the street. "But that's what it took to get that out of my system, to teach me that there was no value there. And in the end I found you," she said, reaching over and squeezing his hand. "One good *karmaphala,* one good fruit of some good action in a past life—the one thing worth living for, the one value, the one meaning that hasn't turned out to be more or less empty. I must have done something right, somewhere along the line."

He blushed, looked down.

"You'll get your time there," she said, "once we're settled where we're going, probably Britain. We'll both be making money. What would be ideal for you would be to spend some long periods there, in India, six months to a year, reading with *paṇḍitas,* and I know you'd also want to walk all over the country, learn Hindi and maybe some other languages—you'd pick them up without even having to think about it, you have such a natural genius for languages. I have relatives up north you could live with, in and around Delhi, though I can tell you right now that you won't find anything in common with them, and they won't like you much, any more than they like me. And we'll find a way to spend time there together. This will be ideal for you. You'll be able to take your fill of the place without wrecking your life. Because believe me, you'll *have* your fill of the place, a lot sooner than you realize."

She smiled compassionately. "Baby, you have no idea, you're just going to have to find out the hard way. I can imagine what you would have done to yourself if you'd managed to get there without meeting me first. I can see. You're a total India-head, baby," she said, lifting her hand to stroke back a strand of his hair, hooking it behind his ear, "a typical white boy who falls in love with his paperback *Bhagavadgita* and imagines that India is still *Jambūdvīpa,* the Isle of the Rose Apple Tree, where everyone's either in *samādhi* or getting there. Even though you've learned Sanskrit so incredibly well and read so much, even though you really know better intellectually, this *is* still your mentality. It's very cute!"

She leaned over and kissed him on the cheek. "But it's obvious that without me to guide you, you'd destroy yourself there, even worse than I did. You'd have jumped in with both feet, and have nothing to step back to when it finally dawned on you. *Jambūdvīpa* is gone, baby. Long gone."

"But I would *never* have gotten there if I hadn't met you," he said. "I would never have gotten anywhere, actually, never been able to do anything. I would have lived and died on these streets. You alone saved me, your absolute understanding and love of everything that I love and am. Without you, there was nothing to save." He looked her in the face. "I'm so sorry. You know ... how sorry I am."

She shook her head, cupped his cheek, and kissed him on the lips, eyes closed. "It was our *ṛṇabhāra,* the burden of some debt in past lives," she said softly. "But we must have done something right, somewhere along the line."

12

"So this is Aditi," said Chamberlain as his wife Kamala wheeled him into the living room, where Ben and Aditi were sitting on plush chairs, looking out over the lake shining under the mellow August sun. "I'm very pleased to finally meet you," he said, smiling warmly at Aditi.

She suffered a moment of confusion, wondering whether it would appear more reverent to remain sitting or to rise and tower over the great man's cruelly reduced form. Ben did not rise, and so she too leaned forward and greeted Chamberlain from her seat. "I'm honoured," she said, "and sorry that it's somehow taken so long for me to get here, at the very end of my time in Toronto."

"Yes, that's a pity," said Chamberlain, "but we all know what writing a PhD is like, and I know how it's been for *you*."

Kamala left them and went into the kitchen.

Chamberlain continued: "But mercifully, your ordeal is nearly over. I have read the final draft of your dissertation. It's a very, very worthy piece of work. I can honestly say that if I were on your committee, I would advise that it be accepted without a single change."

Aditi was flustered, buffetted by a turmoil of gratification and embarrassment. Ben had turned his head to look out over the lake again, his face betraying a hint of the suppressed excitement and anxiety she knew he was feeling at this critical meeting. Kamala returned with a tray of tea, one of them black, for Ben.

"And this brings me to something that I think Ben may not have told you," Chamberlain went on, glancing at Ben. "You might well wonder why I never did offer to be on your committee. One consideration was my health, which is very delicate. Now it's true that nowadays, with email, it would have been possible for me to fulfil the role of a committee member without even leaving this apartment. But I feared that I would have had to face an additional stress besides the pleasant one of engaging with your work. This was the second consideration: the inevitability of conflict with Boylan, whose history with me you know. And because of that history, too, it would have done you no good to have me on your committee: on the contrary, it would certainly have goaded your tormentor to even more determined and extravagant opposition. It now appears that his will to thwart you has spent itself, and that therefore your *viva voce*" (he gave the phrase its Italian pronunciation) "will in all probability be unproblematic. But if at the eleventh hour he turns out to have been secretly plotting some final ambush, it's possible that I *could* intervene in some way, if it's the only way. We'll have to see, but I've been thinking about it, and I have actually written an examiner's report on your dissertation, in case it should ever somehow be necessary for me to become involved."

"Thank you so much," she said, suppressing a laugh of incredulous pleasure. "I'm happy that you think it won't be necessary. It *has* been looking like it won't be."

"Ben will also have been telling you about my meditations on your professional future," Chamberlain went on. "You will be applying for positions at SOAS and Cambridge? I know that world well, and I myself am a Cambridge man. I still have strong connections in indology generally, even though I've been withdrawn for many years, and my contemporaries are retired or dead. So you will have my letters of recommendation, strong letters, when the time comes, if you want them: again, I have already written the text."

"Thank you," she said softly, still feeling that this was all too good to be true.

"You're from the north," he said, "from Delhi ... I was never really a northern man myself, never really learned Hindi properly, and now I can only say the simplest things. You will know ... Hindi, and perhaps Punjabi?"

"Not much Punjabi," she said.

"My wife Kamala is from Pune," he said. "We speak Marathi when we're alone, in our daily life. But my work in India was in the south, in Karnataka and Tamilnadu, and I was once fluent in Tamil and Kannada, and still read them. I have a deep yearning to go back ... but it would simply be impossible at this point. I would never survive the journey. I was last there in 1989, the last time I was able."

He paused, and they looked out over the lake, taking sips of tea.

"Ben," he added, "as usual there are a few passages I'd like your opinion on."

Aditi felt the gentle implication, and said, "If it's all right, I'd really like to lie down on one of these lovely sofas, in front of this spectacular view. As often, I didn't get enough sleep last night." Ben laughed under his breath, sharing a glance with her.

In Chamberlain's office, Ben and Chamberlain first went through the hand-copied passages.

Then Chamberlain said, in a rather low voice, "I have actually received something from Boylan, which is ... troubling."

Ben felt a surge of cold fear. "What ... ?" he asked softly.

Sitting at one of the desk's narrow ends, Chamberlain picked up a large opened envelope and took out several letter-sized photographic prints.

Ben shook his head and looked down as soon as he saw them. "You don't need to tell me," he said in a voice dark with rage and weariness.

"Of course, I already knew about them, and about everything," said Chamberlain, "but I have to admit that that hadn't prepared me for how ... dramatic they are, and damning." He paused. "There is nothing we can do to stop him from sending them to anyone. He doesn't know, does he, where she's planning to apply after finishing?"

"No," said Ben, shaking his head, eyes closed, violently pressing his temples with the fingers and thumb of his right hand, "but of course he can easily guess."

"She was never actually charged with a crime in India, was she?" said Chamberlain.

"No," said Ben, "none of the mere rank and file were, the *kār sevaks,* but that hardly matters. I've sometimes wondered if these pictures might even imperil her citizenship status, since Ayodhya could easily be interpreted as terrorist activity, but probably not, because she was already a citizen by then. But even so, they are obviously very damning, as you say."

"Is there anything he could possibly hope to extort from her," said Chamberlain, "or is this pure vengeful bloody-mindedness? He has never ... actually propositioned her sexually?"

"No," said Ben, "the official complaints she made were about sexually *suggestive* comments ... compliments on her ... anatomy, speculations on her sexual preferences ... And what would he be capable of anyway," he added, immediately realizing that this was a comment that might have offended Chamberlain, and just as quickly realizing that he needn't worry. He lowered his hand and opened his eyes, now red-rimmed and gleaming. "She could say that the pictures have been doctored, but it wouldn't be plausible. And the truth, that her sojourn with the *Sangh Parivar,* with right-wing Hinduism, was just a terrible error of her youth, wouldn't save her from opprobrium, nor the fact that the event documented by these very photographs was the beginning of her alienation from those people. No one would hire her."

"How did Boylan get these pictures?" said Chamberlain.

"Sujay," said Ben, "it must have been Sujay, Aditi's boyfriend in Edmonton. It was mainly through his relatives and connections that she got involved with the *Sangh*. She ditched him years ago, after she left the *Sangh* and started at U of T. I've told you the story of how I knocked him down in Philosopher's Walk. He's bitter, and vengeful." He looked into Chamberlain's eyes. "She's survived everything, fought her way through everything, illusion and disillusionment, isolation, hopelessness. She's my hero." His voice was fervent, tremulous. "Now that we've found each other, we're set for life. This, Boylan, is her last obstacle. *Our* last obstacle, and trial."

Chamberlain held his gaze, evidently moved.

Finally he said: "Boylan may simply want to remind her of his power. He does seem to have mainly lost interest in opposing her, at this point. He might not go to the trouble of mailing these pictures to universities all over the world. And indologists know and despise him ... I believe my recommendation would cancel out the damage."

"That's reassuring," said Ben. "But this is still at least a very bad sign. It suggests that he may after all be plotting some final attack, probably at the viva. It may ... it may be necessary for you to be there ... if you think you can ... "

"I am considering it," said Chamberlain. "I think I would

probably be capable of it. And if not ... this is a cause that would almost be worth dying for."

Ben and Aditi had walked back to the campus, through the lakeshore park, Parkdale, Queen Street West. He had left her at the door of the graduate residence at about five, this being one of his nights out, and gone to the department to read the *Mahabharata* in the South Asian Studies library. As usual, no one else was sitting there, and no one came in. The library was a relic, and Aditi was the last remaining indology student, destined to be the department's final PhD in that subject. Thereafter, the university would leave Boylan on the floor of his office until he died there, or until he reached retirement age at sixty-five, at which point they could force him out, and indology at the University of Toronto, all but dead for so many years, would finally officially die.

As Ben sat at the table reading the verses aloud, his visualization of the story began to be touched by the weird logic of dream. He pushed the large musty volume aside, rested his head on his arms, and drifted down.

As often in dream, he found himself on his streets, in the night, at a point that held some special beauty or comfort for his deep, intimate knowledge of them. Standing on the sidewalk beneath soundlessly breathing trees, he felt the serenity of the scene being contaminated by the old magnetism of dread sucking him towards the ancient object of his obsessive fear, the house where his mother had been living for seven years. It was parallel to where he stood, two streets over, just paces away. Why not walk that way? This was a dream.

He turned left into the lane, down the side street at its end, along the next, strolling under the great dark branches, knowing rather than hearing their cool nocturnal whispering. Reaching the corner, he looked across at the house. Someone was standing on the porch, half-visible above the white barrier with its green capital. Why not go closer? Even in waking life, at this point, what did he have to fear from her? He walked north without crossing, and stopped.

With greying short hair, worn and gaunt, as he had seen her last, she was looking at him with the terrible consuming love of mothers—love and pity. Even through the woollen haze of sleep, he felt nausea begin to rise.

He stepped off the curb onto the empty midnight street, holding her gaze as he advanced, with each step fighting an exasperating sluggishness, as if fording a river in flood. Her expression had begun to shift, a shift more of aura than of the physical disposition of her face. The love had begun to ebb. He stepped onto the curb. She was above him, looking down at him with the faint mocking smile that had once been the harbinger of her violence. And he could feel that he was returning the same smile.

He looked down and stepped onto the first wooden step.

The door clicked. *Who ...*

He felt himself being wrenched out of the scene as if by invisible hands, thrust upwards through black swirling water to the surface. He opened his eyes and groggily raised his head.

Bulky, broad-faced, menacingly crowned with his absurd police cap, officer Ganesh Malhotra was standing in the half-opened doorway directly in front of him, his hand on the knob. He was looking at Ben with cool unsurprise. For a moment they remained frozen, staring at each other. Then Malhotra softly closed the door.

It was so surreal to see him here that Ben wondered if he was still dreaming. He shook his head sharply, testing for the tell-tale physicality of waking life, and seeming to find it, pushed aside his jacket to expose the watch strapped to his belt. 11:07.

He slid the large open volume, the *Udyogaparva,* the epic's fifth book, back into the spot on the table now warm with his recent sleep, paused, staring at the twin columns of verses in the jewelled rectangular *Devanāgarī* script, then pushed his bookmark, a Buddha's Vegetarian Restaurant business card in green Roman and Chinese scripts, to the top left of the page, closed the black-bound volume, and put it back on its shelf about a third of the way through the complete twenty-volume edition of the epic.

Opening the library door, he looked both ways for Malhotra. No one. Something was going on. University cops were never seen inside university buildings unless something was going on. And this was Malhotra, and this was Ben's space and time. He was here for Ben.

Ben went into the washroom, the next door down the hall from the library, pissed in the urinal. The first announcement sounded from the PA system, the familiar mournful female voice: *The library will be closing in forty-five minutes. Please bring all books you wish to sign out to the loan services desk on the second floor before eleven-thirty.* He shook his dick, went back out into the empty hallway, put on his knapsack in the library, came out, turned left towards the offices rather than right towards the elevator: he would take a walk, go the long way round, and come to the elevator by the other hallway. Through one of the gaps in the concrete barrier that enclosed the upper of the two sub-hallways at the floor's periphery, he saw that Boylan's door was closed. Behind him to the left, at a point that he had just passed, the lower sub-hallway's heavy metal door to the fire escape slammed.

He slowed and stopped. An East Asian man in his thirties came round the bend in the hallway ahead, looked at Ben questioningly as he passed him, and disappeared round the next bend. Ben walked back to stand at the verge of the two short concrete stairways leading up and down. The steady roar of the air conditioning was audible through the metal fire escape doors, one on top of the other, at the end of each staircase. He took one step down and paused, listening. There was the stale smell of cigarette smoke. He descended the rest of the way and put his hand on the cold doorknob.

The library will be closing in thirty minutes…

The doorknob turned with cool metallic smoothness, the door opened easily inward, noiselessly, into the echoing roar. Boylan was sitting at the top of the next upward section of grey concrete stairs, at the level midsection where the stairway paused in its triangular upward progress: door, stairs, midsection, stairs, door, stairs ... He was smoking, elbows on knees.

Ben stood for a moment, holding the door open, staring up into Boylan's eyes, then stepped forward and let the door close behind him with a soft clicking thud. In the space to his left, he felt Malhotra standing close, against the wall, but did not look at him. In the dim fluorescent light, Boylan sucked his cigarette, which crackled softly and glowed; then he reached between the two horizontal bars of the metal guardrail and flicked the ash into the triangular shaft round which the staircase centred.

Ben slipped off his knapsack and put it down on the floor to his right with a little thud. "So what's up, assholes?" he said cheerfully, arching his eyebrows and finally shifting his gaze to include Malhotra, whose broad dark face was illuminated by the same chimpanzee sneer it had worn on the morning Ben had first seen it, and again at a later time, in the light of the dim sparse lamps of Queen's Park at midnight.

"Oh, nothin' special," said Boylan. "Me 'n' Ganesh are just hangin' out. We're old buddies, we go way back."

Malhotra chuckled.

"Hm, me 'n' Ganesh go way back too," said Ben, looking at Malhotra.

"So I've heard," said Boylan, taking a drag. "So tell me," he said in a tone of innocent curiosity, "how does it happen that a little street-trash pretty-boy whore who sucks cocks in Queen's Park at midnight comes to be the PhD student of the most eminent professor of Sanskrit in the land? We were just trying to figure that out."

Malhotra chuckled again.

"That's a tough one, I admit," replied Ben, still smiling and supercilious, "almost as tough as the mystery of how the catfish-ugly offspring of illiterate, dypsomaniac trash comes to be the head of the most eminent Sanskrit department in the world. Sorry, the *former* Sanskrit department. *Formerly* eminent."

"You know," said Boylan, laughing slightly and adding just a shade of menace to his voice, "you may not be quite as invulnerable as you obviously think you are. There's still an unsolved assault waiting to get pinned on some suitably suspicious person. And Ganesh here has been seeing you sleeping on campus park benches for years, and even lying around on the lawn dead drunk a few times."

"Yes, and shoving his rubbery smegmatic two-inch dick in my face," said Ben, turning to Malhotra, grimacing with loathing and disgust. "You worthless trash, you worthless trash ..." he almost whispered.

"*You* are the trash," said Malhotra, his voice almost trembling with conviction. His grin had decayed into a menacing oval of hate.

"Brilliant," said Ben, turning away, restored to composure by Malhotra's clownish pathos. "I stand refuted."

He leaned his hip and hand on the guardrail's metal bar, facing Boylan. Boylan took a final suck on his cigarette, flicked it into the void, and rose to his feet on the first step down, exhaling fangs of smoke from his nostrils, putting his hands into his jacket's side-pockets as if casually checking their contents. He descended the four steps, looking down at his feet, and came and stood beside Ben, putting his left hand round his back to press his left shoulder in a comradely manner, and with his right patting and gently squeezing Ben's right arm. Ben felt himself engulfed in Boylan's aura of smoke, booze, and body odour. He could smell his unwashed white locks at his shoulder.

"I think we understand each other," Boylan said softly, with the familiar ironic lilt, gently turning Ben so that they were both looking over the metal railing. "What's your name, anyway?"

Ben realized how limited Boylan's knowledge of him must really be, despite his genius for intrigue. "My name is for my friends," he said, smiling superciliously, holding the guardrail with both hands now as he let his gaze slowly drop down the shaft's vertiginous open wall of bars and concrete ledges to the floor fourteen storeys below. A surge of cold fear welled up from his gut and spread through his limbs. He was about to step back.

"Well, my nameless little non-friend," said Boylan, "I think it's important for you to know at this point," his hand sliding gently from Ben's shoulder to the nape of his neck, "that you are *fucking with the wrong person.*"

At these last words, his voice hardened, and he gripped Ben's neck with surprising strength, forcing him to bend over the bar and look straight down. Ben grasped the rail and tried to step back, but Boylan held him hard, muttering fiercely into his ear: "You really think you're something, don't you, coming out of nowhere, wowing the big professor emeritus and screwing my PhD student, going straight to the top without even getting a BA. You think I don't *know?*"

Ben gripped the bar savagely, clenching his teeth, bracing himself against Boylan's weight and the tremendous gravity he felt sucking him over the edge. Electric terror pervaded his body.

He felt as if his feet were slipping on the smooth concrete, lifting off ... If he unlaced his hands from the bar, Boylan could hurl him over before Ben could seize him, or hit him, or thrust him back.

Through the metal doors, faint, muffled: *The library will be closing in fifteen minutes. Please bring all books you wish to sign out to the loan services desk immediately.*

"You really think you've got me by the balls, don't you, you little half-dick bum-boy street trash nutcase loser, you and your Oxbridge gentleman-pedophile surrogate daddy, and your bony-ass slut of a girlfriend, whose PhD you *wrote,* didn't you. *Didn't you.*"

Boylan thrust down on Ben's neck. Ben half-groaned, half-shouted, and with tremendous effort loosed his right hand from the bar, thrust it back and seized Boylan's crotch, squeezing it in a desperate crushing grip. Boylan roared, staggered backwards, releasing Ben's neck and arm and seizing his wrist with both hands. Still gripping the bar with his left hand, Ben twisted round, coming face to face with Boylan, pop-eyed and grimacing with agony and hate. He could feel the hard and soft little bundle of Boylan's genitals through his pants as he gave one climactic squeeze, then loosed both hands to brutally thrust him back. Boylan bounced off the concrete wall, tumbled diagonally down the stairs, thudded with his shoulders against one of the guardrail's vertical bars, and lay on his side with his head hanging over the stairs' edge.

Stunned, he looked up at Ben. Then he grinned, grasped the guardrail's lower horizontal bar with his left hand, pressed the edge of the stairs with his right, and launched himself into space.

Ben shouted in horror. Through the echo of his shout and the continuous roar of the air conditioning came the soft thud of Boylan's body from fourteen storeys below.

Ben whirled round to look for Malhotra, but he had disappeared. He grasped the guardrail and looked over. Boylan was lying on his side on the small distant triangle of the shaft's floor. Ben cried out again, seized and strapped on his knapsack and, gripping the handrails on both sides, began scrambling down the stairs two and three at a time, despite the pounding weight on his back and the dreadful magnetic pull of the yawning centre.

At the bottom of the last flight of steps, he stood and looked at Boylan. He was lying still, on his side, with eyes closed, as if he had collapsed there in his usual intoxicated stupor, except that the side of his face was mashed against the concrete floor, and his mouth was open in an unnaturally asymmetrical gape, with bloody lips and teeth. Blood had begun to pool round his head. Ben was staring, open-mouthed, scarcely breathing.

Boylan opened his right eye and looked up at him. He made a gurgling, snuffling sound, and the upward corner of his smashed mouth twitched into the suggestion of a mocking smile.

Ben uttered a strangled shout, turned, rammed the handle of the emergency exit, burst through the door. The alarm's bell and throbbing siren screamed, following him as he scrambled down the metal stairs of the fire escape outside, and fled wild-eyed and open-mouthed into the cool summer night.

13

"B-ben, has something happened? You d-d-don't look good."

Ben looked up with a start from where he was sitting on the detached rear car seat that served as a sofa for the carwash's workers. It was Peter who had asked him, Peter the painter, tall, good-looking, incongruously neat and proper and well-trimmed, who lived with his wife in a cheap above-store apartment on the opposite side of Spadina. Ben had been staring straight ahead, at nothing, holding his rag between his knees. He wasn't sure how bad he looked. He must look tired, but perhaps also a bit mad.

"No ... no, I'm alright, really," he said, slowly and softly, unable to force himself to smile. "I didn't get much sleep last night."

Peter smiled. "I h-h-hope it was for a good reason. Were you inside last night? With ... A*dee*ti?"

"No, I wasn't with *A*-diti," Ben said, smiling at last, but weakly, unconsciously correcting Peter's only very slight mispronunciation of Aditi's name—it was always impressive if people were able to remember it in any form at all. "It was one of my nights out. There's just some ... family trouble. Nothing serious."

"Oh," said Peter, looking down.

The small, rudimentary washing machine next to the seat, for the rags, had entered its spin cycle. Larry the hunchback, the most senior of Malcolm's employees in age and historical priority, was standing against the wall smoking, apparently not listening, waiting for the cycle to end. From one of the tall grimy windows, a slash of sunlight fell into the sepulchral space.

"Your mother lives not f-f-far from here, right?" said Peter.

Ben winced slightly. "Yes," he said.

Peter's face always reflected a gentle, sympathetic intelligence, so it would have been difficult to say whether there was now more sympathy in his smile than usual. "Why don't you c-c-come over after work this evening," he said. "And we'd love to m-m-meet Aditi too, sometime."

A car was heard moving slowly into the back entrance, and the first components of the washing machinery's gamut stirred into noisy action. Larry took a rag from the now still washing machine and stood watching as the car inched through the first set of whirling, clattering brushes.

"Thanks, Peter," said Ben, smiling more naturally this time, "but tonight I have to be with Aditi. But we'll definitely take you up on that soon. That would be lovely ... for all four of us to get together, finally."

The cycle's midsection came alive with sounds of hissing water and rumbling machinery. As the headlights loomed through the darkness and rain, Ben slowly turned towards them with harassed eyes that stared as if they could not anticipate what banality or horror they would see.

"Baby, I've never seen you in this state," Aditi said, frightened, as she caressed his head pressed against her breast.

She was lying on her back on the bed, and he was clinging to her, violently, trembling, staring. Since entering the apartment, he had not said a word. When she had opened the door, he had met her with terrified eyes, grasped her hand with both of his, and moved straight towards the bedroom without removing a single article of clothing, his own or hers, a sure sign that something must be terribly wrong.

"What happened?" she said now, stroking his head. She paused. "Did you see your mother?"

She felt his embrace tighten. Then he raised his head and stared into her eyes.

"Help me," he whispered. "Help me to know ... what is real."

He thought he felt her stiffen. Ben's psychological problems had always been a dark zone for her. A major component of their love had always been their shared sense of outsidership. But she knew that Ben's alienation went much deeper: he had been locked up in a mental hospital at fourteen for a suicide attempt, and had been homeless since he was fifteen. And the phobic terror of his mother that had still been riding him when he met Aditi was different not only in degree but in kind from the fears she had known. She studied his face.

"Baby, what kind of help do you need? Why are you doubting reality? *What* seems unreal to you? Before anything, *what happened?* The only thing I can think of is that you must have seen your mother."

"I did," he said, and an encouraging element of reflection now entered his staring eyes. "I saw her ... and ... something else ..." He looked down, thinking. "I ... woke up on the porch of her house, at dawn. I ... don't remember going there." His eyes glistened with terror. "I had seen ... something so *terrible* in the department last night." He again raised his eyes to hers, which were now also wide with dread.

"Call Boylan," he whispered urgently. *"Call him."*

"Ben, it's past midnight," she said.

"What the hell difference does that make to him?" said Ben, a growing excitement and hope in his voice. "Call him! I know he must be there! I need to know right now!" He raised himself from her, got off the bed and took her hand, trying to pull her towards the living room. "I just need to hear his voice. I *know* he must be there, on the floor of his office, like he always is. He won't know it's you phoning him! Aditi, please do this for me. It's literally a matter of life and death."

She allowed him to draw her from the bed to the living room, where the phone sat on its little table next to the sofa. She sat, raised the receiver, and punched in the number as he stood in front of her, arms crossed on his chest, anxiously looking on. She listened for a moment, then handed the receiver up to Ben.

"It's ringing," she said. "Just don't say anything."

He stood listening for about half a minute.

"Ben," she whispered, "he's not there, or he's unconscious."

Ben glanced at her and raised his finger to his lips, shushing her, then turned aside and continued to listen as she leaned her cheek on her fist, looking resigned. The seconds ticked away as he stood listening, hunched with the receiver in his right hand and his left arm crossed over his chest, visibly growing more and more desperate to hear the receiver picked up at the other end.

Finally, after what may have been a full three minutes, he raised his head with a jerk, beaming beatifically, as a sharp burst of enraged squawking was heard from the receiver. He looked down at Aditi with real joy and triumph, and she smiled back at him, looking perplexed but gratified, as another paroxysm of almost discernible obscenities emerged from the phone.

Stooping to lightly put down the receiver, he straightened himself and began to pace around the room, head bent, with his left arm still over his chest and his right fist pressed against his chin. He was smiling tightly, in the grip of the upsurge of some indeterminate emotion of which the main element was joy. He felt tears spill from his eyes as Aditi watched, a look of shock coming over her face. Spinning round at the end of one lap of his frenetic pacing, he burst out in a trembling voice that threatened to collapse into hysterical laughter.

"I could never have imagined ... that I would ever be so glad ... to hear that that dollop of demonic scum wasn't dead!"

And now the wave broke, and he threw back his head and began to laugh, sitting down at last on one of the steel and plastic chairs.

"*Dead?*" said Aditi, sounding frightened. "Why would he have been *dead?*"

Ben rapidly composed himself. "Listen, I've seen ... last night, in the faculty, I saw ... I saw something I couldn't believe, couldn't bear to believe. All day I was wondering ... how much of it was true, could any of it have been true ... I could *feel* that it hadn't been real, or entirely real."

He paused, leaning forward, hands clasped between his knees, and looked up into her eyes.

"I saw Boylan. I saw Boylan and Malhotra, together, in Robarts, in the fire escape stairwell. Boylan ... attacked me. And I defended myself. And then ... he killed himself! He pushed himself off the stairs and ... fell to the bottom of the stairwell."

"Oh my god!" whispered Aditi. She stared at him, stunned. "But ... just now you heard him answer the phone ... ?"

"Yes!" said Ben, again beaming with joy and relief. "What I saw... was a *hallucination!* I know now what has happened. Moksha ... Baby, do you know anything about acid, LSD?"

She shook her head, still staring.

"Look," he said. "Moksha has LSD. A lot of it. I can't explain right now, but ... Moksha has LSD, and so does Boylan. Moksha thought that I should do acid with him, he offered acid to me. I refused, but ... "

"But you think ... that he somehow gave you some *without your knowing it?"* said Aditi softly, staring, horrified. "Oh baby, what is it going to do to you? It's still working, then? Are you going to have more hallucinations? When will it be out of your system? And how could he have done this? When? It's a week since we took him up there."

"I don't know," said Ben, shaking his head, looking down. "I don't know much about LSD, I don't know how it works, or for how long. But I've heard that it doesn't always take effect as soon as you've taken it, that the effect can stop and start, that there can be what they call 'flashbacks,' episodes that come long after you've taken it, months or even years. I really just don't know, this is just stuff I've heard, mainly from Moksha."

"But ... what happens during these episodes?" she said. "What happened to you last night? Were you just sitting somewhere, or asleep, and you had this vision that seemed so real that you remembered it as a real event? So it just makes you hallucinate? I mean ... it doesn't make you *dangerous* in any way, does it?"

He looked up at her, and in her face saw fear struggling with love.

"I ... don't think so," he said. "I just don't know. I've never heard of anyone committing violence while on an acid trip. Apparently it's not like alcohol or cocaine, it's not a stimulant like that. It's a hallucinogen, so, yes, I have the impression that it generally just makes you quite passive, it turns you inward, while you see visions, experience hallucinations. I think the worst that can happen is that you can see something terrifying, and you'll just end up, you know, curled up on the floor, babbling or screaming."

She was still staring.

"Aditi," he said, forcing the words out, "if you're afraid ... I'll go." His face was anguished.

"Baby, no," she said, pained, standing up and putting out her hand to caress his cheek. "I've also heard similar things about it, I'm remembering now. And anyway, I don't care."

She touched his face and kissed him slowly, closing her eyes, and drew back to look at him, her hand still on his cheek. With an expression of tortured gratitude, he raised his hand to caress the nape of her neck under her cascading curls, kissed her, then took her hand, sat with her on the sofa, and lay down with his head in her lap, facing forward, as she stroked his hair.

"I have to see Moksha," he said finally. "I have to go up there. That son of a bitch."

Ben was awake, or he thought he was, looking up at the lights of Bloor and St. George reflected on the ceiling, feeling the cool rhythm of her sleeping breath against his chest, smelling the rich odour of her hair. Sleep felt far away.

Lovemaking had been what it always was, nothing bizarre or visionary, no winding serpentine talking penises or beckoning divine light emanating from her vulva. But now he was haunted by an anxious self-observing vigilance, a suspicion of every perception. At what point had the hallucination begun, last night in the department? When he had woken up from his nap and begun reading again, surely ... though in retrospect, the dream of his mother felt like a prelude to the encounter with Boylan on the stairs, felt like it was made of the same ambivalent half-real stuff. And in fact, he had doubted that the dream was over when he had woken up.

And when had the vision ended? During his sleep on the porch of his mother's house, so that when he had woken up there at dawn, he had been in reality again? But ... he had actually gotten there somehow, in the real world, after bursting from the fire escape into the night, though he could no longer remember beyond that moment, couldn't remember actually going to her house.

There was no obvious seam between reality and hallucination. Was the vision of Boylan and Malhotra a hallucinatory distortion of things that had actually happened? So ... what had he actually said and done to Boylan? And what would he have done to his mother?

He was trying to remember when and how Moksha could have slipped him a tab. It must have been sometime during the trip to the house at Lake Simcoe, but he couldn't think of a moment when it could have happened, or how. Ben certainly couldn't remember ingesting one of the Buddha postage stamps in a recognizable form. Moksha must have shredded it into bits, soaked it ... He couldn't remember. Had he even eaten or drunk anything during the trip? He must have.

Aditi stirred and murmured, pressing herself closer against his hip, tightening the grip of her arm around his chest, resettling her head against his armpit. At last he felt himself beginning to wade into the shallows of sleep, as the images of memory, mingling with the light and shadow on the ceiling, began to assume the vividness and autonomy of reality, in the manner of dream: Boylan, Malhotra, his mother, Peter... He felt a sudden surge of panic as he drifted down: of course there was no reason to think that the drug was out of his system. At this moment he might be entering another hallucination ... or the last one might never have ended. Was he here with Aditi at all? Maybe he was still lying on his mother's porch ... or dozing at the table in the library ... He saw Boylan, face half-flattened, looking up at him with his one still active eye, the unshattered half of his mouth twitching with the beginnings of a wicked grin. The impulse to step forward and grind his sandalled foot into that face, snuff out that worthless life like a cigarette butt ...

Was he really so sure that acid couldn't release murderous violence? Moksha!

And Ben ... what unconscious intention had drawn him to his mother's house? But in any case there could be no danger to Aditi, this woman who was to him the embodiment of all that was worth living for, who had again unhesitatingly put herself entirely in his hands, without either of them knowing, anymore, what those hands might be capable of.

Pain wrested him back into consciousness: spots of crushing pressure on his legs, arms, abdomen, shoulders, invading, feeling out, like hands but more brutal. Someone was walking on him, their feet searching out every point that would bear the full weight of their step. This had happened, in reality, long ago. Now he was dreaming of it, hallucinating it. This time he would remember that it was a dream.

He opened his eyes on his mother's face as she crouched above him, staring intently into his, searching hungrily for the effects of her violence. She looked about as old as she had when he had seen her last, in the street, perhaps a little younger: small figure still spare and vigorous, thin mid-length hair still in the process of changing from brown to grey, face lined and drooping but still pretty. She was wearing a nightdress, as on the night when she had actually trampled on him in this way as he lay sleeping on the floor of his bedless room in the house where he grew up. He had been eleven.

"Ben," she said softly, "why are you sleeping here?"

He became aware of the cold wooden floor, the night breeze, the faint smell of household garbage in garbage bags, his nudity. It was the porch of the house she lived in. A confusion of anger and fear stirred in his gut as he saw her expression soften slightly with love. She reached out and caressed his shoulder, then his face.

"What did you come here to do, Ben? You know, I could call the police. This is what they call stalking."

She shifted her weight on her haunches, and in an instant of exposure he saw the dark flash of her naked crotch. Nausea, fury, the stirring of appalling desire. He wanted to grab her hand and thrust it away, but he felt paralyzed by torpor: this was truly a dream, this time he was aware, he was watching. She was stroking his cheek.

"You never did find anyone else who could understand you, did you," she murmured. "Nobody else understood what a special child you were, so brilliant, so sensitive ..."

Her caress hardened, she gripped and squeezed his cheeks on either side of his mouth, violently pressing out his lips in an undignified pucker. A surge of disgust and panic shook him, a cry died in his throat as a strangled gurgle. Her eyes shone with cruel excitement, searching his face. Her mouth was almost visibly trembling, about to spread into a grin of frank pleasure.

He rasped, "How could you do this to me?"

Her face contorted into a caricature of misery and distress. "Oh! Oh!" she cried in a mocking burlesque of sobbing, *"How could you do this to me?"* Now she openly sneered, the mask discarded. "That's what you tell yourself, isn't it, you little shit? Yourself and everyone around you: the psychiatrists, your father, your worthless crazy loser friends. 'It's my mother's fault, that crazy evil bitch. *She* did this to me.' "

She released his face and poked him in the chest, never shifting her eyes from his, hungrily savouring his anguish. The sneer had wilted into an expression of frank loathing.

"You think you're special, don't you? You think you've got a real horror story of abuse to tell. But there was nothing special about what happened in our house." She flicked his chin with her finger. "If you've got a problem with it, that's *your* problem, *your* responsibility, *your* fault" (poking him in the chest for emphasis, *your, your, your*).

In a paroxysm of rage, he spat in her face. Snarling softly, she seized him by the hair with her left hand and began punching his face with her right, then scrambled to her feet and began kicking him with her naked heel, his face, his genitals, everywhere. He writhed, looking up through tears at the familiar image of her face beaming with the excitement of hate.

He spasmed awake with a cry, shaking Aditi, who was still pressed against him.

"Shh, it's okay, baby", she whispered, tightening her arm over his heaving chest, then cupping his cheek. "It's okay. Everything's going to be alright."

The next morning, Ben and Aditi walked the short distance down St. George to Robarts, climbed the broad steps of the cathedral-like north entrance, and stood waiting alone for the elevator. It was August, the gap month, and the campus was sparsely peopled, summer courses having ended and the new academic year not beginning until September. Ben clutched her hand, expecting at every step to be apprehended by a campus cop, probably Malhotra—or more likely, by a real one. How much of it had really happened? But even if he *had* gone out the fire escape, which seemed likely, they could have no evidence that it had been him, and in any case that on its own was a pretty minor offence, something that people did from time to time, usually accidentally. And Ben and Aditi knew that Boylan was alive—very much alive, to judge from the burst of obscenities and threats that had answered Ben on the phone.

When the elevator door slid open, they walked past the one person waiting there, a young East Asian woman, and turned into the passage on the left.

"How long has it been since we were here together?" Aditi said.

"A long time. Years," he said.

He opened the door to the South Asian Studies library, and they went in. It was empty, of course. Aditi looked around, detached her hand from Ben's, and strolled around the room, touching the tables as she passed, stopping in front of a section of the stacks and perusing the titles on the spines. Ben went to the shelf that held the twenty-volume edition of the *Mahabharata*, slid out the volume he had been reading—the *Udyogaparva*—and tilted it to look at the top: the Buddha's Vegetarian Restaurant card was where he had left it.

He opened the heavy black-bound volume, and the colour drained from his face.

"I can't remember the last time I was in here," she said, her smile audible in her voice. He slowly closed the volume, replaced it in its gap, and turned to her. "Don't be scared, baby," she said, smiling but troubled, taking his hand again. *"he bhagavān,* you look so scared! You're white as a sheet!"

She kissed him lightly on the lips, drew back to look at him again. He was trying to smile, looking down.

"Come over here," she said, drawing him with her towards the space she had just left, between the last table and the bookshelf. "Remember that time in the early days, when you came in, and I was here, at this very table, reading, and you came over, and were just leaning over my shoulder from behind to look at what I was reading, and kiss me, when the door started to open again, and you jumped, and you took, like, two crazy long strides, on tiptoe, over to that shelf, and stood there trying to look like you were searching for some book, while I was over here with my face in my book, trying to look terribly absorbed ... " She laughed, and hugged his arm to her, and looked up at him coaxingly.

"And the person coming in turned out to be just Andrew, who had already figured out the situation between you and me and was cool about it, and he just gave us his usual dopey smile, and sat down over there. So you came back over, and were leaning over me again, and we were kissing, when the door started to open *again,* and you jumped up *again,* and over to the shelf in exactly the same way!" He had begun to laugh now, softly, looking down, as she went on. "And it turned out to be Andrew's girlfriend! And Andrew had figured out what was going on, that we were terrified that Boylan was going to walk in and see us together. So he was laughing, and she was looking perplexed."

She sat down in the same chair at the same table, drawing his hands onto her shoulders, and he bent over her shoulder from behind, and they kissed, eyes closed, for a long time.

"Let's go," she said finally. "Let's go have a look."

She closed the library door behind them, and holding hands, they walked in the direction of Boylan's office. The muffled roar of the air conditioning behind the metal fire escape doors rose as they neared and rounded the corner. Just ahead, above the concrete parapet of the upper sub-corridor, they could see Boylan's door ajar.

Ben stopped. "I'll go," he said softly. "Wait here. Be with me watching."

He left her, caressing and letting go of her hand, walked back a little way to the stairs leading up and down to the two subcorridors, softly climbed, and walked towards Boylan's office.

Through the half-open door, he saw Boylan sitting behind his desk. He had turned his chair towards the window and was sitting with his arms on the armrests and his feet up on the wide ledge below the window, which looked past nearby apartment towers onto the city's vast receding sprawl. Near the western horizon, microscopic airplanes rose and sank, glinting in the morning sun.

Ben stood, silently watching. For a long time Boylan stared out of the window, almost perfectly still. Finally, as if feeling Ben's gaze, he turned his head, and their eyes met. The face that was half-turned to Ben was the face he had seen mashed against the floor of the stairwell. Now there was no sign that that had ever happened: Boylan looked tired and wrecked, as usual, but physically intact. More than tired, he looked defeated, drained: in his weary eyes, Ben saw none of the paranoid defiance that had always smouldered there. His gaze—undefended, even intimate, even pleading—said *Yes, this is what I am, as you know,* and kindled in Ben an unwelcome pity, as on the night when he had found him lying stupefied on this floor, and in the turmoil of his conflicting emotions had been moved to kick him in the gut. Now Ben stood in the gap of the door, and the unsuperior pity in his face was calm and unconflicted. Here was the old psychopath, alone at last, deprived even of his final victim and plaything, and with no object left upon which to project his consuming hate and misery, which would now flow back upon himself alone. *Pity the monsters! Pity the monsters!*

Boylan turned back to the window, and Ben went back the way he had come.

As he descended the steps and came towards Aditi, she was watching him, questioningly, but with confident satisfaction.

"So? He's there, isn't he?" she said softly, putting out her hand, and Ben nodded, taking and caressing it with both his own.

"Let's go," she said as they turned back and rounded the corner. "Let's go to Buddha's. I feel a sudden craving for tofu duck and slimy mushrooms."

He laughed softly, and as they passed the door of the South Asian Studies library, he was sufficiently distracted by his relief and happiness that he almost didn't remember opening the *Mahabharata* to find a torn-off strip of three of Boylan's acid-Buddha stamps neatly placed on top of his Buddha's Vegetarian bookmark, above the last verse read on that half-dreamed night, ending with the words *"Fate is stronger."*

14

Outside the bus window, after an hour of farmland, houses began to appear on what Ben recognized as the outskirts of Seaton. He stroked Aditi's face where she lay in his lap, and she stirred and rapidly sat up.

"Are we here?" she asked a bit hoarsely, shaking her head awake, drawing back her tumbling hair as if to tie it back, and looking out the window.

"This is Seaton," he said, squeezing her knee. "You missed almost the whole trip, Miss Narcolepsy." They both smiled.

They had already reached the town's single central commercial street. "Seaton," the female driver's voice announced over the intercom, just before the bus slowed and stopped in front of the old red-brick post office. Aditi and Ben sidled out of their seats, grabbed their knapsacks from the luggage shelf above, stumbled up the aisle past seats about a quarter full with passengers, and disembarked.

It was about 10 o'clock in the morning, and the main street was almost deserted. Back in the direction from which the bus had come, three or four teenagers in summer wear milled about in front of a convenience store. Across the street, a red *Open / Ouvert* sign glowed in the dark window of the liquor store, a squat red-brick fortress.

"This way," said Ben, looking in the direction the bus had gone, and taking her hand. "It'll take us about half an hour. It'll be a beautiful walk."

They walked out of town on an ancient grass-fringed sidewalk, past one- and two-storey wooden houses separated from the street by yards fenced or unfenced, treed or clear, mowed or fallow, some littered with vehicles and other junk, one with a large dog who inevitably dashed forward, dragging his rattling chain, to bay at them from behind the dilapidated picket fence. The houses thinned, the street became a road, bending to the right. To their left, past lands both cleared and treed, the broad expanse of Lake Simcoe came into view, immense Georgina Island, the distant far shore. Hand in hand, they walked the left gravel margin of the worn two-lane road with its faded yellow line. The coast had drawn nearer on their left, where houses stood well back from the road amidst their expansive lakefront properties, and on the right, farmland: no crops here, but pasture for meat cattle who gazed at them with mild interest from the other side of slouching barbed wire fences. Titanic white clouds occasionally blocked the August sun, which had already begun to weigh hard on Aditi and Ben, despite her white visor and his broad-brimmed hat. Vehicles appeared rarely, arising out of the deep silence as whispers that crescendoed to a brief roar as they passed, crossing far into the empty opposite lane to avoid them, then diminuendoed back into silence. The sharp bend to the left brought them within sight of the MacLeod homestead. Minutes later, the fragrance of countryside swelled as they turned left onto the faded dirt road leading to the house through the fallow fields on either side.

"I imagine he will have been working for hours already, since the *brahmamuhūrta,* before dawn," said Ben. "He must be observing his old monastic routine, like he used to do up here."

They approached the house, passed it on their left, found and followed the faint footpath into the *āśrama*'s wood.

"I have to go in here," said Aditi, putting her knapsack down amid the sparse sun-starved grass and unbuckling her belt as she walked over to the wooden outhouse at the end of an even fainter footpath that branched off from the main one. She slowly drew open the door, which creaked in unison with the rusted spring's metallic sigh. "I'm not looking forward to this," she said, looking at the gaping oval hole in the wooden bench.

"Why don't you just piss out here?" said Ben.

"It isn't piss," she said.

"Wait," he said, "we'll open the house and you can use the washroom there."

"I can't wait," she said, unzipping the fly of her jeans.

"Is there water?" he said.

"Yes," she said, stepping in and closing the door.

Ben stepped off the trail, shuffling off his knapsack, tossed his hat upside down onto the grass, and lay down with his head pillowed against the knapsack, folding his hands over his chest. He looked up through still branches into the sky. His eyes crossed, closed. The branches breathed, rushed like distant flowing water, and as he drifted down, he felt that sound take on an indeterminate menace, like an almost inaudible voice. Far away, the door creaked open and banged shut. The sense of a presence in the breathing branches, dreadful, murderous, watching ...

"It doesn't feel like there's anyone here."

Aditi's voice came to him from far outside, reaching in, dragging him back to the surface. He opened his eyes to see her crouching above him, glancing around, slightly troubled.

"The outhouse doesn't smell like it's being used," she said.

"Maybe he's moved into the house," Ben murmured, still

surfacing. He shook his head and raised himself onto his elbow. "Let's go find him." He studied her face, now turned towards the *āśrama*. "Are you tired?" he said.

"Yes," she said. "But let's find him first."

Leaving their bags on the grass, they walked towards the *āśrama*. Ben knocked. No one stirred within. He knocked again, and again there was no response. He glanced at Aditi, and saw that she was afraid. To her questioning eyes he responded with an amused smile that said *What? What could be wrong?* He turned the doorknob, pushed open the door, and stepped in.

Amidst the darkness, the desk blazed with dazzling sunlight pouring in from the window above it. As their eyes adjusted to the contrast, the scene of Moksha's daily life came into focus: the closed notebook and pen laid neatly in the desk's centre, the volume of the *Yogavāsiṣṭha* nearby, separated from its two fellows among the upright books in the top left corner, the blanket heaped on the bed's bare boards, two paperbacks on the gap of floor between the bed and the bookcase, and on the other side of the bookcase, the shoulder-bag half-buried under a heap of clothes. The window was pushed up and a stream of air was flowing between the window and the opened door. Ben was struck by the unexpected freshness of the air in the hut. He flicked on the light switch, but the light didn't come on.

"That's strange," he said. "Maybe he hasn't turned on the electricity. I guess he wanted to do a harder *tapas* this time, a harder austerity, but ... that would mean that he can only work during the daylight hours. What could he be doing at night, if he can't read? Meditating, maybe. And there's no sign of smoking: the ashtray is empty, there's no smell of smoke ... "

Aditi had gone over to the desk, and was lifting open the notebook's cover as Ben came and stood beside her. She picked it up and began leafing through it. It was old, discoloured, warped with dampness. The earlier pages were filled with what appeared to be Moksha's translation work from years ago, in faded blue ink: single *Devanāgarī* verses followed first by a rough working-out and then by a finished translation. At one point, the ink changed to black, clear and new. After a couple of pages, there was a verse with a longer than usual working-out, and no finished translation. And then, this poem:

I'd go, if not for you.
My name is "Freedom," right?
So easy, to make true
my name, to play the sage,
and run towards the light
that ends this pilgrimage.

I'd go—but here you are.
And you, love, are not free.
And while you linger here,
you falsify my name,
enticing me away
from my long-dreamed-of home.

You are not free. I am.
Love, for the sage self-freed,
means turning, for a time,
from his hard-earned release,
to help his friend in need
win his own final peace.

Thus, for a little while
I stay, to help you sever
the bonds that bind you still,

and when that task is done,
we'll face the light together,
released into the one.

Wide-eyed, Aditi looked up at Ben and handed him the notebook. As she turned and walked over to the bookcase, he read the poem again, then put the notebook back on the table, noticing the clear rectangle of its outline amidst a light film of dust. Gently, so that Aditi wouldn't hear, he eased open the desk's top drawer, and even though it was no more than he had expected, his heart still froze when he saw, atop a stack of old notebooks, the page of Buddha stamps reduced nearly by half, with two remaining at the right corner of the topmost row. He slid the drawer softly closed and turned.

Aditi was looking at the books in the bookcase. He went and crouched to pick up the two paperbacks. Nothing very revealing: Robertson Davies's *What's Bred in the Bone* and Dickens's *David Copperfield,* two of Moksha's old favourites. He raised his eyes: Aditi had picked up the stone Nandi from the shelf and was caressing him in her palms as if he were a delicate little bird. He stood, and she looked at him seriously.

"Ben, how sane is Moksha?" He looked down uncomfortably, and she went on: "I mean, I know what you've told me about his history. So I know he's ... unconventional ... like us. But ... I know he's in love with you. And now we find this poem. And he's nowhere to be found, and doesn't seem to have been in here for a while. And he's up here alone ... This notebook is kind of an *All work and no play makes Jack a dull boy* moment, you know? Do you really think it was such a good idea for him to come up here, whoever's idea it was? And you say he's got LSD, and may even have given you some without your knowing. That's really frightening. Do you have any idea what's going on in his mind?"

Ben was still looking down, shaking his head, more in dejection than in denial. “I don’t think there’s anything to be alarmed about,” he said, though he himself had at that moment been wondering in alarm about the clothes left on the bed. “Moksha has spent long periods up here in the past. The whole point of retreat, of hermitage, is to cultivate a state of mind that is detached from society and the individual’s social identity. And Moksha is already pretty detached from those things, so yes, he will have gotten pretty weird by now. But I know from more than a decade of friendship with him that he’s harmless, he’s incapable of doing harm.”

“But what about this poem!” said Aditi, and this time Ben had no answer, because he was being sucked into a vortex of doubt and self-accusation, having suddenly remembered the drunken Moksha’s oblique expressions of hostility to Aditi over the years in the form of ugly sexual jokes and mockeries. Of course! How could he have agreed to let her come with him! It had been sheer egocentric self-delusion! He had to get her out of here!

He looked up, gently took the Nandi from her hands, stroked the idol’s head as if it were a living animal, and put it back on the top shelf with its small collection of books leaning against one end.

“I should have come up here alone,” he said resignedly, looking aside. “Moksha is definitely harmless, but I wouldn’t have wanted you to see this ... whatever we’re going to see. I guess we’re just going to find him in a very spaced-out and embarrassing condition. He’s probably begun meditating again, practicing yoga—and dropping acid too, but meditation and acid don’t make anyone violent, least of all Moksha. But I’m probably going to have to help him straighten out a bit, before we leave, so that he doesn’t withdraw too far from the exigencies of common reality.”

He looked her in the face now, and found her looking still

concerned but beginning to be a little reassured. He took her hand and stroked it.

"He may have moved into the house," he said. "Hopefully he will have gone into town and gotten an emergency welfare check, which always lasts him a long time. We'll stay in the house for a week or so, you and me, like we planned. I'll kick him out, back here, where he's supposed to be. Forest sages don't live in houses."

He smiled, allowing himself to suppress his dread of Moksha's possible condition, and to hope that, whatever it was, he would work it out of his system while safely isolated from the world. Here they were together, Ben and Aditi, on a private homestead in the middle of the countryside, by a lake, with an ascetics' grove, and a house with a bedroom looking out towards the lake. This was too beautiful, to be with her here. He couldn't let Moksha ruin this completely. She smiled back at him tentatively.

As they walked back through the grove towards the house, the breeze breathing through the high branches, he glanced about, and his hand tightened around hers as his imperfect eyes glimpsed Moksha for half-moments here and there in the flickering undersea light, clad in the tree bark and deerskin of the forest seers of Hindu myth, with long matted hair and beard, standing and staring with crazed eyes red with the dementia of solitary meditation.

Wasn't it true, what he had told her? he thought. What was the worst condition they could find Moksha in? In this solitude, all was peace, beauty, serenity, conditions that the ancient sages had sought out precisely because they conduced to the piercing of the world-illusion that engenders passion and violence. And the poem showed that Moksha had attained that high level of insight—re-attained it, probably. No doubt he was using the acid as an aid to meditation, but this was nothing more than the ancient sages themselves had done with their own psychotropic substances. As he was using it now, it was in effect a completely different drug from the one he had taken back in Toronto. When they found him, he would probably be in a somewhat ridiculous state of ecstatic stupefaction in which he would find it difficult even to talk with them, let alone attack and kill them, even if he wanted to. And why would he want to? He loved Ben, and even though he certainly resented Aditi, it was inconceivable, no matter how insane he might have become, that he could *hate* her the way he hated security guards and the police. And besides, he couldn't be in the most robust physical condition. What was he eating?

As they emerged from the wood and approached the house, he looked up at the windows, the large picture window of the first floor, the smaller three of the second. All were veiled by curtains. Reaching the door, and finding it surprisingly locked, he took out the key from his inner jacket pocket, unlocked and pushed it open. He could feel Aditi's fear again, mirroring his own, which he took care not to acknowledge. He closed the door behind them, paused, then locked it. They found the house in exactly the same condition in which they had seen it when Douglas had brought them in, with the wisps of their trails still visible in the ever deepening dust. He took Aditi's hand and squeezed it, turned and smiled at her, evoking an unwilling answering smile from her half-petrified face.

They looked into the rooms on the first floor: the dining room facing the road, the kitchen, the washroom, the living room facing the lake, all with their furniture and equipment neatly ordered for a long hibernation. A heavy film of dust covered all, including the living room's plastic-wrapped sofa and two easy chairs. Ben opened the curtains first of the dining room, then of the living room, where they stood for a moment in front of the vista revealed: the fallow lawn with woods on either side, the lake, Georgina Island, the northern shore. They turned and climbed the creaking wooden stairs: on the second floor, two bedrooms, a smaller washroom. They pulled the plastic off the double bed in the bedroom facing the lake, lifted open the window, and lay down.

"I'll go down to the cellar and turn on the electricity and water," Ben murmured, lying on his back stroking her hair as she lay against him. She was already asleep, and he followed, sinking through the silence that breathed with the trees' vaguely menacing voice.

Afterwards, they walked down to the lake along the faded footpath, single-file with him in front, the high grass brushing their legs and hands. The hard light of the high sun balanced with the cool air. Near the shore, Ben lay down amidst the grass at the point where it began to fade into beach, not far from the trunk of a large tree, drawing Aditi down with him. They reclined side by side on the sandy earth, amidst high grass, looking out over the lake. It was calm, its surface slightly pulsing with ripples. A scattering of sailboats and motorboats moved about in the silent distance, so far out that their people were invisible. Ben leaned over, smelled her hair, kissed her cheek, and rested his cheek against hers, and they looked out over the water together.

After some time, he nuzzled her ear. "Come on," he murmured, "no one's here. This is *our* āśrama."

She kissed him deeply on the lips, lingeringly, eyes closed. He separated from her, rolled her onto her back, undid her belt and pants, pulled them off her as she raised her feet and knees into the air to help him. They sat up, he tore off his clothes, she pulled off her sweater and T-shirt. He grabbed her sweater, spread it out on the sandy ground, seized her narrow hips and shifted her onto it as she laughed at his fervour, and then he was on top of her and inside her, not even asking her if she was safe. They lay adream in the dappled light of the tree's breathing boughs, with the high grass barely swaying above them. They barely moved, he pulsing against and inside her without friction, she rhythmically clenching and releasing him, caressing his back and buttocks. As he breathed the fragrance of her hair, face, neck, the almost articulate menace in the wind receded. Inhaling the sweet, nearly motionless breath of her nostrils, he looked into her eyes: they were heavy-lidded with serene ecstasy, like his. Seeing him, she closed them and shook with her first orgasm, arching her head back slightly, making a soft guttural sound, clenching him within. He remained poised in the trance of suspended orgasm as she relaxed and their still inner rhythm continued. At last he felt his come rising, and he swelled and tightened below, and began at last to move within her. The friction drove her to a second spasm, and he joined her, shuddering violently as she grasped his buttocks, pressing him into her.

Afterwards, they lay stilled, entwined, feeling their breathing and heartbeats slowing in unison, their joined parts ebbing and relaxing.

"Come on," he murmured, kissing her ear, slipping out of her, still half-hard, and standing up, pulling her by the hand. "Are you ready to swim with me this time?"

She rose with him, laughing, her thighs glistening, and they walked hand-in-hand out of the grass and onto the pebbly beach, and began to wade into the still lake.

"It's cold!" she squealed.

"Not once you're in!" he laughed, moving ahead of her, turning, gently pulling her by her outstretched hand. He let go and fell backwards into the water. "It feels great!" he gasped, re-emerging and shaking his hair, with only his head above the surface. "Come on, before someone sees you!"

"What?" she cried, alarmed, looking around and shrinking into herself, holding her arms in front of her breasts. She took several tentative but rapid steps forward, her hands raised mincingly, and fell forward into the water, eyes closed, going almost completely under, then sprang up again with a shout, gasping and laughing, pushing back her hair heavy with water. Ben laughed, and broke into a thunderous back-crawl, swimming well out, then turned over and headed back towards her, churning and kicking up foam.

"You know how to swim, right?" he said.

She nodded, and began to move out into deeper water in a breaststroke, and he followed, swimming in the same style. Back and forth they swam, together and singly, savouring the water's delicious total caress, from time to time standing on the muddy floor with their heads just above the water's blinding shimmer, laughing. He had stopped and stood, beaming at her with rare serenity, and she approached, pulsing towards him, her back and buttocks shining with hot sunlight, her hair clinging to her head and shoulders. She stood in front of him and pressed herself to him, her arms around his shoulders, and he held her by the lower back, and they kissed, eyes closed.

Opening his eyes, he saw someone standing on the shore. Feeling his body freeze and stiffen, she turned her head and looked, and saw clearly what he could only vaguely see. It was Moksha, standing in the grass where they had left their clothes, staring at them. He was naked except for his glasses and *akṣamālā,* and emaciated. His silvering hair, already fairly long when they had brought him up here three months ago, now touched his shoulders, and was matted: *jaṭā,* the matted locks of the ancient Hindu forest sages.

"Oh my god," she murmured, her arms gone cold against his shoulders.

"Baby, don't worry," said Ben, suppressing his own fear and distress, caressing her hand with both hands under the water as he stepped around her. "Believe me, he's harmless, even if he's spaced out, and so far as nudity is concerned, forget it, you might as well be a tree to him. Follow me."

He began to wade shoreward. *"bho mokṣa!"* he shouted, waving, now waist-deep, *"kim te anayā nagnatayā?,"* *what's with this nudity?*

Moksha said nothing. Ben could see his face now. He was indeed evidently spaced out, staring with eyes that seemed to look from an unreachable distance, frowning. His huge tortoiseshell glasses sat on his face unevenly, and at each ear there was a wild knot of some kind of twine or vine: one or both of the arms must have broken, and he had had to improvise this means of tying them to his face. His withered flesh clung loosely to a wasted, almost skeletal frame.

Now calf-deep, Ben turned and saw Aditi, visibly petrified, still standing where he had left her, with the rippling water concealing and revealing the top of her shoulders.

He turned back to Moksha. "Moksha, would you put some clothes on, just for Aditi's sake? You know, we're still stuck in *saṃsāra,* we haven't transcended such illusions yet. Could you indulge us a bit?"

Moksha was staring at Ben's penis, which shrank into itself under his gaze, until it was as small as Moksha's own, withered and uncut. Moksha looked up into Ben's eyes, and Ben saw that, yes, he had used some kind of vine to make a strap for his glasses: if the forest seers of ancient India had worn glasses, thought Ben, this is how they would have looked, though presumably corrected vision would have been one of the *siddhis,* yogic attainments. He studied Moksha's face. How far gone was he?

"I've been waiting for you," said Moksha, and Ben was relieved to hear that the voice was still the voice of the Moksha he had known, still of this world, human and involved. His eyes, too, had begun to drift back into human range.

"Do you wanna put on *my* clothes?" said Ben, nodding towards the heap of his and Aditi's clothes on the patch of pressed-down grass at their feet. "I don't really need them, at the moment. Aditi's used to seeing me this way. Come on, I have to insist on this," he said, stooping and picking up his T-shirt and holding it out to Moksha, "cuz she'll just stand up to her neck in water till nightfall if you don't put something on."

Moksha stared at the bunched blue T-shirt for a moment, then took it and slowly pulled it over his head and arms. As Ben had hoped, it was large enough that it hung down well past his thighs, completely covering his genitals.

Ben turned back to Aditi, and smiling, made a broad beckoning gesture. *"ehi ehi, gopi! kim anayā te lajjayā niṣkāmasya tapasvinaḥ samakṣam?"* he shouted: *Come on, cowgirl! Why be ashamed in front of a desireless ascetic?*

She smiled weakly, and began to wade very slowly towards the shore, the water descending past her arms clinging to her chest, past her tight abdomen ...

Ben turned to Moksha, laughing. "It's kinda like that scene, you know, with Krishna and the cowgirls, when they're bathing naked and he steals their clothes?"

Moksha smiled, again to Ben's relief.

Ben picked up Aditi's clothes and walked down to the shore to meet her as she stepped onto the sand, her arms still folded over her chest, her dark skin and clinging hair glistening splendidly in the sun. As he watched her clothe herself, he felt his penis swelling slightly, and blushed under the gaze of the palpably not yet quite completely desireless ascetic. When she had finished, he took her hand, and they walked back to where Moksha was standing.

"Moksha, Aditi. Aditi, Moksha," said Ben with ironic formality, and then doubled over in a paroxysm of laughter at the ludicrousness of the scene: Moksha the insane ascetic dwarf with his vine-tied glasses, clad only in an oversized T-shirt, staring blankly at Aditi; Aditi, not much taller than a dwarf herself, with her wet clothes and dripping hair, staring back at Moksha, terrified and embarrassed; and Ben, still naked, towering above both of them, and courteously bringing them together like two dignitaries at an ambassadorial cocktail party.

"Hello." Moksha sounded stoned.

"Hi," Aditi replied coldly.

Repressing another seizure of hilarity, Ben bent down and picked up his underpants and began to dress himself, talking the while. "Aditi and I have come up to stay in the house for a week or so, as Douglas said we could. We both have some time: I've taken some days off, and Aditi submitted her dissertation last week. We've already been in the house. Evidently you haven't gone in at all? Our tracks were still there from May, but no new ones."

Moksha shook his head, staring.

Now fully clothed but for his T-shirt, with his torso naked under his open jacket, Ben continued: "But our main reason for coming up now was to check up on you. And I need to talk to you about a ... an experience I've had, which you might be able to cast some light on."

Ben thought he saw a slight ripple of interest in the blankness of Moksha's face.

"Listen, Aditi and I are going back to the house," said Ben, taking her hand. "Then I'm gonna come and find you in the *āśrama*. Would you go and put on your clothes? I hope I'm not asking you to make too great a concession to our bondage to the illusions of *saṃsāra* if I ask you to wear clothes for the few days we're here? You know that we're nowhere near to your level of liberation."

"Well, you both seemed pretty liberated when you were lying here a few minutes ago," Moksha said, smiling slightly and looking down, again sounding completely like his un-stoned self.

Aditi flushed darkly and scowled, and Ben took a deep breath.

"Come on," he said, embarrassed for her, moving forward and drawing her by the hand. "Moksha, I'll come and find you within half an hour."

"Baby, let's please be happy here," he pleaded with her gently as they walked back along the trail to the house. "Look, this is beautiful: we have our own *house* to live in, in these beautiful surroundings. It's a preview of what we're gonna have in the next few years. And as for his seeing us: you know the guy is one hundred percent queer, not to mention liberated from mundane illusion and desire." He smiled. "So when he looks at you, you should regard it as no different from being looked at by a dog."

She was still frowning, but seemed somewhat mollified. "It's true that he doesn't seem dangerous," she said, "but I'm not going to want to spend much time around him. But ... look, he's completely stoned, completely into this acid. He *must* have slipped some to you. Otherwise how could you have had that experience, that hallucination and blackout? That's very scary, that he did that. What could he have been thinking? And why wouldn't he try to do it again? Be careful around him."

They were walking past the house, round to the front.

"Well ... I don't know anymore," said Ben uncomfortably. "Maybe it wasn't him who gave it to me."

She glanced at him as they reached the door. "What do you mean?" she said.

"I don't know yet," he said, shaking his head, as he took out the key and unlocked the door, "but ... just don't worry about Moksha."

She stepped up onto the floor inside, and turned, half a foot higher now, but still not face to face with him, as he remained standing on the concrete slabs outside. He bowed his face to meet hers, and they kissed lingeringly.

"Sleep some more," he murmured, his face still touching hers. "I can see you still need it. Wait for me in bed. I won't be more than an hour."

Instead of walking directly to the *āśrama* by the trail through the woods, he returned to the lakeshore the way they had just come, turning off of it to the right just before he reached the beach, then walked along the edge of the grass until he came to where the feral remnant of the ancient farm's orchard came down to the shore. Before he had even reached the uneven vanguard of squat trees, he began to smell the sweet late-summer miasma of rotting apples. This must be what Moksha was living on, he thought. What else? Grass? Was there any other edible thing growing around here? He clearly wasn't going into town to shop, and thus had probably never gotten an emergency check from the welfare office there.

Passing between two of the first outlying trees, barely taller than himself, Ben began to step around the apples in the grass. Wasps loitered and darted, and clung to apples fallen and unfallen, pocked with brown concavities. The warm air was heavy with the cloyingly sweet aroma. And ... he was suddenly aware of another sweetness mingled with that of the ripe and rotting apples. He looked down in alarm, and sure enough, he was barely in time to redirect his step to avoid a sun-baked mound of unmistakably human shit half-hidden in the grass. He stood and surveyed the ground, and now noticed several scattered piles of brown, interspersed with rotting apple cores.

He stood for a moment with lowered eyes, coming to terms with this new evidence of the extent of Moksha's withdrawal from common reality, then struck out straight for the open grass to his right in a jerky irregular stride, scanning the ground in front of him, clownishly overleaping or stopping short with foot raised, ducking and leaning to avoid the branches of the closely-set trees. Once out of the orchard, he walked along its margin towards where it faded into the main wood, his eyes still vigilantly lowered. The *āśrama* was now visible through the woods. He waded into the shadow of the high trees and reached the hut within a minute.

Moksha was sitting on the sparsely-grassed ground in front, straight-backed, cross-legged, eyes closed, his hands folded together in his lap: the posture of meditation. He had put clothes on, a ruined pair of dress pants and a grungy no-longer-white undershirt. Ben's blue T-shirt lay neatly folded on the ground beside him. He opened his eyes and glanced up, smiling slightly, as Ben approached. He again seemed his normal sober self. Ben smiled in return, took off his jacket, spread it on the yielding branches of a nearby bush, put on his T-shirt, and sat down beside Moksha in the same position.

"Moksha," he said quite softly, with a slightly perplexed, ironic smile, leaning forward a little, "what exactly are you doing up here?"

Moksha's smile broadened, and he looked down. It was the half-innocent, half-impish smile of his sobriety or very early drunkenness.

"It looks like you're probably not stoned right now?" said Ben.

Moksha looked him in the eye, still smiling, but serious. "I'm not stoned anymore," he said. "I'm never stoned anymore."

"Well, I can see that you've dropped a truly superhuman quantity of acid since you've been up here," said Ben. "If acid can be used as a vehicle for attaining higher realms of consciousness, well, I guess you must be ridin' around light years above us by now. Maybe you don't even need to take it anymore. I, *we,* read your poem. That leads me to the question that was really the main reason I came up here: The last time I was up here, did you slip me a tab, somehow? Because I've had an experience, a terrifying and baffling experience, that can only be explained as the effect of a drug or insanity."

Moksha had not lowered his gaze, but his smile had faded. "What was the experience?" he murmured.

"I met, I *thought* I met, Boylan and Malhotra in the stairwell in Robarts," said Ben. "And I thought ... Boylan attacked me, and then ... threw himself off the stairs and fell to the bottom of the stairwell."

Moksha looked at the ground, straightening his posture. Ben was nonplussed to see that his expression of intent interest had melted into indifference, but he continued.

"Malhotra simply disappeared, like an illusion. And when I ran down to the bottom of the stairwell, I saw Boylan lying smashed against the floor. But then he opened his eyes, and smiled at me. It was like a nightmare, a waking nightmare. I pushed open the fire escape door and ran out, and then I don't remember where I went or what I did, but in the morning, at dawn, I found myself lying on the porch of my mother's house." Moksha looked at him again with what may have been a flicker of rekindled interest. "But all this couldn't have been real, not all of it anyway, it must have been some kind of dream or hallucination, because the next day I saw Boylan again in his office, and there was no sign that anything like this could have happened to him, no trace of any injury."

He paused, then said finally, "Did you slip me a tab of acid, Moksha? Or am I finally going mad?"

Moksha straightened his back again, scratched his nose and sniffed. Ben was dismayed and humiliated: Moksha was by now completely back to normal; the benevolent distant serenity he had been radiating when he had appeared had completely evaporated. And he was clearly bored.

"Well," said Moksha, not looking at Ben, "this isn't the kind of experience I thought you were talking about. Yes, it sounds like you were hallucinating. It isn't every day that one gets to hallucinate. One should make the most of it, if the opportunity comes. And it sounds like you missed the opportunity. This was a boring hallucination."

"Fuck you, Moksha," said Ben, his voice low with controlled rage. "I'm not *interested* in any kind of hallucination. I'm interested in *sanity,* in maintaining as much of my fragile sanity as I can. I'm interested in the boring, predictable sanity that will let me build a life with the woman I love."

Moksha had met his gaze. His expression was a familiar one that Ben feared: cold, disdainful, a forerunner of brutally dismissive words. But Ben was animated by a righteous outrage against him that he had never felt before, not even at times, years ago, when he had awoken from drunken sleep to the killing cold of a clear winter night, under the Troll Bridge or on the frozen concrete floor of a Bloor Street storefront, to find Moksha spooned against him from behind with his rough pawlike hands down Ben's unbuttoned pants.

"You slipped me a tab, didn't you," said Ben.

"How do you think I could have *slipped* you a tab?" said Moksha with savagely disdainful curtness. "I don't need to *slip* you anything, any more than I needed to slip my cock into your mouth the times you sucked it."

Ben looked at him darkly, but doubt and confusion mastered his rage.

Moksha's gaze softened slightly. "Even I know that you're not the type to go mad that way," he said. "You're not a schizophrenic. You're not going to go mad by seeing what isn't there. You're going to go mad by not seeing what *is* there."

"Then ..." Ben began.

"Then do better than that," said Moksha scornfully. "You remind me of the moron hippies in San Francisco who gave me my first tab. They told me it would make me, like, see all kinds of groovy colours when I listened to Jefferson Airplane, man." He mimicked the dreamy, imbecilic diction of the stoner.

"So you *did* give me ..." Ben began again.

"Would you get your mind out of that gutter?" snapped Moksha, again holding his gaze hard, then said softy, almost pleading, "Look around you here. Look at the *opportunity* you have here, *we* have. How could you even have *dreamed* of getting an opportunity like this in this miserable incarnation you're stuck in, born in this Age of Decline on the opposite face of the globe from the Land of the Gods, and born crazy? It's an *āśrama,* the classical locus of liberation! In *Canada,* in the twentieth century!" He paused. "You musta done something right, in some incarnation along the way. Karma has brought us together, guru and pupil." He lowered his head slightly to look him more closely in the eye: *"This is our last birth."*

Ben looked at the ground for some time, then said, "What about Aditi?" His eyes were still lowered. "If you love, if you *still* love, even from where you stand at the edge of the abyss of *mokṣa* ... then you must understand." He looked at Moksha again. "This is not *my* last birth. I may *loosen* the bonds of *saṃsāra* in this birth, I may lay a *groundwork* for *mokṣa* the next time around. But this time around, it's my destiny to be a householder, not a renouncer. In this birth, my destiny is Aditi." His eyes were locked with Moksha's. "You do not hurt her," said Ben softly. "You do not hurt her."

They remained in this posture for some moments, until Moksha's look softened, and seeing this, so did Ben's.

"We'll be here for about a week," Ben said, straightening his back a little. "I've come to spend time with both of you. And I want to walk into town with you and get you set up at the welfare office, the way you've been when you've lived up here in the past.

You've been surviving on nothing but apples, haven't you. I came via the orchard. You look like you're starving. Well, I guess that's what forest sages do, starve themselves, but I didn't know that shitting in the grass was also a mark of enlightenment. I mean, for god's sake, Moksha? Is this really an effect of liberation?"

Moksha was looking down. "Yes," he said, "actually, it is."

"Tomorrow I'll walk into town with him," he said to Aditi. Mellow evening light cast a shifting rectangle on the wall, illuminating the bedroom where he lay on his back, and she lay against him, her head on his shoulder. "I hope you'll come with us?" he said, turning his head slightly to smell her hair. She was silent. "Baby, I know this isn't ideal for you," he said, "but let's make the most of it." He caressed her hair with his left hand.

"Did you at least find out if he slipped you acid?" she said.

He paused. "He didn't really tell me," he said, "but ... the *way* he didn't tell me amounted to an admission, I think."

"How can you trust such a person?" she said.

"I don't," he said. "I don't trust anyone but you."

The three of them walked into town the next morning, taking much longer than Ben and Aditi when they had come the same way the day before, since Moksha could only stroll at about half their natural pace. Dark-topped clouds covered the sun at intervals, suggesting a thunderstorm later in the day.

Despite Aditi's initial discomfort and distrust, it turned out well. Moksha had combed back his matted hair and was dressed in his usual urban attire—brown tweed blazer, shirt, pants, shoes and socks, and a wide-brimmed brown cloth hat like Ben's, all somehow clean. His weird remoteness of the day before had continued to evaporate, and by now he was completely and consistently his normal sober self, reticent but charming and funny, so that even Aditi relaxed and began to laugh, and Ben allowed himself to hope that, whatever Moksha might have done and might be going through, the critical phase was past, and he was not going to end up being more eccentric or dangerous than he had been before. Their arrangement shifted as they walked: now three abreast, Ben and Aditi hand-in-hand on the gravel shoulder and Moksha on the pavement's margin, since only rarely did a vehicle pass in either direction, now broken into a triangle, with Ben walking alongside Moksha or Aditi, according to the fluctuating demands of the conversation.

It was only at this late date that Aditi finally got to know Moksha directly, having heard so much about him over the years, but having spent very little time in his presence, and only in passing, when Ben was parting from one or the other of them. And what she heard from Moksha cast a new and sympathetic light on Ben, rendering his strangeness more comprehensible and less absolutely unique. The belief systems into which Ben and Moksha had been born had failed them, and they had come to India's literature in search of answers to the urgent ultimate questions that that collapse had thrown up, running just ahead of the devouring void. Their conversation today was the continuation of one that had been going on since long before Aditi had arrived, and that had been radically disrupted by her arrival. Moksha's perception of her as a threat had proven to be valid: she had brought to Ben her own crisis of belief, which at once recalled his own alienation from his birth religion and mirrored his devotion to his adopted one, and the fascination of this recognition, mixed with eros, had been irresistible to him. Old, ugly, a predatory pederast, another mere apostate and convert, Moksha hadn't stood a chance. Ben's destiny had reserved for Aditi the role that Moksha had dreamed was his, and so here was Moksha, alone again, again seeking solitary refuge in philosophy and other drugs.

The welfare office, ominously adjacent to the police station, occupied half of a typical government building set back from the main road at the edge of town, single-storey, red-brown brick, perpetually new, the other half being an employment centre. There was no sign of life from the outside this morning, and indeed, in a town like Seaton, both halves probably never did much business. Through the welfare office's dark window were visible the waiting room's unoccupied steel and plastic seats, and the service window, framing the indistinct shadow of a head. Outside the entrance, there was a heavy wood-and-concrete bench and a concrete ashtray with a single butt mashed into the fine white sand.

"We'll leave you here?" said Ben to Moksha.

"Yes," said Moksha. "This will probably take about an hour, if the system hasn't changed much in the last ten years, since I last did this in Toronto."

Ben held aside the left wing of his jacket and looked at the watch strapped to his belt. "Okay, we'll be back at around quarter to noon."

Ben and Aditi strolled into town on the main road. A ravishing young woman briskly descended, mail in hand, the concrete steps of the two-storey red-brick post office, an ancient building for this region at about a century old, got into her idling car and drove away, leaving the scene devoid of visible human presences other than Ben and Aditi. As they walked past the façades—a clothing shop, a restaurant, a variety store, a hardware store, a pharmacy, an art gallery—figures could be seen lurking in the darkness beyond the display windows. A superabundance of offices of lawyers and financial advisors, occupying what had clearly been more shops years ago, quietly indicated the town's decline to a returning native like Ben, who knew how to read the signs, but anyone could interpret the ancient gravestones that had been the

Empire movie theatre and the Algonquin Hotel, both boarded and hopelessly for sale. The sign in the window of the monumental stone library, a first-generation survivor, declared it open. In the adjacent cenotaph park, two old men sitting on a bench set back from the sidewalk with their hands atop their canes looked up with some interest at the unusual spectacle of a beautiful brown woman. Further in, a teenage boy and girl, she sitting on a bench and he leaning against it with one raised foot, alternately talked and sucked on jumbo soft drinks from the convenience store just up the street. The sunlight faded, blocked by one of the thunderheads gathering over the lake to the north.

"This must be similar to the town where you grew up?" said Aditi as they strolled on arm in arm.

"Yes, very," said Ben. "And they're both dying in the same way. I haven't been back to New Cheltenham since I escaped more than a decade ago, but it was already going this way. You know, the economy here is still fine, but most young people don't want to spend their lives in a place like this anymore if they're middle class and have middle class tastes and needs. My case was extreme and unrepresentative because I was crazy and my parents were crazy, but even so it actually did fit into the trend ... Your relationship with your hometowns must be very different. Edmonton was a city, and ... it wasn't your hometown. And Delhi?"

"My relationship to Delhi would be roughly analogous to your relationship to New Cheltenham," said Aditi a little distantly, "insofar as I never want to see it again."

"I sometimes wonder where you'd be today," he said, "if your father hadn't decided to emigrate."

"Thank god I'll never know," she said.

As they were walking back towards the welfare office, they heard Moksha's voice behind them:

"Ben!"

They turned, and saw Moksha walking towards them, with his shoulder bag evidently full.

"It took hardly any time at all," he said, "and so I just came over to the grocery to pick up some things before you came back. Not much, because I can't get another check. But ... a few things."

They began to walk back, talking as before, but now with long intervals of silence. By now, Ben had ceased to marvel at how completely like his normal self Moksha seemed, and so he almost didn't notice when, well out of town, he zipped open his shoulder bag, pulled out a small bottle of Bushmills, cracked it open, and tipped a swig into his mouth, barely pausing in his discourse of the moment, as thunder thudded and rolled in the gathered darkness over the lake.

Ben opened his eyes to late-morning light from the bedroom window, and for a time remained lying on his side, lightly clinging to Aditi's arm, inhaling the scent of her shoulder, as she continued to breathe the deep breath of sleep. He remembered being half-awakened by a second thunderstorm in the night, but now the sky over the lake was cloudless. Their midnight lovemaking, and the interruption of his sleep by the storm, had made him sleep well beyond his usual dawn waking time. Rain-chilled air wafted from the half-open window, slightly stirring the curtains on either side. He let go of her with the greatest delicacy, softly rolled over, lightly stepped onto the creaking wooden floor, stood for a moment looking at the glowing landscape of her dark body and the white water of the bedsheets pooled around it, turned away and slipped on underpants and pants before he could be aroused again.

Outside, the grass around the trail, protected from the strong morning sunlight by the grove's trees, was still heavy with the night's rain, and his pantlegs were soaked below the knee by the time he reached the *āśrama*. Moksha was gone, but although this almost made him despair for Moksha's safety, it did not really surprise him, nor did the new poem lying on the desk.

Where the barely trodden grass
revealed the way beyond,
I turned from my own peace
to offer you my hand,
but you did not respond—
and yet, you understand.

I read the silent plea
that shimmered in your eyes,
the longing to break free
from the last bond of hate.
Our mingled destinies
stand on the threshold. Wait.

15

Aditi had heard the news at the department on the afternoon of the morning of their return, and had walked straight back to the residence, and gone to bed, and watched the remaining daylight age, fade, and die on the ceiling and wall. It was Tuesday. She knew that Ben would not appear again until Friday night. She rose in the ghostly light from the street, left the apartment and building, and walked along Bloor towards Philosopher's Walk. It must be ten, eleven. He must be in the department, she thought, reading in the library. She descended the steps from the street into the Walk, reflexively glanced towards the Troll Bridge as she passed, walked on through the fatal spot where he had saved her from Sujay years ago, down to Hoskins, and along it to the Robarts Library.

She leaned against the corner of the ascending elevator, her blank defeated gaze fixed on nothing, did not even look up when the door slid open and she walked past the person who was standing waiting on the fourteenth floor. She rounded the corner and opened the library door. Ben wasn't there, but his knapsack and the open volume of the *Mahabharata* lay on the table in his usual spot. She paused in the open door. He must have gone to the washroom. Leaving the door open behind her, she walked over to the open book, and touching the table edge with her fingertips, absently read the verse marked by the Buddha's Vegetarian Restaurant card placed beneath it:

kecidīśvaranirdiṣṭāḥ kecideva yadṛcchayā
pūrvakarmabhirapyanye traidhametadvikṛṣyate

Some act at the command of the Lord, some act by chance,
and some act under the influence of their own past deeds:
but all three are drawn against their will.

She stared at the verse for a moment, then removed the black plastic hair clasp from the back of her head, letting her curls tumble free, placed it on the page next to the card, and left the library, turning to the left and climbing the stairs to the upper sub-corridor. Approaching, she saw that Boylan's door was ajar. She heard him talking to someone, animated and cheerful. Her heart was pounding. What was she doing, what was she about to do ... She smelt the familiar odour of unwashed body, cigarettes, booze.

Sitting at his desk, Boylan looked up when she appeared in the door. He beamed at her, radiant with a chilling, incomprehensible amalgam of malice, triumph, pleasure and goodwill. Sitting across the desk from him, facing away from Aditi, was a tiny person, silver-haired, a man, in a brown tweed blazer. He too was animated and cheerful, talking in a nasal voice, and concluded a phrase with a burst of sniffling laughter.

"Hey Aditi!" said Boylan, grinning. His interlocutor stopped talking.

She was about to faint. She stumbled away from the door, back the way she had come, down the five steps, holding the metal handrail, with the air conditioning roaring behind her through the fire escape's metal door. She almost fell through the library door. Ben still wasn't there. She stumbled down the hall to the men's washroom and burst through the double doors.

Washing his hands in the basin, Ben looked up, startled.

"What ... ?" he said, alarmed, standing facing her, holding his dripping hands in front of him as the water continued to hiss into the basin.

"It's all over," she whispered, leaning against the wall, looking down, and strangely not touching him. She sighed heavily, and tears spilled from her eyes, though her face remained inert.

"What is it, baby?" Ben said softly, turning off the faucet, wiping his hands on the seat of his pants, and advancing to hold her by the shoulders.

She looked up. "Chamberlain," she said. "He's gone."

Ben lay staring at the ceiling, palely lit by the still lights of the midnight street, with the slow rhythmic breath of her sleep at his shoulder.

The medics and police had reconstructed the scene afterwards. Kamala, Chamberlain's wife, had collapsed to the floor, felled where she stood by a massive heart attack. Chamberlain had either seen her fall, or had rolled into the room afterwards, perhaps drawn by her cry or the sound of her collapse. Seeing her, he had had a heart attack himself and slumped onto the floor in front of his wheelchair, comatose. They had been lying there for more than forty-eight hours when a maintenance person let himself in after vainly attempting to get them on the phone, alerted by other tenants' reports that Kamala had not been seen for two days on her usual daily round in and around the building. Kamala was dead, and Chamberlain was almost dead. He now lay in the St. Joseph's Hospital in Parkdale.

Aditi had despaired at the news. Her viva was next week.

He would visit Chamberlain tomorrow, in the evening—he

had already taken too many days off work recently. Chamberlain and Kamala had had no children, and both had outlived their families in England and India. Ben had no idea who else might care about Chamberlain's state. There were innumerable former students and colleagues, but how many were still in or around Toronto, how many would find out, and how many would care enough, had known him intimately enough, that they would want to visit him in this condition? Chamberlain was revered, and he was liked and loved, but the reserve of the British Brahmin enveloped and insulated him, whether he meant it to or not, and deterred overtures of more than formal friendliness. His relationship with Ben may have been unique in his life, and was certainly unique now, at least. There might be no hope that he would ever wake up again, and he would certainly not wake up when Ben would be there tomorrow. But Ben would go.

Though of course, this would do nothing to help Aditi. They had been counting on the silent warning menace of Chamberlain's availability as she walked into the possible ambush of her viva, an ambush that had become probable rather than possible now that Boylan would know that he faced no consequences, during or afterwards, for lies and distortions that only another indologist could perceive. Now she would have to face this without an ally, and without an ally she would not be able to survive. The slimness of her hope had been reflected in the weary defeat in her face this evening, during which she had spoken a total of maybe twenty words, words which had sounded to him as if they were coming from further and further away.

"What is your relation to Professor Chamberlain?" asked the nurse behind the glass, an elegantly attractive woman in middle age.

"I'm his PhD student," said Ben. "I can show you my student

card, and I can ... tell you all sorts of things about Professor Chamberlain and my relationship with him, but I don't have anything on paper: that would take time, and trouble with bureaucracy, and I—we—just wanted to get down here and see him as soon as possible, after we heard the news yesterday."

"And this is ... ?" said the nurse, glancing at Aditi.

"I'm his—Ben's—fiancée, and fellow PhD student," said Aditi, barely raising her tone from the monotonous, devastated dullness with which she had been speaking since yesterday, "and Professor Chamberlain was also helping me with my PhD, but that was unofficial, still, at this point."

The nurse looked down at what must have been some relevant piece of text on the desk in front of her. Ben had judged her to be a reasonable person, and her answer did not disillusion him.

"It seems that the professor had no family in the world but his wife?" she said, looking at Ben. Her voice and eyes were slightly tinged with pathos. "That's what his faculty at the university told us." She looked down again. "The department of ... East Asian studies?"

"Yes, that's right," said Ben. "He had been very well known and influential, during his career, had known everyone, but of course he had to retire many years ago, so he had fallen out of touch with his colleagues, and most of his contemporaries had died."

"Hm, that's what we thought," she said, "but we did have two people inquiring about him... another professor, a ... Ian Boylan?"

The merest shadow of disgust flitted across Ben's face. Aditi's registered no change at all.

The nurse glanced at Ben, and went on: "And the other... a former colleague of his at the university, he said. He actually came and visited. He lives very near, he said, just over on Roncesvalles."

Ben's eyes became almost wild. "Who...?" he said.

"A ... Saul Rosselli?" she said.

Ben's face took on an expression of intense concentration. "I don't remember the name, actually," he said.

"He must have been in his forties," she said.

"Did he give you a phone number?" said Ben.

"Yes," she said, "and he asked us to call him if there was any change in the professor's condition. He sat beside his bed for about half an hour. I think he was talking to him, too, for a while."

"Could you give me his number?" said Ben with guarded eagerness.

"I'm ... not sure if I can do that, actually," she said, "but I can certainly call him and give him yours."

Ben glanced over at Aditi, who was looking down with blank eyes and had clearly stopped hearing the conversation. Then he looked back at the nurse. "I'll give you ... *our* number."

He softly suggested to Aditi that she wait for him on one of the chairs in the hall, and she did not protest. The nurse then led him to Chamberlain's room. The walls were yellow-orange with the light of late evening before she turned on the light. Chamberlain was hooked up to the machinery of life support. The window looked out over the flashing traffic of the Queensway and the Gardiner Expressway, and beyond, the coast of Lake Ontario curving round to the monolithic apartment tower at the mouth of the Humber some kilometres to the west, which had been Chamberlain's and Kamala's home for decades, and where she had died.

"Let me know when you leave," the nurse said gently, and left, leaving the door open.

Ben sat down in the chair next to the bed. He had been prepared to be more or less overcome by emotion. Morbidly self-aware since childhood, he was conscious of his reasons for feeling the things he felt, and so he knew what Chamberlain was for him, knew the historical wounds and deficiencies of the soul that drew him to Chamberlain, starving for redress. In the years before Aditi appeared, Ben had been almost in love with him, in a way that he could not be with Moksha, whose flaws and limitations were daily before his eyes, and who was sexually dangerous besides. Ben was a superior linguist to both of them, but Chamberlain's enormous experience, and the fact that he *knew India,* gave him something that he could revere and aspire to.

Their first meeting had set the tone for the whole relationship. Ben, seventeen years old, was sitting in a carrel in the undergraduate library, Sigmund Samuel, copying out verses from the *Mahabharata,* upon which he was already obsessively fixated. As he fluently filled line after line of his notebook (found in a library trash can) with *Devanāgarī* script in blue ballpoint, he became aware of a presence behind and above him, but he continued without pausing to look, determined to accomplish as much as he could before being challenged or thrown out, as he expected, by whoever this was, probably a library technician who had caught a whiff of his stink. This was before Ben's discovery of the Harrison Baths, and of the pleasure of being at least as clean as circumstances allowed.

"That's a very fine *Devanāgarī* hand," said a deep patrician British voice. "Where did you learn?"

Ben stopped writing and turned to look up at the voice's source. "I taught myself, from books," he said with cautious simplicity to the stooped but still tall patriarchal figure, already ancient, but a decade stronger than the man who lay all but dead before him now.

Leaning slightly forward on his cane, Chamberlain studied the script, then looked at Ben, whose almost neutral face was just touched with a defiant confidence. "You're ... not a student here," said Chamberlain, stating rather than asking, noticing his extreme youth and his hobo attire and odour. "That's very extraordinary, that you've been able to teach yourself to this level, that you were capable of wanting to, for that matter." He paused. "I'm the head of the university's Indian Studies department. You ... seem like someone I'd like to get to know."

Now, reflecting on his friendship with Chamberlain so soon after his sojourn up at the lake with Moksha and Aditi, Ben was struck for the first time by how indifferent Moksha had always been to Chamberlain, in contrast to his simmering hostility to Aditi. The reasons were not hard to guess. Aditi enjoyed Ben's love and body, both hopelessly out of Moksha's reach, and as such was an existential threat to his relationship with Ben, besides being a cause of agonizing jealousy.

Although he must have been cowed by Chamberlain's authority and power, Moksha would have known that Ben was almost certainly too mad and alienated ever to be tempted away by the prospect of a legitimate academic career. It was possible that Moksha had never even uttered Chamberlain's name, and Ben reciprocated by only rarely mentioning his meetings with him, to which Moksha responded with lack of interest, or perhaps some guardedly catty general comment on the inauthenticity of the academic approach to India. So Moksha came to know little of this other region of Ben's life. Even if Moksha were now to be found in one of his familiar old haunts, he could have offered Ben no consolation, even if he had been willing to. And Aditi was so shattered. There was no one to see Ben's tears.

When he came back to the desk, the nurse looked up, paused on seeing his red eyes, then said, "I forgot to mention something—I forgot to mention it to his previous visitor, too ... Rosselli. The medics brought some things they had found on the floor near them, the professor and his wife, when they brought them both here. They thought they might have some significance, but the police weren't interested." She held up what looked like a small collection of papers with a couple of pages folded round them. "Some pictures, photographs," she said, "old ones, it looks like, and these two pages, which look like a letter written in some foreign language. You can take them, since the police didn't want them, and you and Rosselli are virtually his next of kin, it seems."

Ben took the small bundle, unfolded the outer pages, which he immediately saw were handwritten in Hindi, then looked at the pictures. They were letter-size black and white prints, new prints of what were obviously very old photographs, showing two men, Indian and white, in their twenties or thirties. They were clearly close friends, lounging against each other with the physical closeness that was normal between male friends in India, and which tended to convey an uncomfortably strong suggestion of homoeroticism to Anglo eyes.

As Ben looked, within moments the features of Professor Chamberlain surfaced through the waters of the years. In Chamberlain's apartment, and in Boylan's file on him, he had seen pictures of him in his forties and fifties, but never as young as here: tall and robust, unbespectacled, with unruly longish hair, not yet bearded, but with the same mustache as his friend, of a type common to most Indian men.

His friend was dressed in the same formal suit as Chamberlain, with hair oiled into the tight, shining coiffure of the Anglicized Indian of the time. Five photographs, probably taken on the same day in some place in the countryside, perhaps in one of the so-called "hill-stations" Chamberlain had told him about, the Britishers' high-altitude retreats from the lowlands' brutal summer heat.

He opened the letter again, glanced at Aditi to find her slumped dejectedly in one of the joined padded metal seats that stood against the wall, then looked back at the letter. He knew almost no Hindi, but dozens of sanskritic words immediately sprang out at him, enough to suggest to him that this letter—addressed to Kamala but unsigned—purported to explain the photographs. And when he had formed this general sense of the letter's meaning, he returned to one word—*dosti,* "friends"—that had at first only touched him, but which now combined with another—*ṣaṇḍh,* "eunuch, homosexual"—to inspire a sickening upsurge of dread.

"Yes," said Aditi, putting the letter down on her apartment's small dining table, "it tells her that Chamberlain was having a physical sexual relationship with his friend Dilip, in the thirties, when they were both working in the bureaucracy of the Raj. It says that these pictures were taken in Lonavla, a hill-station near Pune, when they stayed there together for a few days ... The language is ... coarse and full of hate, and has errors, or at least patches of less highly educated usage."

"But ... it *is* the language of a native speaker?" said Ben. "The errors aren't the errors of a foreigner?"

"No," she said, "they're not that kind of error. So it couldn't have been Boylan who wrote it, if that's what you're thinking. Not the faintest chance. He can't do anything in Hindi." Ben was silent, but she soon read his thought: "Well, it could have been Malhotra."

She was better today, insofar as resignation is better than distress and despair. Over and around the buildings visible from her window, the sky was grey with dawn. They were sitting nude at the table, drinking coffee he had brought from the kitchen.

"What else does it say?" he asked finally. "There's much more there."

"Hate," she said. "There's a lot of hate, like I said." (She spoke from memory, without lifting the letter from the table.) *"Your marriage has been a fraud from the beginning, he only wanted you for the status and mystique of marriage to a native, the deeper familiarity it would give him with Indian language and culture, the convenience it would afford him in India. No wonder you never had any children. Did you never guess? Did you never wonder where his desire was?* That kind of thing. Probably all lies—it hardly matters. It's openly malevolent; it makes no attempt to mask that. It offers no hint of the writer's identity." She paused. "It *is* hard to imagine that it could have originated with anyone but Boylan. Where else have we ever encountered such evil." She took a sip of coffee from her large green mug, and spoke softly, defeated, looking down at nothing: "Professor Chamberlain was such a beautiful, good man. *Is*. If he dies ... while this worthless creature lives ..."

He looked at her in quiet anguish, then spoke. "The nurse will probably call today, about this person, this Rosselli person who came to visit Chamberlain before us." He reached over and stroked her hand where it rested on the table, still lightly holding the mug. "Baby, I can see you hardly care anymore," he said tenderly. "But you're still going to go through with it, aren't you? You're still going to try, at least?"

"Oh, sure," she said, almost succeeding in sounding a little hopeful. "It's still possible that he doesn't care anymore, the way it was seeming before this happened. It's not impossible that I'll live through it."

"It is *very far* from impossible," said Ben with controlled fervour, looking her in the eyes and holding her hand by the wrist. "You've lived through this much. *That* was impossible, and you did it. And think of us. Even ... even if he should die, *we* have to live."

Under the intensity of his gaze, the resignation in her eyes softened into a sad tenderness that might even have seemed to reflect a little bit of his hope. He rose and came over to stand behind her chair, where he put his hands on her shoulders, bent to smell her hair, then wrapped his arms around her, laying his face next to hers. She raised her hands to hold his arms, and pressed them, hard.

"Ben, your lady called," called Malcolm from the office door, across the roof of the car that was rolling out of the last set of brushes, as the machinery clattered and howled.

"What?" shouted Ben, pausing with his rag in his hand as his colleagues advanced to begin drying the car.

"Your lady," repeated Malcolm, louder this time. "She called. She's coming to meet you. She said the call came."

Ben nodded and smiled with unusual warmth, and followed the car out onto the sidewalk to join the others in polishing its shining surface in the mid-afternoon sun.

"Saul Rosselli ... *Doctor* Saul Rosselli," she said as they walked up the east sidewalk of Roncesvalles Avenue in the darkness just after sunset. "*Doctor* is on the name sign, he said."

Ben was comforted by what appeared to be a note of interest in her voice, a hint of recovering spirits. They passed Polish groceries, bakeries, butcher shops, closed at this hour, counting the building numbers.

"Five seventy-nine" she said, stopping at the door to the apartments above a flower shop. "And here's his name."

She pressed the round doorbell button, the upper of two, and they stood back on the sidewalk, looking up to the third floor, where a window scraped open, and a strikingly handsome middle-aged man's head appeared, leaning out over the street.

"Aditi?" he said, pronouncing it correctly, which never happened: this was an indologist. "Aditi and Ben," he said. "I'll be right down."

Within moments the door opened. The figure that appeared confirmed the initial impression of beauty. Rosselli was probably in his mid-forties, with silvering black hair, still youthfully abundant and carefully coiffed, and a lean but strong build, well shorter than Ben's six foot two. He radiated a youthfulness and vigour that almost made him look younger than Ben and Aditi, both rather dour at the best of times, and presently looking quite worn down. He smiled a perfect cinematic smile at both of them, then looked at Aditi and spoke to her in fluent Hindi, which so flustered her that she could only respond, after a pause, with a stammered English "Yes!" He smiled with evident pleasure at the effect he had had, then looked at Ben and said, "Let's go up."

They climbed the two flights of creaking stairs in silence and came through the still-open door into a living room lined with bookshelves, with a large window looking out over Roncesvalles and the florist's glowing sign. Ben and Aditi immediately perceived a canine scent, and in the next moment its source met their eyes: a largish dog with white and orange-brown mottled hair lay on a plush armchair, apparently asleep, except for a brief gentle thumping of the tail which seemed to be a response to their arrival.

"Please sit down," said Rosselli, closing the door behind them. "This is Ghatotkachi," he said, noticing their pleasure at his companion. "She'll probably want to meet you later, in her own good time. Can I get you ... tea? Juice?"

Ben glanced at Aditi. "It's not too late for tea, is it?" he asked her. "We'll be up for a while yet."

"Yes, tea," she said, looking at Rosselli. "But ... no milk or sugar for him: he's vegan."

"Ah, vegan," said Rosselli. "I've been meaning to go vegan myself for quite some time, after a lifetime of mere vegetarianism. Maybe you've finally inspired me to do so."

Ben and Aditi sat together on a sofa while Rosselli went into the adjoining kitchen. *"Ghatotkachi!"* she half-whispered to Ben, laughing at this strange feminine form of the name of a famous *Mahabharata* demon.

"Aditi told me that neither of you had ever heard of me," Rosselli called from the kitchen over sounds of tea preparation. "That doesn't surprise me. I can't think of anyone who would have mentioned me to you. As I told you, Aditi, in our brief phone conversation, I was in the old Indian Studies department for years. But everyone's gone, and my publications weren't in your area. And this was all long ago. I did all three degrees at U of T: the indology department was the best on the planet in those days, late seventies, early eighties. Chamberlain and I were very close, at that time, though he didn't supervise my PhD, because I was working on the grammarian Panini, linguistics ... which I came to dislike in the course of writing my dissertation, but ... I was locked into it. Chamberlain and I came to know each other well from the time I took my first courses with him as an undergraduate. We used to talk for hours, over the years, in his office, at his home. About literature, philosophy, India. Everything. He took a strong interest in me and my career."

He came and stood in the kitchen doorway. His voice was rather high and creaky, his manner of speaking relaxed.

"My real love was always poetry, literature, from adolescence, even though my parents were Indian spirituality enthusiasts, and raised me in their California version of Indian religion—not that we were in California, I'm a born Torontonian, I just mean that that was the tradition they followed, that peculiar cult of Western India-heads, who were at that time very few, very eccentric people. And all that did deeply form me, even though I didn't end up being religious, like they were. But vegetarianism, belief, or near-belief, in things like reincarnation, pantheism—things like that stayed with me."

He turned his head for a moment to look into the kitchen, then continued.

"So my parents started teaching me Sanskrit when I was just a kid, first the little that they knew, then they brought in sanskritists to teach me, even an authentic Indian *paṇḍita*—there certainly weren't a lot of those around in Toronto in those days! And I learned all that mythology, all those stories, the epics and *Purāṇas,* which I adored, but my parents' focus was on spirituality and philosophy—that set's *idea* of Indian philosophy. Panini was a kind of escape hatch for me. I turned out to be extremely good at grammar and Indian linguistics, the Sanskrit grammarians and philosophers of language."

The sound of a kettle boiling came from behind him, and he turned and disappeared into the kitchen.

"What have you been doing since then?" Aditi called from the sofa. "Did you teach somewhere? At U of T? Somewhere else?"

"I taught Panini for two years at U of T, after completing my PhD," he replied from the kitchen, then appeared carrying three mugs on a tray. "But it just wasn't for me, the academic life ... teaching, writing in that style, conferences, administration ... especially not administration, especially not after what I'd already seen of the workings of an academic department during my three programs. You will probably know something of what was going on during those years, the situation in the department. I was beginning my doctorate when Boylan arrived."

He looked for and saw the moment of agitation in their faces.

"Yes," said Rosselli. "More on that in a moment."

He sipped his tea. "So, I left the university, left Toronto, lived in Europe and Israel and India, wrote, published, got into all sorts of trouble—getting married in India was the worst of it. And when that was over, the marriage, I came back here to Toronto, shattered and demoralized." He laughed weakly. "Got this apartment, got a job as an editor in a publishing company, and devoted myself to my own reading and writing."

"What are you writing about?" asked Aditi.

"Animals and reincarnation," he said. "It's a book I've been working on for years, since India. I have a good hope that it'll sell nicely, actually. If I ever finish it. I could certainly use the money. A few years ago I had a house built up in Uttarakashi, in the Himalayan foothills. That made more than a dent in my savings."

Ben had left his tea on the coffee table and gone over to the largest bookshelf, where he was perusing the spines and the photographs and Indian artefacts that stood in gaps between the rows of books. Ghatotkachi, now visibly awake, was complacently surveying the humans with her head comfortably propped on the chair back.

Aditi said, "So, how did you find out what had happened to Professor Chamberlain?"

"Since I left Toronto," he said, "I've quietly gotten in touch with the secretaries of the department from time to time—first Indian Studies, now East Asian Studies—asking them to let me know if anything serious happened to him. I'm in touch with a few of the others from those days, professors and fellow students, none of them in Toronto anymore. But I've always been an outsider and a rogue, and I dislike the majority of indologists as I dislike the majority of humanity. I have the impression that this isn't a confession that will scandalize you two too much?"

Still standing in front of the books, Ben looked round, smiled, and shook his head, catching a glimpse of Aditi as she blushed again with lowered eyes under Rosselli's gaze.

Rosselli went on: "If you're wondering why I kept a distance from Chamberlain during those years, until now ... I was ... difficult in those days, and they were difficult times. He had had very high hopes for my career, wanted me to replace him as head of the department. He saw me as the department's only hope for the future. So did I, but we had completely divergent views on how to accomplish that end. My nature is such that I couldn't just stand by while that psychopath Boylan set to work dividing and destroying that great department. I was for Chamberlain ... but ... I just had a very different style, and that's not the way Chamberlain wanted to fight that fight. In fact, that was the problem: it was *beneath* him to fight, beneath his, you know, patrician Oxbridge highmindedness. He thought he could defeat Boylan by simply refusing to respond to him. But if you take the high road with a creature like Boylan," he said, shaking his head, "he'll just dig the hillside out from under you while you've got your eyes fixed on your noble high goals, he'll destroy everything behind your back. I came from a different background, Jewish, Italian, and I've got a touch of the street in me. I knew what I was dealing with, with Boylan. He fucked with me at his peril. And he found out." He paused. "It came to violence, actually."

Ben had turned with a book in his hand. He and Aditi were visibly shocked. Rosselli looked down.

"I was a great disappointment to Chamberlain. To a lot of people, actually."

He finished his tea, and held the empty cup. "But enough about that, for now. I'm very happy to have met you two, sad though the occasion is. Aditi told me a bit about you, the two of you, your situation," he added, looking at Ben.

"Then you know about our relation to Professor Chamberlain," said Ben, "and about the emergency that his condition may have created for Aditi."

"Yes," said Rosselli, "and I've been thinking hard about possible ways to help you. The most obvious one is for me to propose myself as a new member of Aditi's committee—which would make me the only other member of your committee besides Boylan who is actually qualified to serve in that capacity; let me rephrase that: the only other *indologist* besides Boylan, and the *only* qualified and competent member of your committee. I think there's only the slightest possibility that he'll oppose this. I hope he does! But it's far more likely that the mere sight of my name will be enough to send him slinking silently back to his warren."

He laughed, softly and darkly, a new shade of laughter that made Ben uncomfortable, a glimpse of the face of Rosselli the intellectual street fighter. What they needed right now *was* a street fighter. But brilliant rogues make dangerously unpredictable allies. Ben glanced at Aditi, and felt a stab of pain: she was looking at Rosselli with a mix of fascination and hope.

Ghatotkachi roused herself, jumped off the chair, and with an old dog's leisurely step walked over to Aditi, who beamed with delight, put down her mug on the coffee table and began caressing her head and tufted ears, cooing to her in Hindi, to which Rosselli responded with some phrases in the same language.

"I brought her all the way from India, believe it or not," he said, "from Pune, where I lived and worked for a few years. She was a street dog who just attached herself to me. I left the house one morning to walk to work, and there she was, strolling into our housing society from the street. We looked each other in the eye, and that was it: *daivam,* it was fate, unfinished business from a past *janma,* a past birth." He laughed, came over, and scatched Ghatotkachi on the rump, and she turned her head and looked at him gratefully, whimpering softly with excitement and affection. "Now she's old," he went on, as she sat down, "very old, fifteen years at least. You don't know it," he said to Ghatotkachi herself in a solemn tone, only slightly ironic, "but soon you will have to go to the abode of Yama."

As Aditi continued to stroke her, Ben came over and sat next to Aditi on the sofa. Ghatotkachi looked up at him with a brief renewed burst of tail-thumping, but did not rise to come over to him. *"kim idam, aham api na te roce?"* Ben said, *What's this, don't you like* me *too*? He gave a fake smile, conscious of how pathetic and obvious was this attempt to coax Aditi back from Hindi, which she never had occasion to speak in his presence, to the Sanskrit that they shared. Aditi smiled, but said nothing.

"So the first order of business is for me to read your dissertation," said Rosselli in a *let's get down to business* tone, going into the kitchen to leave his cup there, then coming out and sitting in the doghair-covered chair vacated by Ghatotkachi.

"I can bring it to you tomorrow," said Aditi.

"Why don't I pick it up from you on campus," said Rosselli. "I'll have to come to the department anyway. I work from home, so my schedule is flexible. You've told me enough about it that I already basically know what my written comments will be and what I'll say during the viva. Obviously I won't recommend any changes. If *Chamberlain* said that it was excellent ... You know, it's just criminal, that they gave this job to these incompetent outsiders who have no idea what you're talking about. *Criminal* professional misconduct! It's a tragedy that this has happened to you. You belonged in a first-rate department."

He was growing more and more fervent, apparently truly outraged. Aditi looked gratified, but confused, and embarrassed—and no doubt not only for herself.

As she and Ben walked the long way home together, she frequently hung on his arm, and when they reached Kensington Market, she invited him to stay the night—which they had not been planning: in recent months, with their departure looming, he had begun to stay over more nights than not, and there had been complaints and warnings.

Her usual style in bed was a passionate passivity, but tonight she was notably forward. She began by sucking him, which she did not usually initiate, and while he was riding her from behind, she reached back, drew him out of her, raised him. "There," she whispered, with her other hand reaching for the small plastic bottle that he now noticed on the bedside table. He pressed into her, at once troubled and guiltily excited by this strange new intimacy with its dark mingling of desire and anger, feeling in her inner embrace the anxious self-sacrificing tenderness that he could not see in her face pressed against the pillow, her turned-up eyes, her sweating brow, her jaw clenched in the confused pleasure of love and pain.

16

Tonight he had to sleep outside. He *had* to.

This thought stood in the near background of his conscious mind this evening, frequently intruding, as he sat in the library reading. Aditi would soon be moving out of the graduate residence, but they still weren't sure when, and in any case it wouldn't be so soon that they didn't still have to consider the evil eye of her fellow residents and the building's management. They had to pull back a bit. It would still be a disaster if he were formally barred.

The first closing announcement on the intercom, at 11:15, had already been made. He was finding it unusually difficult to remain focussed on his reading. Aditi would have met Rosselli today to deliver and talk about her dissertation. She would have come to the department in the morning to submit a petition to have him added to her committee, and he would have come on his own in the afternoon. If Rosselli was right, the process would be smooth and uncomplicated, and Boylan would probably offer no obstructions once he saw Rosselli's name.

Rosselli was a magnificent creature: Ben and Aditi were both well aware of this, and of each other's awareness of it. Aditi was far less given to brooding on the past than Ben was, and so Ben might have been the only one to wonder what would have happened if Rosselli had appeared in their lives sooner. It was impossible to imagine that he had not been a womanizer in earlier years, and was probably still. Aditi would know that there could be no future with such a man. She had told Ben that her fantasies of relationships had never involved older men, and she was very comfortable with the seven-year age gap that divided them.

But what was Ben, that he should so presume? After all she had given up for him. For him, who was nothing.

With a burst of effort he concentrated his attention:

yadgataṃ gatameveha śeṣaṃ cintaya mānada

In this world, what is gone is *gone*. Think of what remains.

The intercom came on with its usual sound, like a single knock on a door, followed by the female voice. *The library will be closing in thirty minutes. Please bring all books you wish to sign out to the loan services desk on the second floor immediately.*

Ben rose, went to the washroom, unbuckled and opened his pants, pumped a handful of liquid soap into his palm, locked himself in the stall, and awkwardly pulled down pants and underpants with his left hand alone.

He was on the cusp when he heard the outer door boom and the inner one open and remain held open. He shuddered and gasped.

The door fell closed and the outer door boomed.

After some time, he pulled up his pants, came out of the stall, and began to wash his hands. From the washroom's own speaker, the clear voice filled the little room: *The library will be closing in fifteen minutes ...*

Descending alone in the elevator, he reflected on how little he cared who had stood and half-watched him from the opened washroom door. The same person, perhaps, who had removed the strip of three Buddha stamps from his volume of the *Mahabharata* at some point between the last time he had seen them and his discovery a few days ago that they were no longer there: Boylan, Malhotra, Moksha, some extremely unlikely, unknown person who had just happened to want to read the *Mahabharata* one day at this university where no one read Sanskrit anymore.

Who cares? he thought, then immediately realized that he had to step back from the abyss. It still mattered. He had not lost her, they had not lost their future, and within days they would have won.

Reaching the bottom of the library's south stairs, he paused and looked up St. George: he could just barely see that her window was lit. A few others who had left the library at midnight were dispersing in several directions. He thought of going and lying down to sleep on the side porch of the Department of Religious Studies, where he had encountered Malhotra for the first time eight years before, long before Aditi appeared. He had stopped sleeping on campus years ago, when Chamberlain had obtained his fake student card for him—a tremendously powerful asset, but one whose power he had not wanted to needlessly squander on the university cops. But he didn't want to be far from her tonight. The department was right next to the graduate residence; sleeping there, he would be close to her, close enough to hear her voice, if she were to shout. But the risk would be too great. He finally decided to compromise: he would just go and sit on the porch steps for a while, not lie down, and then he would go south to sleep on his usual bench in front of the church.

He crossed St. George and walked north, turned into the unlit lane between the department and the next building, put down his knapsack on the porch and sat on the stairs, stretching out, crossing his legs and leaning back on his elbows, tipping his head back and closing his eyes. It was a beautiful not-too-cool September night. Her window would be open, as usual. He listened in the trafficless silence.

"Mr. Doheney?"

Starting violently, he opened his eyes on Malhotra, who stood massively above him. He was not grinning: his mouth was slack and expressionless as he looked at Ben through huge eyeless lenses that reflected distant lights.

"What are you doing here, Mr. Doheney?" he said, stepping forward slowly to stand with the toes of his boots almost touching Ben's sandalled feet.

Ben looked up at him with cool defiance. "After an evening of working on my PhD dissertation in the South Asian Studies library," he said evenly, as if reciting a ritual text, "I'm sitting here enjoying the night before I go home to bed."

"Mr. Doheney," said Malhotra with an exaggerated calm and civility that could not conceal the excitement of his triumph, "you are not a student at this university, and you have no home to sleep in. You are what you have always been: a homeless piece of shit, and a trespasser on university property who I once kicked off of this porch itself many years ago, before you obtained the fake student card that you have used to deceive the university authorities ever since." His teeth were now displayed in an unsmiling grin.

Ben's eyes were dark. "I would show you my card again," he said, "which you have personally examined in the past, and found to be authentic, but I know better than to trust you with it tonight. What's happened, Malhotra?" His voice began to rise, hard and controlled, as he held Malhotra's invisible gaze with his own. "Did your master unleash you and give you the go-ahead because Professor Chamberlain is no longer able to protect me? Did he tell you that he'd killed him, or as good as killed him? I'm calling your bluff. Arrest me, take me in, investigate me, and I'll walk out of your pseudo-police station within fifteen minutes and barely miss my bedtime."

Malhotra paused, then said, with a sternness that barely masked his confusion, "Yes, come with me."

"So arrest me," said Ben. "I'm not coming willingly. Arrest me!"

Malhotra didn't move.

Ben smiled, with a calculated touch of pity. "You *can't* arrest me," he said, in a tone of patient explanation. "You don't have the authority to make arrests, any more than you're allowed to carry guns, or clubs, or handcuffs, or even to have lights on top of your cars. If you want someone to be arrested, you have to call the city police. The *real* police."

He was smiling ironically, eyebrows raised.

"So call them," he said calmly, still leaning back with his legs stretched out. "Call them, and have me arrested, so that the real police can conduct a real investigation into the only real crime that's happened on this campus in years, and so that you glorified security guards can get back to the serious business of beating up homeless people and diddling street kids in Queen's Park (which is in the jurisdiction of the real police, by the way), and spying on masturbators in university washrooms."

With a grunt of rage and exertion, Malhotra swung back his foot and kicked him in the underside of the knees. Ben cried out and bent forward, drawing up his legs and grasping them at the point of impact. Malhotra kicked again, hitting him in the side of the abdomen, and Ben again cried out, and scrambled blindly to his left, off of the stairs, falling onto the pavement on his knees, holding his side with both hands. As he tried to crawl away, Malhotra kicked again and again, in the legs, ass, back, until Ben fell on his side and curled up, holding his arms together in front of his face. He lay there, breathing in gasps, waiting for the next blow.

It didn't come. Instead, Malhotra screamed.

Ben rolled rapidly onto his back and scrambled into a crouching position, ready to spring. At some distance, back at the foot of the steps, in the darkness compounded by his myopia, he saw Malhotra on the ground, thrashing about, gasping, grunting, trying to shout, maybe in the grip of some kind of convulsion. No, it was two figures.

Ben stood up and approached slowly, limping, horrified at what he already knew he was seeing.

In the dim light of a distant streetlamp, Moksha was sitting astride the belly of the now motionless Malhotra. His newly shaved head and face, free from glasses, were strangely small and round, giving him the appearance of some demonic infant. Frenzied, open-mouthed with childlike excitement, he raised his arm high again and again, rapidly and without pause, bringing the knife down on Malhotra's neck, face, chest. Blood sprang and bubbled from the ragged, pulpy wounds, trailed from the flying knife, spraying Moksha's face, bathing his clothes.

Without surprise, he looked up at Ben standing before him, and stopped, letting his arm fall at his side. He looked at the mangled mess of Malhotra's face and neck, again looked up at Ben.

"tathā smārayitā te'haṃ kṛntanmarmāṇi saṃyuge," he said, smiling, breathing hard. *"I'll remind you of this when I mangle your guts in battle*. Right? Did I remember that right?" He sounded sober. "Now get out of here," he said. "Shut up, and get out of here, now, or we'll *both* go to jail. That way. And careful you don't step in the blood."

17

It had begun to rain in the afternoon, not very heavily, while Ben was at work. Now, as he sat beside Chamberlain's bed, cars swished past on the Queensway below. Under the almost lightless grey sky, Chamberlain's apartment tower was visible only by its lights. Beyond, the Golden Horseshoe shone dimly as far as Hamilton, a crescent of urban and industrial lights.

It had been a second day without Aditi. Tomorrow night was theirs—unless Ben were arrested. He felt an abyss of doom and despair looming at his back, just out of sight, creeping nearer, to suck him under. Yet he had been able to function today, as if on automatic pilot, because what was the worst that could happen? Moksha was doomed, but what could they pin on Ben? Moksha would never implicate him, would deny that Ben had even been there. And Ben had seen no one else around.

The murder had been front-page news that morning. Ben had called MacLeod in the evening, after work, before walking to the hospital.

"What if one of your friends was in trouble?" said Ben.

"I don't do murder cases anymore," said MacLeod without missing a beat. "Not in court, anyway. *Uh-uhm.*"

"I thought you might be here," said Rosselli's voice softly from behind him.

Ben turned to see him standing just inside the door. Rosselli met his gaze with a warm but subdued smile, then looked at Chamberlain, and his face was suffused with quiet anguish. For a moment, nothing was audible but Chamberlain's slow breathing.

Then Rosselli took another chair from where it stood against the wall, put it beside Ben's, and sat. Ben looked at him with mild surprise, and an affected pleasure which did not very effectively conceal his distrust, envy, humiliation.

"How are things going with Aditi?" he asked in a somewhat sullen tone, conscious of the question's comical ambiguity, and unable to avoid glancing at Rosselli's crotch.

Rosselli caught the glance, and smiled with a mixture of unmalicious amusement and sympathy. "Things are going very well," he said. "We initiated the paperwork without a problem. The viva won't even be delayed. I told them I had already read the dissertation, which was almost true. I read very quickly, and as I expected, there's nothing to object to. Of course, if *I* had been supervising her it would have ended up a very different piece of work, but not because the present work is bad—far from it. As you know."

He paused. "Aditi told me that you both discussed everything—even though the work is wholly hers, of course, and you don't have your own background in feminist theory. She's told me everything. It's an extraordinary story, an extraordinary relationship, very beautiful and inspiring ... Like your relationship with Chamberlain. Which began, I now realize, at exactly the same time that my relationship with him was ending."

His gaze was steady, serious with admiration, goodwill, compassion, sadness. Ben held it for some moments, visibly taken aback, then looked down.

You'll be seeing Aditi tomorrow night, right?" said Rosselli.

Ben nodded.

"It will be all right," said Rosselli seriously. "This is going to work. You and Aditi have a destiny together, a bond formed in past lives. Like you and Professor Chamberlain." He laughed. "Like me and Ghatotkachi."

Chamberlain's slow breathing and the swishing of cars on the wet Queensway rose to fill the silence.

They walked up Roncesvalles in the rain, which had by now become no more than a light spray. At his door, Rosselli said, "Do you want to come in for a while? Have tea, something to eat? Have a better look at my library? You could even sleep on the sofa. Sleeping outside ... I can't imagine it, even on a summer night, never mind when it's raining, or winter."

Ben paused, then said, "Alright, yes, I will, that will be nice."

Entering the apartment, they were met by Ghatotkachi on her lion throne, still curled up, but with eyes open, thumping her tail. *"he bhagavati!"* Rosselli addressed her with affectionate mock reverence, "milady on her *siṃhāsana!"* She leapt down and trotted over to them, whimpering softly with affectionate excitement. Ben bent down and caressed her ears and face with both hands as Rosselli took off his jacket, hung it on a hook by the door, and went into the kitchen.

"I'm making coffee for myself," he called. "I'm a night-owl, I'll be up till dawn. What do you want?"

"I'll have tea again," called Ben, walking over to the largest bookshelf and resuming his survey of its titles. Besides Sanskrit, there were large sections of English, French, German, and Italian, smaller but still substantial ones of Hebrew and Hindi, and, particularly fascinating to him, a beautiful sky-blue bound copy, ancient but perfectly preserved, of the famous eight-volume Chitrashala Press edition of the *Mahabharata* from Pune. He roamed the collection, taking out a book here and there, opening it and perusing the text, even if it was in a language he didn't know.

He had felt a similar admiration and longing the first time he saw Chamberlain's personal library, but here the element of aspiration was stronger because of Rosselli's relative nearness in age. He could feel his attitude to Rosselli beginning to shift. Why distrust him? Why resent the power he clearly had over Aditi? Why not appreciate it as a beautiful thing, a positive aspect of a powerful personality whose goodness was already beyond doubt? Aditi was fascinated by and attracted to Rosselli. But she loved Ben. And Rosselli's powers were Ben's own, they were already there within himself, if he could only find the courage to admire himself for the strengths he admired in others.

The kettle whistled from the kitchen.

Besides the Indian artefacts that stood in gaps between sections of the collection, there were also a few framed photographs. In one, black and white, a handsome smiling boy of about fourteen in an Indian loincloth, evidently the young Rosselli, was sitting cross-legged on the floor next to a typically grim-faced Indian swami. Another black and white one showed an older Rosselli, probably in his twenties, standing between an elegantly beautiful late-middle-aged couple whose features unmistakably identified them as his parents. Their Western-style hot-climate clothing and the landscape and Hindu temple in the background placed the scene in India. A colour picture showed a sombre Rosselli in late youth, wearing a formal *kūrta* outfit and a peculiar headdress with light cords hanging over his face, arm-in-arm with a beautiful, notably dark Indian woman in a splendid sari, abundant jewellery, and identical headdress. Her tall, strong physique and almost arrogant smile suggested a commanding personality.

"Ah yes, that was my marriage day," said Rosselli, coming out of the kitchen with two cups on a tray. "I don't look very happy, do I. She does, though." He laughed rather bitterly as he sat down on the sofa. "What's that final quarter-verse that occurs again and again in the *Mahabharata? daivaṃ hi balavattaram,* 'fate is stronger.'"

Ben looked at him, stunned. "Yes... I know that *pāda* well," he said softly.

"Fate so often seems to be the only explanation," said Rosselli, lifting his coffee from the table and taking a sip, "fate and karma, the unfinished business of past lives. Your own desire leads you into a situation where you find nothing but suffering and misery, and nothing but your own desire keeps you there. You're in hell, and you keep telling yourself, railing at yourself, *Why can't I leave, why why why?* But you just can't want it enough. Your desire for hell, your own proper personal hell, is stronger—because it's right: horrible as it is, it actually *feels* right; it's fate, it's what you deserve, the just fruit of your own unremembered action, which brings you together with people whom you've harmed, or who have harmed you—maybe even by loving you too much. But in any case, there's something unfinished, some situation that's working itself out, that demands resolution."

He looked intently at Ben. "You believe this, don't you?"

"Yes," said Ben, softly but fervently, holding his gaze.

Rosselli picked up Ben's tea and held it up to him, and he took it, still standing in front of the bookshelf.

"Well, Sudeshna and I worked out our karma together," said Rosselli. "That was resolved. One of the fruits of *that* action was that I realized that *gārhasthya,* domesticity, is not my *svadharma,* not my role: I was not born to be a husband, this time. So the house I built for me and Sudeshna up in the Himalayan foothills near Uttarakashi turned out to be for me alone."

Rosselli smiled sadly, looking down at his coffee. "But me and Ghatotkachi here," he said with ironic jauntiness as she looked over at him from where she still lay on her throne, thumping her tail, "me and Ghatotkachi are still living on the fruit of some kind of good karma."

Ben smiled, though his eyes were still serious, as if pregnant with some unformed question.

"You can *feel* when something is fated. You *know,*" Rosselli went on, "whether it's good or bad, whether you want it or you don't." He looked at Ben. "The way this is happening now is the way it has to be, the only way it *can* be. And I know it's going to be good."

"Your cop, Malhotra, was murdered just a few steps from here, the night before last, Tuesday night," said Aditi, "close enough that I could've heard something if I'd been awake. Some others in the residence *did* hear something, a scream, but they thought it was just some drunk. He wasn't found till morning. It was gruesome, he'd been stabbed more than twenty times, his face and neck were pulp. It was the top story in the *Star* yesterday morning. Did you see?"

"Mm," Ben murmured, with his head cradled in her lap, facing her. Her voice was present and interested again, after the days of despair following Chamberlain's fall. She was stroking his hair and neck.

"Do you have an alibi" she said finally, "if the police question you? I'm thinking of Boylan, obviously ... if he tries to frame you. It's too much of a coincidence, that this should happen now, to this minion of his. But ... what to think."

"No, I don't have an alibi," Ben said, "because I wasn't here that night, and I wasn't with anyone else. But there's nothing to connect me to his murder."

"Except for what Boylan presumably knows about your history with Malhotra," she said, "Boylan and any other university cop Malhotra might have told over the years." She paused again, then said, "Do you have any idea where Moksha is?"

"No," said Ben, shifting onto his back, leaning his feet over the sofa's armrest, and opening his eyes, looking into hers. "No, I haven't seen him since the *āśrama,* or heard from him. I don't even know if he's in Toronto, though I can't imagine where else he could have gone." He paused, and his look sharpened. At this critical moment in his and Aditi's story, on the eve of her viva, the ordeal on whose outcome their shared future depended, he had to free her from fear and suspicion of Moksha once and for all. "He didn't do it, just in case you're wondering about that. Nor did he assault the Hart House guard, just in case I haven't thought it necessary to be so explicit in the past. Bizarre and fucked up though he appears, Moksha *is* actually *mukta,* liberated. He has transcended the world we know. He has no use for violence."

Aditi looked up, away from Ben's gaze. "No... of course not," she said. "But I'm afraid he could again be in danger of becoming a suspect, like you thought he might after the assault. And if he's still stoned, what will he be able to say in his defence?" A shade of desperation moved across her face. "And of course I'm afraid for you. And for Chamberlain. I'm afraid."

Ben sat up and put his arm around her shoulder. "Listen," he said softly, kissing her, "forget Moksha, forget Malhotra. Forget Boylan, and even Chamberlain and me. Just think of what you're going to say in your viva next week—if you even need to think about it. Because what is there to think about? All you have to do now is what any PhD candidate does in her viva: present your work to a sane, reasonable, expert audience. Because now, that's the audience you're going to have."

He began to suck her lower lip. He stood up, lifted her into his arms, and carried her into the bedroom. He caressed and devoured her with the thoroughness of a search, and what he found was all his own, because he knew that she loved him alone, and therefore he feared no other.

Had Ben seen this man from this angle in the department, sitting in the lounge, maybe, facing away from him, he would have realized immediately that it was Boylan from the unkempt hair, the shabby jacket, the lowered head and slouched shoulders of the seated drunk. But when, walking down St. George Street, he found his gaze lingering on such a figure sitting on one of the benches in the little Innis College plaza, he didn't recognize him: all he recognized was the striking dejection that the attitude suggested, which moved him to say whatever he could to console such an obvious brother in mental suffering, whoever he was. He turned off the sidewalk onto the plaza.

It wasn't until he had nearly reached him and heard the soft, distinctive snuffling sound that he realized that it was Boylan. But today, this was not the sound of cruel, mocking laughter. It was the sound of weeping. And Ben knew this even before Boylan turned his head and looked at him from an abyss of such pure despair that Ben froze mid-step, just as he was about to lay his hand on his shoulder from behind. Boylan's eyelids were red as lacerated flesh, his face was streaked with tears. But it was the scream in the eyes themselves, their terrifying hopelessness, that told Ben that Boylan had finally been destroyed, probably by whatever intolerable memories had been awakened by the reappearance of Rosselli, memories now shared by them alone.

Ben withdrew his hand, and stood. Boylan remained still, head turned, staring at him, weeping in soft, irregular gasps. *Yes, this is what I am, as you know.*

Ben smiled, a smile of brotherly pity for the monster—and if he was more monstrous than Moksha, Ben's mother, Ben himself, it was only through whatever twist of karma had denied him the empowering consolation of some kind of love. Ben did not hold out his hand, and did not need to, before he turned away.

He was working on a car that had just rolled out onto the sidewalk, he and two of his colleagues, polishing it with rags, wiping off the dirt left in corners and shadows by the huge imprecise mechanical brushes, and was reaching across the car's roof, when he saw a dwarfish figure standing on the sidewalk a few paces away: Moksha, obviously, yet strikingly changed in the single transforming detail that Ben had noticed on that night: the unprecedented absence of his beard and hair and the resulting infantile roundness of his head. He was wearing his glasses again, the vines tied at his ears just visible at this distance. He had changed his clothes, somehow, because his shirt, pants, and suit jacket, though evidently not brand new, looked clean and showed no trace of blood. At first, his expression was blank, but when he saw that Ben had seen him, he smiled with a warmth that Ben had rarely seen in him. Ben's hand went still on the car roof. The astonishment in his face became a questioning smile, and as his hand resumed its labour, Moksha turned and began walking back the way he had probably come, towards College Street.

The feeling stayed with Ben all day, a fragility that was indeterminate but vaguely tender, close to tears. That evening, sitting in Buddha's Vegetarian, he realized that he had never before felt anything precisely like *tenderness* for Moksha, whose embarrassing infatuation—and in the early days, occasional molestations—had always put him on his guard and hardened his attitude to him. And then there were the times—two that he could remember—when the drunken adolescent Ben, deeply and terrifyingly alone in those days before Chamberlain and Aditi, had responded to Moksha's love, the only love that had ever been openly offered to him, by surrendering himself to the role that Moksha dreamed he would assume, and sucking his withered smegmatic dick.

The morning after the first time, a bitter bright cloudless February morning, he woke under the Troll Bridge to find Moksha embracing him from behind and with his hands down his opened pants. As Ben tried to recover and organize the confused traces of the night before, like the fragments of a fading nightmare, his first impulse had been to kill himself, and he had said so, to which Moksha had replied, murmuring with post-coital tenderness, with the Latin maxim *In vino veritas,* "there is truth in wine," and a quotation from Thomas Hardy's *The Ruined Maid,* with its blaming mockery of the hypocritical seductress.

Suicide had continued to haunt Ben for some time, and again with renewed intensity after Malhotra—already his nemesis after kicking him off the stairs of the Religious Studies department—had molested and beaten him one summer night in Queen's Park. Now Malhotra was dead. And Moksha had certainly killed him not to avenge himself, but Ben. What should Ben feel, but some twisted and desperate form of love?

In the library, he found the strip of three Buddha stamps under his Buddha's Vegetarian Restaurant bookmark, with a note written in *Devanāgarī* script on one of the paper slips from the catalogue room on the fourth floor: *ehi,* "Come."

In the night, Moksha's rough hand on his cheek awakened him. He opened his eyes to see him crouched beside him, face to face, where he lay on one of the benches in front of the church. He felt no surprise. He had been dreaming of Moksha just now, of walking with him through the *tapovana,* the ascetics' grove around the *āśrama*. Opening his eyes on Moksha, he might almost have been opening them in his dream. Moksha smiled, the same strange new intimate smile Ben had seen in the afternoon just hours before, and Ben smiled back. The same desperate tenderness, haunted by the certainty that everything precious was potentially on the verge of collapsing and being lost, freed him from the disgust and sense of violation that such intimacy with Moksha would have inspired in him only days before. Moksha had been talking in the dream, but already Ben couldn't remember about what. He began to talk again now: Ben saw him talking, heard his soft even syllables, but it took some moments for his words to come into focus:

"... because I know now that you can't join me. You're bound too strongly to this world, and you don't *want* to be freed. I'm bound too. Strongly."

His eyes were unwavering, beatific.

"But I want to be freed. I'm about to free myself. Because unlike yours, my bondage is for pain alone."

He paused again.

"You *do* have the renunciant's hate in you, the hate of life, consciousness, existence, the world. That was obvious from the beginning, the first day. And that was what made me love you, the way I could never have loved for physical beauty alone. But by now it has become equally obvious—you told me so yourself, and I saw it for myself, but I didn't want to understand—it has become equally obvious that this is not your last birth. But I don't blame you. Because you can't *will* yourself to want what your karma has not yet fully prepared you to want, you can't hasten your own destiny. And because what you are bound to is the most beautiful thing that *saṃsāra* has to offer. I don't believe that anyone even begins to long for *mokṣa* before he's had the experience that your actions in past lives have made available to you in this one. You can't want to leave the world, you have no *need* to leave the world, unless you've had that experience. Unless you've had that, the world is not worth renouncing. And you, my dear mad young friend and lover and savior, my guru, have given me that experience. And before I go, I will complete my role in our shared destiny, and make that experience possible for you. I will sever your bonds. All but one. The beautiful bond. The bond that frees."

Tears were streaming from Ben's eyes, wetting his hair and the paperback book that was his pillow.

They strolled down deserted Augusta, past the cardboard boxes full of rotting fruit and vegetables. On the other side, Reg Hartt stapled two posters to a poster-covered shopfront boarded for the night, then disappeared down Oxford Street. Moksha was talking, softly and evenly, but now Ben was unable to understand, or even to hear what language he was speaking. On Baldwin, a woman Ben's age appeared before them. She had a quietly beautiful leonine face, long matted carrot-red hair, and penetrating psychotic eyes, and was dressed in motley thrift-store clothes fragrant with cigarettes, piss, and sweat. It was Ben's first girlfriend Elizabeth, the only woman he had ever had sex with before Aditi. "Hi Ben", she said melodiously as she passed, grinning to reveal large, perfectly-ranged, tobacco-stained teeth. And then she was gone.

Suddenly, without having crossed Spadina or any of the other intervening space, they were on the west sidewalk of his mother's street, silently looking across at her house, where she was standing on the porch, half-visible above the white barrier with its green capital. Moksha took his hand and began to lead him across the street. As she watched them approach, her familiar faint mocking smile darkened with fear and rage, and this was the face that Ben saw above him as he and Moksha stepped onto the house's bottom step.

"No ... no," he half-whispered, closing his eyes. He felt himself being engulfed by almost audible darkness, swirling around him and sucking him under like water. Moksha's hand was gone, the steps were gone. Then Moksha was talking, softly and evenly. Ben opened his eyes, and saw him crouching on the ground in front of his bench. He still couldn't understand what he was saying, but now he knew. He reached out and laid his hand on Moksha's.

"Moksha, no. Please, no. There's another way. Wait."

18

In an earlier age, in the great days of the Department of Indian Studies, Aditi's viva would have been witnessed by an audience of at least five of her fellow indology students. But on this September day, at this viva of the last PhD in Sanskrit ever to be completed at the University of Toronto, the only member of the audience was Benjamin Doheney, whom Aditi now introduced to her departing committee members as her future husband, the last student of the late Professor Anatole Chamberlain.

Besides Rosselli, the members of Aditi's committee were almost strangers to her. There was a professor from Comparative Literature and a female professor from Religious Studies. Aditi had heard nothing from them over the years. They were mere official placeholders on her committee, appointed to fill the absence of scholars who would have been qualified to supervise her work. They knew nothing about indology and had no idea what her dissertation was about. The brief questions they had read out today, after Aditi's serenely masterful presentation of her thesis, were meaningless and harmless. Aditi had known Professor Victoria Chen a little better, since they were both in the Department of East Asian Studies. Chen's contribution over the years had consisted mainly of embarrassed sympathy, and today her questions, too, were a mere formality.

Rosselli read out the assessment of the external examiner, one of Cambridge University's Sanskrit "readers," as they are called there, a genuine and serious critique which noted a handful of minor weaknesses and unanswered questions, none of them serious enough to require rewriting. Rosselli's own assessment was brilliant, thrillingly laudatory yet uncompromisingly critical and objective, at every step supporting his praise with solid reasons and examples, and again identifying a few minor deficits she should address in her future work.

And finally there was the assessment of Chamberlain, which Rosselli also read out, and which, in the tragedy of the situation, would have swept away any objections by sheer dramatic force, even if its praise, less grandiloquent but no less powerful than Rosselli's, had not all been irrefutably true.

19

“They want me,” Aditi said, repressing her exhilaration with an ironic smile. Ben had just walked into the balmily overheated kitchen of their Kensington Market flat after his workday at the carwash and seen the letter lying open on the table. “Cambridge,” she said. “The postdoctoral fellowship.”

He smiled with a gentle glow of unsurprised satisfaction as he took off his mittens and picked up and read the brief letter. Putting it down again, he embraced and kissed her, tipping her slightly back and cupping her head from behind, being careful not to touch her neck with his cold hand.

“It could lead to anywhere,” she murmured. “It’s already like Boylan never happened … ”

“yadgataṃ gatameveha śeṣaṃ cintaya mānada,” he murmured back. *“What’s gone is gone. Think of what remains*. Everything. Our whole lives.”

He woke at around midnight, gently extricated himself from the embrace in which they had fallen asleep, and silently went and sat nude at his desk in their study. *His* desk. *Their* study. It still seemed unreal. With only a single shelf of books, most of them Aditi’s, it was still nothing like Rosselli’s study, and now it never would be, not in this city. But their eventual departure from Toronto had always been all but inevitable.

He turned on the desk lamp, intending to read a few verses from the volume of the *Mahabharata* that Aditi had checked out of the library for him, when he noticed, shining glossily where he had left it under the lamp, the postcard that had come from India two days before, postmarked from Uttarakashi and showing the *āśrama*-lined banks of the narrow Bhagirathi river just below Gangotri, the Ganga's source in the Himalaya. He picked it up and contemplated it again. To the left of the address was written a single word in *Devanāgarī: acireṇa,* "Soon."

20

"Saheb," he heard, a child's voice this time, and felt the familiar tapping on his foot.

Leaning on his elbow out of the open train window, he almost didn't bother to look, but he knew there was no point in trying to ignore it. He turned his head to the right and saw, standing in the aisle, a boy of about ten, filthy and rag-clad, whose right arm was spectacularly deformed, violently twisted back onto itself by what had probably been a deliberate break inflicted when he was an infant. With his left hand, he continued to alternately tap Ben's foot (he was sitting on the seat cross-legged, Indian style) and make the conventional gesture of begging, at once a beckoning and a miming of the act of eating.

"Saheb," he croaked, his voice and face almost lifeless. Ben winced. Aditi, sitting in the single seat across from his, was searching in her purse. She took out a twenty-rupee note, a true jackpot for any beggar, and handed it to the boy, gently speaking to him in Hindi.

As the boy moved on down the aisle to the next row of seats behind her, she glanced at Ben with an expression of quiet compassion that had become familiar to him as his disillusionment had deepened over the course of these three months of the monsoon, now coming to an end in September. He was grateful to her for never once reminding him that she had told him so. Across the aisle, a young man sitting at the window, dressed in the standard modern outfit of Western shirt and pants and Indian sandals, glanced sideways at Ben with a soft sneering laugh, and murmured to his companion opposite him a word that Ben had by now heard so many times that he rarely even noticed it anymore: *goryā,* "whitey."

In Dehradun they stayed the night in a hotel near the train station, and at dawn set out in a taxi for Uttarakashi to the north, taking the road that ascends steeply into the Himalayan foothills, then windingly follows the valley of the young Ganga where it is still called Bhagirathi, clinging to the foothills' vertiginous upper slopes. Through the day, they watched the snowcaps loom ever larger, losing and catching sight of them again and again as the road rose and plunged and twisted through the rocky, treeless terrain of the foothills' crests, through rare cliffside-hugging villages, past small remote roadside restaurants like the one where they stopped around midday to eat with their driver the region's peculiarly delicious fare. Once, as they rounded a massive, towering spur of rock, a vast vista opened itself to their view, with the river valley, foothills, and mountains stretching endlessly to the north, and Ben wept, squeezing Aditi's hand, and she wept too, seeing this landscape for the first time in twenty years, and seeing it now, for all she knew, for what might be the last.

Late in the afternoon, as they descended to the forested lower slopes near Uttarakashi, their driver stopped at a mountain stream that plunged from a rocky precipice, and they drank, washed their faces, and filled their plastic water bottles with the preciously rare pure water. Passing through the town without stopping, crossing the narrow but already powerful young river, they again began to climb into the hills on the other side. After a short ascent, they turned off the paved main road onto a narrow dirt one with a saffron-flagged temple perched on the rock high above. Rounding a corner, they saw Rosselli standing on the roadside ahead of them, with Ghatotkachi.

He smiled broadly as the car came to a stop, and as they got out, greeted them all in Hindi. When Ben didn't respond, Aditi looked at Rosselli with a significant smile, cynical and regretful. "It hasn't happened," she said softly.

Rosselli paid the driver, whom he knew and had hired, and chatted with him in Hindi. When he had left, the three of them climbed the steep steps to the house, accompanied by Ghatotkachi, who whimpered and whistled with excitement and affection. It was a large single-storey house built on the hillside, with Rosselli's book-filled study, and a bedroom each for himself and his woman, currently a ravishing Indian thirtysomething named Sneha, who greeted them warmly but a little shyly in a pure California accent. For as far as could be seen all around, the hillsides were covered with the green of the region's characteristic terraced fields. Low, rapidly shifting clouds occasionally obscured the sun. The Bhagirathi was visible at the valley's bottom. The dirt road could be seen continuing to the next village a couple of kilometres away. Uttarakashi was just out of sight round the side of the next foothill. And as they stood on the front balcony, the Himalayas themselves loomed before them, filling half the sky.

As they sat drinking tea at the heavy wooden table in the kitchen-dining room, Rosselli said, "The *āśrama* is on the next terrace up, a bit further west."

Ben and Aditi climbed the steep unpaved track alone. The *āśrama* was a one-room wooden hut, plainly newer than the house, well-constructed, austere but not wretched. Rosselli had told them that they could knock, so Ben knocked on the simple wooden door with a carved, brightly painted demonic guardian face, typical of the region's folk art, set above the doorframe. When no one answered, he gently pushed the door open, and they stepped into the room. It was well lit by a large window in the opposite wall, which looked over the terraced fields towards the village. Below it were a wooden desk and chair. Open on the desk were what they found to be a large edition of the *Yogavāsiṣṭha* and a notebook in which each individual copied verse was followed by a working-out and a final translation. There was also an Apte Sanskrit-English dictionary, and a framed photograph of the south Indian sage Ramana Maharshi. Against one wall there was a simple pallet with a blanket, and against another, a bookcase with a number of Sanskrit, Hindi, and English books, including *What's Bred in the Bone* and *David Copperfield,* and in one of the gaps, a little black stone Nandi.

They set out along the track that Rosselli had told them about, which led between terraced fields to the village. They could see no one either below them towards the road or above them towards where the fields ended and the hillside rose sharply in a steep rock face. A heavy curtain of fine late monsoon rain swept across the hillside from above, yielding to the sun again before they were more than superficially wet. As they neared the village, the descending track joined a stone-paved path that led them through a narrow gap between rows of concrete houses. Two monkeys looked at them without much interest from the branches of a tree in a grassy lot. The path turned sharply into a steep stone staircase, now perilously wet, that brought them down to a temple square, where some children stopped playing to stare at them curiously. The oldest girl, a beautiful, intelligent-looking child of about thirteen with her hair in pigtails, asked them in Hindi where they were from, and appeared mystified when Aditi answered that they were from Canada.

"Is that somewhere near Chennai?" she asked after a pause.

"Further," said Aditi, smiling, but without condescension.

Ben kicked off his sandals and entered the temple—to Hanuman—then immediately came out and looked at Aditi, shaking his head.

"Have you seen a little old man with a grey beard?" Aditi asked the children. "Very small, with glasses ..."

"*Moksha-ji?*" said the girl. "No, big sister, not today."

Following a zigzag course, they descended the rest of the way through the village, passing several people who noticed them with only a little surprise. When they reached the road, they stopped and looked east towards Rosselli's house, visible as a small bright form high on the distant hillside.

"Shall we go on to the next village?" said Ben. "Or should we just go back and wait for him?"

Before he had finished saying this, Aditi saw his eyes narrow myopically at something behind her, and turned to follow their gaze.

There was Moksha, strolling towards them from the direction of the next village. He was wearing a long-sleeved saffron-coloured shirt, a loincloth, sandals, a bright new *akṣamālā* next to the faded, stained old one, and the typical small round metal-framed glasses of the poor villager. His hair and beard were trimmed short, and better tended than they usually had been in Toronto. But the old sharpness in his eye and smile qualified his now even greater likeness to Ramana Maharshi.

"Hello," he said, with the familiar friendly upturn of his voice at the end of the word, nodding genteelly at Aditi.

"Hello, Moksha," she said, smiling a little sadly. "It's been a while since we last met."

Moksha responded in Hindi, addressing them both, and Ben looked down with a sad, irritated wince of a smile.

"yat iṣṭam tat na saṃvṛttam. devabhāṣayā āṅglabhāṣayā vā saṃvaditavyam," said Aditi in Sanskrit: *It hasn't happened the way he hoped. We have to converse in English or the language of the gods.*

Moksha looked probingly at Ben, who looked up at him with a defeated eye that told him everything.

Aditi spoke in English, answering the question Moksha had asked in Hindi. "We arrived about two hours ago. When we didn't find you in your *āśrama,* we walked here by the path. Saul told us how to get here. He said you usually take a walk here in the evening, but that you sometimes go on to the next village."

"I did that today," Moksha said. "There's another Hanuman temple there, larger and more beautiful than this one. Sometimes I go even further. There's a steep path up the cliffside to a Brahmin village on the hilltop. I have a couple of friends up there with whom I can speak some Sanskrit, but it's pretty basic stuff, they aren't *paṇḍitas*—actually, Saul speaks it better than they do—so I've never become fluent. Sometimes I walk back the long way from there, by the paved main road."

Ruggedly and still girlishly beautiful, trim with the fitness of working people, an old sari-clad woman appeared on the road before them, walking swiftly in their direction. She smiled broadly at Moksha, including Ben and Aditi with a glance, and as she passed spoke briefly to Moksha in Hindi, animatedly and with pleasure. He replied with the same good cheer, and with what again struck Aditi as native fluency.

"Your Hindi is extremely good," she said, audibly impressed. "If I didn't know, I'd assume that you must be a native. You know ... you don't especially look white. You'd really never studied it before you left Canada?"

"No, never," he said. "As soon as I arrived, I began working through a primer that Saul had in his library, but it came to me very easily, supernaturally easily, without much work at all. I often think I was really just remembering, actually. It was always Ben who talked about learning Hindi, I was never that interested. And now look how things have turned out."

Ben smiled with a touch of sad resignation, and spoke, immediately following the Sanskrit verse with his spontaneous translation:

anyathā cintito hyarthaḥ punarbhavati so'nyathā
anityamatayo loke narāḥ puruṣasattama

We conceive a purpose in one way, but it turns out in another. In this world, people change their minds.

"Holy shit!" murmured Moksha, smiling, awed. "No wonder you didn't have any space left in there for Hindi."

They all laughed, a complex laughter with hints of darkness and regret.

By now the sun had passed behind the western hills. Saul's house stood above them to the left, still in sunlight, close enough that they could just see Saul and Sneha leaning on the balcony's railing, looking down at them. To the right, the land below the road fell away sharply in a cliff before the terraced fields resumed, descending towards the river. A herd of goats began to trickle round the next bend, soon followed by the goatherd, a man of about sixty dressed in long-sleeved shirt, loincloth, and loosely bound turban, whose sun-baked face was adorned with a magnificent white mustache and stubble. He too smiled at Moksha with recognition, acknowledging Ben and Aditi with a courteous side-to-side tipping of the head. Moksha spoke to him, miming the act of smoking with twinned fingers, and the goatherd produced a pack of *bidis* from his breast pocket and handed him one, with an uncertain glance at Ben—and at Ben and Aditi's joined hands—apparently considering whether to offer him one too, but finally deciding against it. These were city folks. Who knew what they liked to smoke, if anything? He moved on with a benedictory tipping of the head, and the remainder of his flock streamed past their legs.

"You're happy here," said Ben with a touch of sadness and envy, though his face glowed with quiet joy. "I can see that. Very happy."

Moksha smiled. "If I'd had a choice, at the time, I would've preferred Arunachalam, or even Varanasi, but of course I had to follow fate. Saul and I will eventually visit those places, but it's safer for me to be here, and simpler. And in Varanasi there would have been ... distractions ... such as *gāñja* ... And from what Saul tells me, Arunachalam is virtually a spiritual tourist trap at this point. So ... I think I can manage to reconcile myself to an *āśrama* in the Himalaya." There was quiet laughter in his voice. "After all, the whole point, originally, was *śānti, samādhi,* peace, union with the divine. For a while, people have considered this to be one of the better places to go looking for it."

He took a gentle drag on his *bidi,* exhaled, and glanced up at Ben's troubled face. *"śāntaḥ bhava,* be at peace," he said with a quiet earnestness, an intimate intensity, that had been rare for him. "You'll be back, back here in the *devabhūmi,* the land of the gods, back up here to see me. You're only ... what? twenty-seven, something like that? I'm sixty. And this isn't really my first time here. I'd had a while already—a long while—to get used to this place." He paused, looking at Ben intently. "You have no idea how long life is."

Ben looked into his eyes, now more inscrutable to him than ever before, and felt an upsurge of anguished love and compassion for his old friend, despite everything: the harm he had once done to Ben, the terrible deeds that he had shown himself capable of in the pursuit of what he had conceived to be Ben's liberation, at least at that time. How much of what he was saying was truth, how much of it was insanity? All Ben knew was that according to his own truth, he had done what he had to do for Moksha, what love owed to love. And didn't he really owe him even more than that? Was it not Ben who had brought Moksha Boylan's acid, thereby unbalancing his delicately balanced sanity?

Ben was weeping, and Aditi, too, quietly wiped a tear from her eye.

Rosselli was standing with Ghatotkachi at the bottom of the stairs. *"bho suhṛdaḥ," hello, friends*, he said with a quiet smile that registered his awareness of the situation. "I'm glad you found each other." He scratched Ghatotkachi's ear as she looked around at all of them with love. "That has a way of happening, in this world."

Ben sat with his elbow on the sill of the open train window to his left as the hilly rural landscape rushed past in the mellow light of the sun hanging minutes above the horizon. Yes, he was thinking, how strange and unforeseeable that it should have been Moksha who ended up here, and so at home here. It had always been Ben himself who was determined to eventually come to the homeland of the language and literature that obsessed him—to live here for as much as possible of the rest of his life, in this country about which he really knew nothing. But India had turned out to be related only in a very complicated and indirect way to the great ancient civilization described in his beloved *Mahabharata,* and to the Indo-Canadian woman he loved, who had had no desire ever to see it again.

Fate! Where would they all be now if Ben had not brought Moksha Boylan's acid? Certainly not in the Himalayan foothills. And Boylan would not have ended up smashed against the floor of the Robarts Library fire escape, and the police would not have found the knife encrusted with Malhotra's gore in the bottom drawer of Boylan's desk, as an anonymous caller told them they would. Malhotra's fellow campus cops had been able to testify to his vaguely unbalanced temperament, and to the fact that he had for years had a mysterious, uneasy love-hate association with Boylan, whose dangerous insanity was finally proven by the contents and condition of his office.

With the case thus closed, Moksha might still have safely retired to the *āśrama* at Lake Simcoe, or even stayed living in Philosopher's Walk. But there was still the assault on the Hart House guard, unsolved. There was a more appropriate refuge for him than Lake Simcoe, safer for him, and also more acceptable to his two oldest friends, Ben and David McLeod, the only people who would ever have to know that he had killed Malhotra, and make some kind of peace with that knowledge. It would be better if Moksha were removed to the Land of the Gods through Ben's providential new connection with Rosselli, who now remembered seeing Moksha in the halls of the old department, an age ago, and conceived a characteristically big-hearted interest in him, as he had in Ben and Aditi.

Moksha was *jīvanmukta,* finished with the world while still alive. He had been looking forward to nothing more than liberating himself from the body after liberating Ben from his most limiting and painful earthly bond. Leaving Canada was no loss to Moksha, and despite the completedness of his work in this incarnation, spending the remainder of it in the Himalaya was, after all, something gained, for him, and for Ben. And this was so even if, as Ben now thought probable, he would never see Moksha again, even if he finally came to feel that his oldest friend's liberation had brought him to a place that was beyond what Ben was able to understand and accept. Whether it was the result of philosophy, or meditation, or LSD, or insanity, this was not Ben's liberation. Alienated though he was, ultimately illusory though reality might be, he was now surer than ever that in this incarnation, at least, he was destined to accept the values of a world in which it was better to forgive evil than to destroy it.

Ben glanced at Aditi in the seat opposite him, and saw that, inevitably, she had fallen asleep with her head leaned against the wall. The train had slowed and was rolling into the station of a village in the rapidly fading light. The platform was far less crowded than the ones they had seen during the day, and so travellers, vendors, and beggars stood waiting at the margin for the train to slow to a stop instead of chasing after the still-moving doors in a panic and grasping the handles to hoist themselves in ahead of the rest of the swarm. The moment the train stopped, vendors' chants—youthfully strident and engaged, or weary and resigned—began to sound from the two ends of the car, the clearest being *chai, chai,* "tea, tea." Ben looked up the aisle and saw a tea vendor, a youth of about seventeen, carrying his spigotted metal tank and a stack of paper cups, stopping at each unit of seats, filling cups, handing them to his customers, taking coins and notes, giving change. Behind him, a small, worn, sari-clad woman carried a basket of toasted rice which she mixed on the spot with spices and chopped onions and tomatoes to create a snack called *bhel*.

Seeing this food which they both loved, Ben was about to touch Aditi on the knee and wake her, when he felt a tapping on his left elbow. He looked and saw a boy of about thirteen on the other side of the window's horizontal bars, alternately tapping him and raising his fingers to his lips in the beggar's dumb show of eating, smiling the aggressively coaxing, faintly mocking smile that always inspired in Ben an irritation and resentment that he could not master, and which he could not now conceal. Aditi would handle it, as usual. He withdrew his elbow from the window, leaned forward, and touched her knee.

"*Bhel,*" he said softly, gesturing with his eyes towards the aisle behind her, and added, "and do you have a few coins for this kid?" But when he looked back at the window, the boy was gone.

The *bhel*-vendor arrived, chanting the name of her merchandise, and at Aditi's request, mixed two portions in newspaper funnels, then took a ten-rupee note from her and moved on. The train's horn sounded. Ben poured out a handful and emptied it into his mouth.

"*Saheb,*" he heard from the window, a boy's voice. He turned, and only had an instant to recognize the same boy before he felt a splash of hot liquid hit his eyes and face: tea. He cried out and raised his hands to his eyes, spilling the *bhel* onto his lap and the floor. As the train bumped into motion, he opened them to see the boy laughing and pointing mirthfully—"*Goryaaa!*" *Whitey!*—in the instant before he slipped from view.

Aditi leaned forward and pressed her face against the window's bars, screaming something menacing in Hindi. As Ben collected the remaining *bhel* from his lap into his right hand, the passengers on the other side of the aisle, including two large sari-clad sisters, stared, murmured, laughed. Aditi shot them a glance of disgust, settled back in her seat, took a handful of *bhel,* and muttered, "Let's get the fuck out of here."

Ben surfaced from sleep to the plane's soporific low rumble and looked out the window at a barren mountain landscape that might have been Afghanistan or Iran. Caressing but still, his hands lay on Aditi's head and shoulder as she slept in his lap, leaning across from her own seat to his left. He resisted the urge to stroke her tied-back hair, fearing to wake her. He glanced at the middle-aged Punjabi-dressed woman in the aisle seat next to Aditi, and saw without surprise that she was again looking at them with cold disapproval. He turned away, and in that moment of distraction stroked Aditi's hair. She stirred in her sleep, and languorously resettled her head in his lap, nuzzling the outlined form of his erection. The woman turned to look up the aisle, and began gesturing, not too subtly, to a flight attendant, a tall, slender young woman with dark hair bound tightly back, who immediately approached, smiling, and solicitously bent down to listen. As the woman muttered to her without looking at them, the attendant glanced over at Ben and Aditi, and he met her look of guarded perplexity with a resigned, conspiratorial smile.

"Just a moment, I will see," said the attendant softly in a strong Italian accent, then stood up, looked around, and moved down the aisle towards the rear. Ben turned back to the window, and within a minute heard the attendant return and say, "This young lady is willing to change places with you," followed by a muttered "Thank God" and a bustle of movement.

For some moments, Ben continued to watch a large lake or sea inch into view and dominate the lifeless Martian landscape kilometres below, then turned to look at the neighbouring seat's new occupant, an Indian woman in her early twenties with long straight hair and in fully contemporary dress.

"That's sweet," she said, glancing at Aditi sleeping in Ben's lap, and smiling at Ben. "Where are you headed?" Her accent was Canadian, but Ben couldn't pinpoint the region.

"London," said Ben, "and then up to Cambridge, Cambridge University. We'd love to stop in Milan for a few days, but ... not this time."

"Yeah, me too," said the young woman. "I'm flying Alitalia just because it was the best flight I could get, but yeah, I would have loved to stop in Milan. But as it is, I'll be going straight on to Toronto from there."

"And you're going to...?" Ben asked. "I believe I'm hearing the accent of a fellow Canadian? We're Torontonians."

"Oh wow!" she said. "Amazing! I would never have imagined that I had a Canadian accent, or that there even *is* a Canadian accent. Yeah, I'm from Edmonton, I'm flying back there via Toronto. Was this your first time in India? Is your girlfriend from there?"

"Yes, my wife is from Delhi, originally," said Ben ("Oh, your *wife*. Sorry," she murmured), "but now she's Canadian," Ben went on, "from Edmonton, actually." ("Oh wow!") "And yes, it was my first time. You?"

"Yeah," she said, "it was my first time too ... visiting relatives." She paused and looked ahead, a faint shadow darkening her smile. "I can't wait to get back home. I love Canada."

Aditi stirred again, her eyes opened, and she turned her head slightly to look up at Ben. He smiled at her, and she sat up, blinking, suppressing a yawn, pulling her hair back with both hands.

"Oh... hello," she said, a little hoarsely, when she noticed their new neighbour, who smiled at her, staring a little, before discreetly finding and inserting her earphones and becoming demonstratively absorbed in her music. Aditi turned back to Ben, laying her head on his shoulder.

"I keep thinking of that verse you quoted," she murmured, "on the road back from the village to Saul's house. How did it go... *anyathā cintito hyarthaḥ...*"

"*punarbhavati so'nyathā,*" he said. "'We conceive a purpose in one way, but it turns out in another.'"

"Yeah," she said. "And then... *anityamatayo loke narāḥ.*" She stroked his arm pensively. "'People change their minds.'"

"And we have, haven't we," he said, "about India, about religion, about our life's mission, about ... some people." He stroked her hand that lay on his thigh. "And about others, not. And never."

"Yeah, baby, I know. Some people never." She kissed his shoulder through his jacket and shirt. "And that makes the things that change, the things we have to lose, easier to live through." She paused. "England, Cambridge, academia generally... I don't know. Just at the moment, they seem less than inspiring. I only did it for us, and we made it, here we are. But after this trip, and everything that's happened, I'm less sure about where I'm going to want to go, ultimately. But... at least I know that I don't have to go there alone."

"People change their minds," said Ben, "but then there's fate, destiny, *daiva*. People meet and separate, find and lose—each other, roles, missions, faiths—according to *daiva*. But *daiva* is not completely inscrutable. Sometimes, it insists on something over such a long time, through all its apparent vagaries, that its intention becomes clear. Look at us." He turned his head slightly to meet her eye.

She smiled seriously. "Remember this one?" she said. "You recited it to me, once, long ago, and I've never forgotten it, I've held on to it through everything, because I had to believe that someday it would turn out to have been true.

sarvaṃ duḥkhamidaṃ vīra sukhodarkaṃ bhaviṣyati
nātra manyustvayā kāryo daivaṃ hi balavattaram

"'All this suffering will end in happiness...'" she began.

"'And you should not rage against it, this suffering,'" he said, squeezing her hand, before she joined him, eyes shining, to speak the last quarter-verse in unison:

"'Because fate is stronger.'"

They closed their eyes on a cloudless western sky dim with the day's last light.